Acclaim for *A Crash Course On the Anatomy of Robots*

"*A Crash Course On the Anatomy of Robots* reads like a collision between Hunter S. Thompson and Pico Iyer. Expect to be surprised."
–Elana Bell, author of *Eyes, Stones*, winner of the 2011 Walt Whitman Award

"*Crash Course* travels on the wings of poetry, autobiography, relationships and humor to cross-examine modern reality and cultural rebellion. Stemming from a lyrical voice, the chapters range dizzyingly from a desire to handle real objects, real people and real experiences to the realization of its actual impossibility. Humans, robots, love, music, and the globe collide and ultimately develop into a rich, lively and stimulating inquiry into existence itself."
–Inés Ferrero Cándenas, author of *Gendering the Marvellous* and *El Caracol de Arena*.

"Kent Evans has blasted the picaresque novel into the 21st century, melding sex and travel with some seriously roguish suspense."
–Stephanie Elizondo Griest, author of *Mexican Enough* and *Around the Bloc*

"Gonzo word artist Kent Evans sets the words a-kindle, running the line where they turn into music, spinning the tale of his character Damien out along the frayed edge of being. A harrowing, smart, lyric report for our time."
– Tony Cohan, author of *Valparaiso, Opium, Native State,* and *On Mexican Time*

Like the robots in his title, Kent Evans' new novel is an ingenious mash up of well-oiled parts. A melding of bildungsroman, trippy travelogue, journal entries, and song lyrics, *A Crash Course On the Anatomy of Robots* is the story of a young man grieving the loss of his parents. Wrenching, insightful, and wholly original, this book beats with life, fueled by Evans' wry wit, poet's eye, and generous heart."
–Jillian Medoff, author of *I Couldn't Love You More* **and** *Hunger Point*

"A step beyond where *Malas Ondas* left us, *Robots* is a thick, compelling and spiraling journey with a fearless writer. I wanna say 'flawed' in the right way here...like heroic but not as sexy. *Crash Course* is Evans' successful foray into what today's fiction needs - a skillful mash-up, if you will, of genres. He deftly mixes the scientific, travelogue and confessional into an original narrative style."
–Kevin Brink Nielsen, author of *Club Fascistland* **and the** upcoming *Lightweights of Babylon*

Praise for *Malas Ondas: Lime, Sand, Sex, and Salsa in the Land of Conquistadors*

"Kent Evans is one of the best young writers alive today. If Rimbaud, Henry Rollins, and Hunter S. Thomson collaborated with Arthur Frommer on a Rough Guide, you might get some idea of what you're in for: a brilliant, wickedly satiric, low-budget tour through the seamier and sexier parts of a third world culture. Kent has nailed the Zeitgeist of our times. I couldn't put the book down."
–David Ishay, Founder *YRB Magazine*

A Crash Course
On the Anatomy of Robots

Δ Δ Δ Δ

Kent R. Evans

ISBN-13: 978-1-938545-01-6
ISBN-10: 1-938545-01-X

For information regarding permissions, bulk purchases,
or additional distribution, write to
Pangea Books, PO Box 818, 31 Vose Avenue
South Orange, NJ 07079-0818
www.pangeabooks.net

Cover Design and Art:
Katie Clancy EStudio473
http://studio473.wordpress.com/

Author photo by Yasemin Rodriguez

Acknowledgment is made to YRB *Magazine* in which a version of
"They'll Get You For $25" first appeared.

**Original soundtrack for the novel available from
cdbaby.com and all other major distributors**

Dedication

For my mother who passed too soon
Stubborn to the end
Jess who helped to pick up the pieces
Or what was left of them
And my brother Bob

God knows, one day we'll get it right

Contents

Parents (A Crash Course on Death, Family, and Fallout

Where we get some *Origins (Not Like Heroes and Hiro, like umm... Damien)*, he does some *Re-writing for you with FreeCell and smokes* till he gets *Back to Earth* and has *A Momentary Poetic Interlude on top of the giant* and gets back to *The Asian Journal of Damien Wood.*

Portrait of an Artist as a Not So Young Man (A Crash Course on Survival)

Where we find out how *Work and South of the Border* fit in Damien's life, followed by *Anatomy of a Poet Parts 1, 2, and 3* which cover his odd profession and path to it. We again head to *The Asian Journal of Damien Wood and get A Quick Guide on the Art of Traveling* before hitting the *Journal* once more.

Escape from New York (A Crash Course on the Anatomy of Relationships)

We learn about *Test Drives* and Damien finds himself *Fucking bored and censored in the city of lost angels* with *The daytime lover.* This was preceded by *The call from J* which got him *Back in fucking New York* where *The apartment, Penny, and unpaid bills* lead him to *A casual drink to destroy all self-worth* and *Dinner with J and the concept of sharing.*

After going out with **Adena and Kienyo and stalking an Ex** he gets to deal with **Fraudulent shippers, Jeepers Creepers trucks and storage space shittiness.** He learns about the problem with **Chasing demons in Harlem and why Damien should have just kept his mouth shut,** not to mention **Amorous custom guys named Oscar, An unexpected email and the problems of drinking alone on a pier.** After **The unnecessary brunch to move suicide up the options** he's thinkin **"They keep pulling me back in" and off we go** to California but in no time at all he's **Leaving LA** and **Bikers and the Battle of Lost Angeles** only to find himself once more **Dead in central Mexico** and comes to the conclusion that he and his buddy Alex – well **Chippendales they are not.** He then finds himself **Back in LA, off to Bangkok, and feeling quite aftermathy...**

We kick you some knowledge on **Blogging, Journals, and Poetry**, then Damien hits the road to Southeast Asia and this novel become s a bit more chronologically than thematically arranged. Among the sights are **Thailand**, dirty dirty **Soi Cowboy, Cambodia** – where Damien starts feelin his **Mortality** and finds himself a bit **Lost in Translation** before heading to **Vietnam (but first has to deal with a little more Cambodia)** till he takes a rather radical **Detour (where fate's wicked sense of humor catches up).**

ix

Where Damien is once more *Back in LA and Beyond.* We tie up some *Loose Ends,* find *There is a church* across from Damien's new home and again he is *Boldly Going* to somewhere warmer or at least *As Damien would imagine it...*The beginning of *(A NEW Damien Wood Novel).*

Where we give you the **complete poems** *and a short story about Damien that could be an* **Epilogue** *if you like. This is followed by the credits, better known as* **Acknowledgments***, where the author thanks everyone this book is probably about - ha ha just kidding, lawyers... and finally* **Propaganda on the Writer***, where we get some egregious exaggerations and embellishments about the author.*

So here I am in the middle way, having had twenty years -
Twenty years largely wasted, the years of *l'entre deux guerres*
Trying to learn to use words and every attempt
Is a wholly new start, and a different kind of failure.
Because one has only learned to get the better of words

—*T. S. Eliot,* Four Quartets

A Crash Course on Using the Manual

This section is designed to introduce some concepts to better your understanding and enjoyment of your new novel.

Definition of Primary Terms:

Main Entry: Crash course

Part of Speech: N

Definition: a fast, intensive training in or study of a subject, esp. on the basics; also called cram course

Webster's New Millennium™ *Dictionary of English*

anatomy   (ə-nāt'ə-mē)

1. The structure of an organism or any of its parts.

2. The scientific study of the shape and structure of organisms and their parts.

The American Heritage Science Dictionary

1398, "study of the structure of living beings," from O.Fr. *anatomie,* from Gk. *anatomia,* from *anatome* "dissection," from *ana-* "up" + *temnein* "to cut."

Online Etymology Dictionary

ro·bot   (rō'bŏt', -bət)   n.

1. A mechanical device that sometimes resembles a human and is capable of performing a variety of often-

complex human tasks on command or by being programmed in advance.

2. A machine or device that operates automatically or by remote control.

3. A person who works mechanically without original thought, especially one who responds automatically to the commands of others.

This is a manual but not quite a how-to.

You may have some questions.

Ground rules

This book occurs over many years over many countries.

For the most part it is from the mid 90s till the present Millennium.

But it will occasionally leap a bit further back.

For the most part it is in the US and Southeast Asia.

But Mexico and Europe may pop up.

As in life, many people will pop up once
And never be mentioned again.

The protagonist is a Poet who has enough money to travel.
Deal with it.

The protagonist is Asian American,
But this is not the *Joy Luck Club*.

A Crash Course On the Anatomy of Robots

There is death and family,
But this is not *Ordinary People.*

There are relationships,
But this is not a love story.

There is horror,
But the author is not Stephen King,
Although he is quoted

There are, as mentioned, many countries,
But this is not a travel narrative.

There are journal entries,
But this is not a memoir.

It is autobiographical,
But it is not an autobiography.

The author is not Damien,
Though I suppose Damien is the author.

This is a Crash Course
On one life
In a brief span of time

A Crash Course On the Anatomy of Robots

On a tiny planet

And there are no mechanical Robots.

Not the way you're thinking anyhow.

Try to keep up.

Prologue

In 1978, Japanese scientist Masahiro Mori coined the phrase "Uncanny Valley." A specialist in robotics, he found that creating humanoid characteristics in artificial life forms had a bell curve of human reaction to them. Statistically, up to a point, the more human robots appear the more endearing subjects find them. (Think of Yoda, the Smurfs – really any clearly non-human entity that elicits a positive response. You may insert your warm feelings toward E.T. here.)

Mori discovered that at some point however this growing mountain of goodwill takes a sharp dive toward disgust that does not start climbing again till you have an actual human being once more.

The reason is simple. The robots become too human. Whereas subjects find artificial-looking things with some personality are cute or draw the subject into human comparison (look he's smiling), once a certain threshold is passed they simply find it freaky, or more specifically they stop noticing how human the robot looks and start noticing how inhuman it appears. The general consensus at this crossover goes from one of endearment and adoration to one of fear and repulsion.

Running into death can be like a bad memoir you picked up mistakenly thinking it was experimental fiction. No one gets too worked up about *did you hear about John? You know John? He used to deliver pizza and date Joan. You remember Joan right?* cause it's been relegated to the realm of gossip, verbal Jerry Springer. Actual death stinks. It literally burns the eyes and causes ordinarily sane people to break into unexplained tears or nervous inappropriate laughter. Whereas we all contain the foolhardy assumption that we can all relate to or even have a clue about mortality outside of a concept, those actually touched seem to have a particularly distasteful odor to them. It is akin to the rot of damage that comes off someone from a recent horrible break-up or heroin crash. Somewhere in the sub-conscious alarms go off screaming *run* while our conscious socially adapted selves scramble for a polite excuse to get the fuck out of there.

We like cute robots that look like Muppets not humans with robot parts. Humans let's say like inveterate traveler, performance artist and confessional writer Damien Michael Wood. A particular specimen blessed with an unfortunate amount of death in his life and in and on his hands in too many places around the globe.

The Uncanny Valley (A Crash Course on Social Isolation)

"What do you think," he asked, "you get social academic brownie points for deliberately staying out of touch with your own culture?"

-Stephen King at the National Book Awards 2003

The Asian Journal of Damien Wood Part 1

Los Angeles waiting on a flight to Bangkok - April 16, 2006

13 towns and cities in three countries in ten weeks, or why Thailand is like Mexico, but less dangerous and sleazier. The new novel by the author of how I tried to kill myself in Latin America but ended up with a bar and a book...

Your name is Damien Michael Wood and you were born in July 1975 about three decades ago. An emergency C-section in New York Hospital, you were already difficult from jump. You are a pathological liar and always tell the truth, usually when it's least convenient. You are a coward and a leader. Wildly insecure, and illogically self-confident. You are almost 31 and you know not who you are.

You have grown sick of Canadians and their polite arrogance. American fools on tour, minus the guilt. Sick of the French and Israelis, their unwillingness to learn any other language or break out of insulated groups. You are done with travelers, of which you are one, who like chauvinists mistreating women, create an uphill battle for you wherever you go. You are sick and tired of seeing yourself in all those assholes, who just like you, are killing time. You would tell them your name if you still knew it. It has been lost in years and self afflicted deceptions. You are a middle class kid from the Northeast, gifted in some ways, and lazy in most. You have played roles and worn masks, those that fit snugly and those that were worn loosely, and you have never stopped looking, never

9

stopped searching to the ends of the earth for the face behind them, and someone who would love it.

It's one in the morning in LAX in the most prefab bar/deli you've ever been in. The music and staff is Mexican despite the fact that all boarding gates are headed to somewhere in Asia. You sip a vodka soda with a touch of Roses Lime and pretend you're not scared shitless of being alone in yet another foreign land in less than 24 hours.

Your thoughts don't exactly fixate on Ivy, but definitely include her. It was with some relief that you shut down the Internet and your mobile some hours ago eliminating action through communication. There is no more you can do – or more accurately, proactively obsessing over a dead relationship is no longer logistically possible.

The bar is now closing. You'll be boarding in 20 or 30 minutes. You sip your drink, think maybe you shouldn't have eaten a soggy turkey and cranberry digestion bomb – Easter or not – then go back to not thinking about Ivy and the fact you are going alone on a trip whose timing and itinerary were determined by the both of you. You most definitely don't think about your other ex Marie and four years ago and breaking up in India and taking off alone to Mexico and Jesus is she really getting married now?
Your mind is a calm clean blank slate.

April 19, 2006 - Bangkok to Southern Thailand
It's Election Day. You know this since it is illegal to buy or drink alcohol till midnight. The walls of buildings are plastered with

portraits of well-dressed men and women (power suits or military uniforms) in addition to one blind smiling candidate with his cane and dog, all with numbers in the lower corners. The fact that candidates are identified by number rather than name, and all booze is banned for the length of the elections, tells you a little bit about the voting process and populace in the monarchy.

You spent the day traversing the river on overloaded boats, riding on modern elevated metro, and battling sub-Mexico city bus lines all in the search of cheese. It had never occurred to you its absence in Asian diet (Mongolian fermented mare's milk aside). Nursing a Thai whiskey hangover with honey green tea and iced coffee you've found Bangkok to be a visceral assault, most definitely in the olfactory sense. Durian, duck, rotten fish and spice mingle freely with every culinary and refuse smell one can imagine as you wander through the crowded and currently oppressively hot metropolis. Thousand year old temples run into 7-11's; Tuk-tuks (modern day rickshaws with motorbikes attached) and BMW's battle for automotive dominance; and Europe casually blends – occasionally collides with local culture (i.e. fat old men with impossible young pretty things, all bought and for sale in the vigorous sex industry).

You are thinking again of the soft curves of Malaysian skin and barely felt moist lips gliding through sweat and sound in a dark village hut with no ventilation and minimal fans contrasting with Chinese classical strings and extreme cable, a full third of its stations labeled "future channel" and another third rubbish.

A Crash Course On the Anatomy of Robots

This is the new Asia, ancient in words and customs and eyes, wearing the emperors' new clothes just like you. You find the general attitude toward you is one of polite indifference. There is little curiosity or offense, mostly the cool Asian line of separation. This despite, or perhaps exacerbated by the fact you are half Chinese, but clearly American.

You feel very much like a mid-westerner in midtown Manhattan.

You haven't stopped wearing the shirt she hates for being too busy and distracting; lacking, according to Ivy, simplicity, taste, or obvious focus. Got a bandanna and sunglasses and sandals on all the time, the trademarks of hippy – not punk-rock at all.

And the linen pants are rolled to the knees.
And the 3-day shadows slips into 4.
And the smells of sheesha mingle with whiskey.
And you begin to wonder,
if she knew you at all.

There are lights that hum over the city of Bangkok, fireflies glowing bright luck candle orange, phosphorous blues and milky whites. The locomotive on which you ride runs south, and the river runs black, and we are all simply alit in the florescent glory of halogen and Thai.

The lady sitting across from you, all of a foot and a half, won't return a nod and grips a water foot massager like one your mother Joan had when you were young. You keep seeing decorations and trinkets – habits and customs that remind you of near forgotten pieces of her. Ones she herself had parted with before the end, pieces you only remember now as you see them and feel something you cannot place.

You are in an upper bunk and ergo there is no window. As an insomniac in a sleeper car, this absolutely sucks. You are also not sure where you can smoke. But you sure as hell need to take a piss.

Now in Thong Nai Pan Noi – you think (your Thai is not really expanding beyond "hello" and "thanks"). It's a beatific cove with crystal clear calm water. Two couples, Brits, arrived with you on the back of a pickup. There appears to be an abundance of couples which has spawned an imaginary dialogue between you and all of your past lovers and companions. You see Marie flirting with obnoxious Israelis, Jez sunbathing with the occasional dip, and Ivy either eating a salad or making commentary on how gorgeous it is or bitterly complaining. You know both of those versions fairly well, the latter, which would most likely involve insects and heat, all too well.

In travel situations Jez was always the most reliable, the most kindred in spirit. How strange nearly a year and over 9,000 miles away you realize how good you could be when your feet weren't nailed down.

And there you suppose is the rub. Ivy was perfect in stability and Jez in instability. You and Marie were, quite simply, too similar. You would have made great companions in all realms, if only you had not been in love.

In Thai there are no tenses, and because of that a sense of time becomes complicated. Phrases are arranged in elaborate order to create various effects, the poetry is said to be nearly untranslatable. In a way it's the truest test of the Sapir-Whorf hypothesis – the idea that language itself can define reality.

You are not a linear thinker, not exactly anyhow. You see the world in terms of relationships, many of them occurring and changing continuously and on many levels, but all intrinsically connected. The pop term "multi-task" comes to mind. Man may be an island, but he is within a sea on a world in a universe that acts and counteracts.

In interpersonal transactions you seem to end up with far more literal-minded, often linear, people than yourself. Their lives seem contained in a framework of minutia and in denial of the larger picture. Your dismissal of these detail-oriented specifics is well – dismissive, leading inevitably to your break-ups. Again and again, things you have done or said are quoted verbatim while you struggle unsuccessfully to remember doing or saying them whilst attempting to retort to exact lines of dialogue. By then you are fully aware of the big picture and could give a fuck about any particular details, responding to the accuser with your own brand of denial.

Human beings possess an amazing capacity for denying the inevitable, from minor tiffs even to death. With the exception of Marie you have never had any doubts from the first moment where a relationship would lead and how it would end. With Marie, it was simply that she was your first and you were blindly in love – some slack should be cut.

You suppose that anyone could argue that with a vision of where these relationships would lead that you had perhaps manifested that vision. Were you so powerful in your skills of manipulation you would surely be a politician or cult leader by now. The more likely truth is that you denied those gut instincts and tried to avoid or change what can only be described as fate – inevitability.

In every case you saw a different 'possible' outcome. In the end you did not give enough weight to the 'probable.' Call it idealism.

You do not know if you can fall in love again. You want to, but that's like getting laid – the more you think about and crave it, the more likely you are to fuck it up when the opportunity presents itself.

You feel damaged. Marie once said she never wanted a bond as intense as the one you shared, which you said was sad, and moreover meant it. Intensity need not be synonymous with stress and conflict, and mediocrity is hardly the state in which you'd like to spend the rest of your life in, being mistaken for a robot without enough independent programming to have the sense to get out of the rain.

Δ   Δ   Δ   Δ

The Southeast, "The Beach," and Why Dave Eggers Received Damien's Ire (The author's note to the author's note for a yet as untitled and unfinished novel)

For those of you unaware (as surely as Damien was in the summer of 2003), Mr. Eggers wrote a little book called *A Heartbreaking Work of*

Staggering Genius. It is quite fantastic and Damien would have surely loved it if not for the fact that sometime around the fall of 2004 he had started writing his own new novel.

In July 2003, practically coinciding with the launch of the tour for his last novel, his mother Joan had succumbed to stomach cancer. That he had found out she had cancer of any kind only weeks before did little to prepare him for it. He had lost his father at 19 to what he thought was hepatitis, which he would continue to believe till a shit St. Paddy's two years ago.

Having had quite an unreasonable amount of tragedy in his life for a middle class Asian kid who spent his teens in the wilds of Connecticut Damien took this new horrible development as an inevitable function of the cycle of life. Of course that kind of horseshit logic only works if you write self-help books or have miraculously found Jesus (*sorry Bro, still looking*).

That he grew tired of discussing, reading, and promoting his last book may seem a bit whiny to all the struggling writers out there. However, one must explain that at some point the gleeful romp through Latin American self-destruction and self-discovery had inextricably become linked with dealing with an estate, his parents' unfinished lives, and a younger brother whom he dearly loved, but wanted to strangle at times.

Therefore as an act of keeping busy (i.e. non-suicidal) and productive (i.e. working) Damien began writing a novel about an artist whose parents had both died and was saddled with caring for his younger sibling. He was idealistic, though being an artist, not entirely competent, and he and Ronnie's fictional cipher raged out against the world and all it could throw at them whilst colliding with the sort of pop culture nonsense and societal folly that had come to dominate Damien's own little life. It was told with black self-referencing humor that very much fit his state of mind at the time. He got started on the project and was even feeling a bit better about himself since the act of writing was helping him deal with some of the issues that he was facing in his all too real life.

But that is not the novel he is currently working on.

You can imagine Damien's dismay at finding that the book had essentially already been written by Mr. Eggers and his further frustration at discovering *Staggering Genius* was actually pretty damn good. To top it all off it opened with a massive tongue-in-cheek introduction and author note which basically put the one in Damien's last book to shame.

As retribution for such rampant pre-cognizant plagiarism of his life for fiction (ignoring the fact that the book came out before any of this happened to him, which simply indicated that the author was a psychic) he proceeded to take a page out of Mr. Eggers' book and inserted a warning in the intro which went something like this:

Hey all, thanks for picking up the latest opus and let me assure you I will be having many drinks and smokes on you. That said however I feel the need to offer a few bits of warning.

Ahem.

A Crash Course On the Anatomy of Robots

Principally I would advise those looking for another Extranjero *to simply skip the entire first 2 sections of the book. They contain only one poem that I am aware of and no journal material whatsoever let alone email updates. They also have quite a bit to do with depression and death and danger and introspection and all that messy nonsense you can do without.*

In addition, if straightforward narrative is your deal then I would say probably most of section three and all of section four won't be your cup of tea. You would probably hate my last book and I can assure you that you'd be completely justified in doing so. Confessionary writing is lazy stuff indeed. Just ask Harold Bloom. Section five has lots of verse, so you may wanna give it a miss. Since poetry is the ultimate in literary sloth.

I'm confident you will be thrilled to have taken my advice and skipped it.

As an added bonus I might add that section six contains absolutely no poetry – not one verse.
The book opens with quotes, a eulogy, and an introduction that was short listed for the Glimmer Press Short fiction award. I ask you: is there ever anything as boring as quotes or depressing and phony as eulogies? And could someone please tell me why the fuck do there appear to be more awards than writers? Sounds like a scam to me.

Come to think of it, authors of my generation have recently been responsible for an awful lot of sarcastic hip books, often dealing with interpersonal relationships or lack thereof. Most of them don't seem to go anywhere. Who really wants to hear about the trials and tribulations of whiney spoiled twenty and thirty-somethings of first world nations when there are people starving, STARVING I tell you, all across the globe? With this in mind you might as well just skip the second half altogether.

I stand by the Epilogues, even if a fictional protagonist writes one.

As with my last novel, 'Extanjero: Mexico on a Shoestring', names and places and events have been changed to protect myself from libel. Should you find yourself within and disagree let me assure you that you are entirely mistaken. In any case why should you care since you probably make more money than me anyway? Please continue sitting in your cubicles avoiding number crunching and coming up with new ways to create edible plastic. You are doing the world a great service.

Oh, and I live in Mexico so I'm outside the law anyhow so piss off.

(And finally, a bit cryptically)
And if you're reading this Dave I loved your book but please stay out of my head. Enjoy.

This was not the first time Damien felt the plight of all artists, which is essentially to create something new. He had long ago abandoned the idea of a truly original work as defined by narrative, since as with his opinion of music, there were only so many chords to be played. One could leave one's own footprint of style, perspective, and contemporary referencing then hope for the best. Neither was he immune to this in other mediums. Around the same time he read the Eggers's work he watched the film *Garden State* which more or less captured his experiences returning to a small town (Connecticut not Jersey) as a semi-famous artist (Spoken word author music guy as opposed to second rate actor) for his mother's funeral and those left behind. Course he didn't have a living father in that empty house (especially not one as subtle as Ian Holm), his friend MOC wasn't quite as eccentric or close-minded as Peter Sarsgaard's character, and there was no meet-cute with a local girl - rather a string of drunken hook-ups and Jez's eventual arrival to try and save him from complete nervous breakdown.

That's why people love fiction: its neatness is seducing. Characters are well defined and extras are summarized in one word or background, the narrative is engaged to show you something new or take you somewhere, and the end of a book or film is generally final (unless you happen to be in a series which mysteriously manage to end up focused on one main character anyway). Real life can be fairly soul-sucking, tedious, and doesn't make a hell of a lot of sense, which in literary works can turn a whole lot of people off (were she alive you could just ask Joan). A truism or philosophy may sound corny, delusional or immature on paper, whilst in the mouth of Tom Cruise advancing the plot in a sci-fi flick it may be positively inspirational.

Damien remembered an editor's criticism of his last novel set in Mexico. He said it read too much like a memoir, contained too much poetry, and seemed to endlessly list details that had already been covered by other travel authors. He had no interest in memoir writing, hated poetry (even if Damien's more or less was prose with spaces), and kept mentioning *The Beach* as a more successful attempt at setting a contemporary novel in a foreign setting. That the editor himself had never been to Latin America, failed to realize the poetry was of narrative use (he was one of those for whom the simple act of dividing a paragraph into spaced lines had an adverse effect), and that any peer Damien ran into on the road or at shows (his target audience) loved and found it absolutely authentic was all the proof he needed to fire said editor. It did not however diminish his gut feeling that the guy was right. In the end he had heavily edited out poetry or converted it to paragraph format and converted all first person sections to third to reduce the impression of memoir writing. There was even a cheesy unfulfilled romance added to the end (he could not credit Alex Garland for this as having neither read *The Beach* or been to Thailand yet).

As 2005 approached Damien had begun to appraise the major themes of his recent life. Three years of death and doomed relationships in various countries had defined life more or less since the Towers had fallen. On the night before the world changed Damien had dropped Marie on a flight to India. At the time they had an apartment in Brooklyn, two cats, a car, and what had seemed like a mildly promising future. Marie was a successful graphic designer working in midtown and modeling part-time on the side. Damien was a contributing writer for several major pop-culture publications as well as a highly paid academic and corporate freelancer writing mind-numbing prose to make billionaires and bureaucrats sound intelligible. He had plans to head off to Southeast Asia to meet up in a month after finishing work on a Matrix management implementation in a large German Bank (a terminally paranoid one that monitored their employees like Big Brother and Damien was fairly sure had an enormous solid gold Hitler in their basement but at almost $200 an hour he could hardly turn down). They had kissed nervously before the midnight flight and he had driven home alone, doomed to stay up working on information capture templates and watch infomercials till he had to head to his midtown office around 9.

In less than 24 hours he would be staring at the debris from offices floating through the streets and looking at the gigantic dust cloud that enveloped lower Manhattan from his rooftop. He had fled his midtown office after barely getting his car into a lot and observing just how big the WTC looked down Fifth Avenue when completely engulfed in flames. The first had collapsed as he had headed west toward Kienyo's pad. His later arrival at St. Vincent's to donate blood was clearly unnecessary. By the time he got back to his office that afternoon his roommate Jasper was laying on his office floor covered in dust (Damien thought he had done Jasper a favor by outsourcing his work on Liberty Street that morning, only nearly to have killed the poor man). That night as it rained and the atmosphere moved over the East River Damien swore he could smell burning flesh and metal.

His major clients: Fortune 100 banking institutions, government, and non-profits would have little need for freelance writers focusing on organizational design after this. Marie decided to stay in India and eventually they broke up thousands of miles apart as she explored her end of the world sexual freedom and Damien eventually abandoned New York for Mexico where he would meet

Jezebel and finish his last novel. Joan's death and the revelation of his father's past would quickly crush his triumphant return to the city and book deal in 2003. The stumbling reconstruction of a book tour and his parents' lives while living once more in a city he had sworn off all but killed him these last two years. Soon he would be back in Mexico with Jez, another casualty of his patterns, and by the summer another would have risen in its place, with a girl named Ivy and different, if connected and perhaps slightly more tragically comic, pitfalls.

It is close now.

In some ways it is as if time had never moved since that cold night in September when he dropped Marie at JFK on a flight to Madras. Damien still longed for the Southeast. He wanted to roll back time and make it right, for his soul, his sense of self and time and history - if for nothing else a sense of completion.

He needed it to move on.

Δ   Δ   Δ   Δ

They'll get you for $25

It's summer 2001, just months before the towers, and I'm riding down Bowery with DJ Jasper, two bros from Cali and my girl Marie. We're below Delancey, almost at the bridge and on to boogey down Brooklyn. Jasper is talking about watching DVD's, he just picked up two new joints and he's convinced us to head home rather than cruise the city. We've just come from Drinkland, and we're a little hurt up, so we say why not. We can always go to Lego's old crib and spin some records if we get bored. At this point an unmarked car pulls behind us and mutters incoherency over the megaphone; it takes a second to realize that the black caprice classic is addressing us. We pull over just before the bridge entrance. One of the Cali kids asks if it's a monument or something. My girl Marie says it's just the entrance.

"Can I see your license and registration?" this little Indian cop demands.

His partner is shining a flashlight on my hands to make sure I ain't hiding nothing. We all mutter and laugh cause we've been joking tonight about Giuliani's upper middle class "quality of life" bullshit and how you get fined for fuckin breathing. It figures tonight a burned out tail light would be our undoing.

It occurs to me just for a second while we're talking that Jasper might have something on his record. I ask him and he says no way. We sit. The kids from Cali ask what's taking so long. We just figure it's the cops writing a ticket. We talk about what bullshit it is that they must be writing a ticket for a busted taillight. After all that's the most clichéd fuckin segue way into police nonsense ever conceived. And how can you tell you got one of those anyway? I mean, when are you actually at that vantage?

Anyhow we're sitting there and we start to hear sirens and everyone jokes about how it's the cavalry coming for us. I know at that moment that we're fucked. I mean after you've dealt with the Gestapo enough, you just know these things. When the unmarked sister car and undercover cab pull up, I know the DT's are gonna roll out like a fucking clown car and start some shit.

A Crash Course On the Anatomy of Robots

After the typical what the fuck shit, we get silent and the cops ask us to step out of the car. My girl has already started spouting some shit about the land of the free, but I keep quiet cause I know things are about to get really stupid. They explain to Jasper that since he has $25 dollars in outstanding fines that his license is suspended in New York. Cause of Giuliani iron grip that means there's zero tolerance for driving without a license, and that means Jasper is headed to the tombs.

I don't really see J for the rest of this police action except to watch him cuffed and give him a heads up when they truck him away but he's always in my peripheral looking tired and confused. I'm pretty sure he has some "yeh" in his pocket and they're probably gonna really fuck him over when he gets to the station. The man just wanted to watch some DVD's, that's what I keep thinking.

So anyhow let me describe the scene. The six cops at the scene are preoccupied with inventing myriad means of fucking with us. This excludes the arresting officer who is with Jasper the whole time, and seems like the only decent man among the whole mess of fuckers, even though he won't let me have a word with J after I sign for his car. It all starts with the dicks telling us to wait on the sidewalk while they push Jasper against a car and cuff him. Marie is crying and pleading with a particularly fuckhead pig. He tells her to shut up and asks me if she's been drinking cause his puny fucking brain can't fathom that throwing someone in the tombs for $25 in fines is actual injustice.

Don't get me wrong, there are many reasons we could have been arrested that night, and despite the fact that I believe that all of them were victimless crimes, I would have preferred that we had gotten fucked with for any one of them more than this piddly petty unbelievable shit.

So anyhow the cop yells at Marie to hit the curb and my friends from Cali are in shock that we have landed in NYPD Blue (when you come from the land of Rodney King this is a real social statement). I am calmly trying to ask the cops what fine Jasper could have possibly incurred that would be a mere 25 dollars since the smallest ticket I've ever gotten was double that, years ago. At this point this short little redhead bitch with a 70's mustache and probably no fucking dick proceeds to snidely ask me if I'm a judge or a lawyer. He actually starts yelling at me and getting in my face. I'm thinking of NWA. Without his gun and his badge I would've pulled his fucking tongue through his asshole and told him to find the chewy filled center. If I see this fucker off duty I still may. You hear me bitch? Anyone can be tough with a crew. Your mommy probably likes to fuck vegetables cause your daddy was too busy with you right?

Anyhow I volunteer my license cause someone's gotta take the car. They tell us that technically they should impound it and make us walk home. They also mention that my girl should calm down and yet again claim that she must be drunk. The truth is that there's no way they want to spend the time and paperwork taking the car. The fact is that Marie is clearly the most sober of us all but they'd rather choose to ignore this and paint her as a drunk hysteric. Not to complain, but it would have almost been better to go to the tombs for DWI that fulfill these cocksnots "quality" quota. On top of this, while I'm trying to ask about my friend this fucker is now hounding me about some shit from three years ago that I paid like:

A Crash Course On the Anatomy of Robots

"So I see that you got some shit on your license Damien," he grins nastily.
"Excuse me," I say.
"New Rochelle, speeding," he announces in triumph.

For a second I think that maybe I have forgotten to pay some age-old debt or still have some bench warrant for smoking a cigarette in the subway or some other such fascist nonsense. It takes me a second to realize that the dude is referring to some ancient speeding ticket, incurred in a bumblefuck town not even near here, which I already paid and he just wants to break my balls about.

Anyhow, there is no hope of bail for Jasper tonight. He sits in the tombs probably eating doped cheese sandwiches and getting fucked with by minor herb dealers and escorts. All I gotta say is that Giuliani is a spineless Nazi catering to the upper white middle class, policing neighborhoods that don't need policing, and seriously fucking up my quality of life. I live in Brooklyn, and it ain't no safer cause of fuckface #1. But since his bitch ass came into office I obviously ain't no safer anywhere else in the city. I hope your candy ass alpha male no dick Klingon looking ass dies a horrible painful cancerous death. The cops, as big of fuckheads as they are, wouldn't have the power to turn into such mob mentaled pigs without you.

Fuck you bitch. You can take your 25 dollars and whatever else the people owe you, and shove it up your dirty little ass till you're puking change.

Baile Funky and Star-Studded New York

February 2005

K hands you a brew to soften the edges and points out some trendy little urban culture mag folded in half to balance an amp. It looks familiar so you pick it up and open right into an article called "They'll Get you For $25" you did a few years back. It brought you joy at the time to hear that the magazine lost a sponsor because of it. This was of course right around the time the towers happened and Rudy Giuliani became an international fucking hero. The War on Terror (which you'll notice is the acronym t.w.o.t.) had yet to begin, and Rudy's fascism would soon be replaced by Bloomberg's imperialism—more or less buying himself the position of mayor. You get a wave of nostalgia, embarrassment, and a bit of a grin, absentmindedly thinking of Marie's hollering and Jasper's current distaste for you.

So fucking young and stupid, a silly story from a sillier time you say and leave it at that.

So try this. Your name is Damien Michael Wood, a not terribly respected spoken word artist but at least marginally well-known author. In the years since your last novel, *Extranjero: Mexico on a Shoestring* (essentially a poetry-laced, drug fueled sex romp through down South), the book sold well enough to buy a house and bar in central Mexico, but not well enough to guarantee a follow-up.

A Crash Course On the Anatomy of Robots

At the moment you're in a Chinatown studio listening to a remix of an obscure Brazilian throwback and Kienyo is trying to convince you this is the wave of the future and you cannot imagine trying to put poetry to it.

Originally there was singing in the *favellas,* the ghettos of darkest Rio. Picture street kids and professionals, all damned with the worst equipment imaginable: boom boxes, headphones for mics, old mixed tapes with tape over the record protect – that sort of thing. Now think of the decadent early 80's ripping that sound into beloved Miami. Think Sheena Easton. Think Freestyle.

Now think of that dying with the rest of that decade's pop and being resurrected in those same South American streets it was born; re-adopting the mongrel spoils and making it ghetto again. Quietly it goes unnoticed throughout the 90's, the odd *hoopty* (a beat up ride with the trimmings) cruising through Bushwick aside.

Now think it's 2005, the middle of the first decade of the millennium and a talented producer has the wise-ass yet genius idea of taking what was and remixing it yet again with hip-hop and house, bridging the generational and continental gap.

Simple.

He takes the deaf-mute screaming into a boom box, the 70's divas that never were, an 8-year-old boy singing about the boogey man – he gives them a voice in a country that can't speak the language or understand the lyrics but likes to shake their hipster booties to the newest craze. He takes what amounts to countless generations of recycling of a product that was questionable in the first place and makes it palatable to the dance floors and private parties of Manhattan, and convinces them it's actually enjoyable.

Simple. Brilliant.

Now Kienyo is writing more poetry than me. This guy has some audacity. A mere DJ, yet effortlessly luminous – hell I should kill him on general principle.

Of course K points out that you've been watching far too much cinema. *Maybe I've lost my ability to distinguish between brilliance and immediate hackery – immediate in its imminence to make you believe you've seen something brilliant.*

You just realized that if Kienyo did in fact die and this journal was found you'd be blamed for murder rather than literary humor. You don't kill him though, even when he accuses you of racism. You just drink whiskey and smile.

Funny, prophetic.

The guy who just walked in the studio… you can't place who this fucking guy looks like. He's got on a bandana and on the whole is dressed for Southern California summer 15 years ago, despite the fact it's clearly winter in New York in the new millennium. *I've got it – he's a dead ringer for that extreme sports guy on MTV — the one who's been on Melrose Place or some shit like that.*

That's bad... I shouldn't do that. Despite the fact you've been compared to Brandon Lee, Johnny Depp, and once an amalgamation of the entire cast of 21 Jump Street (yes including the plump one) you'd like to believe we are all unique looking beings. All that shit about 20-something facial templates being the composite for every person on earth is just a bit disheartening. *I guess with like 7 billion people that's either likely or impossible, then again maybe ants think they all look unique. Maybe robots do too.* Even if this guy looks like Dan Cortez on a harrowing bender, he still might be cool... Nope. X-treme Sport man just nearly unplugged the whole damn studio. The guy's like a nemesis. *No projecting here. There may have been a time, probably in the early 80's, when I wanted to be that guy, but I most certainly have never been fortunate or unfortunate enough to be him.*

Drunk as hell leaving the studio then securing two slices of the worst pizza Delancey has to offer you hop in a cab after unintentionally being a hypocrite *(you know you should slow down on the speed K)* to pay $20 to make it back to the upper east. Let off a block from home you walk past the obnoxious frat bar you live above and Christian Slater leans out the window and starts yelling at you *Hey man, you're beautiful. What are ya? Korean?*

You stop, stare in disbelief at your childhood idol from *Heathers* and say *no I'm Chinese and Irish.*

Chinese and Irish, Jesus, that's beautiful, hey come on inside and have a drink he says whilst his two of his friends mumble disapproval.

It looks dead in there man you say glancing into the empty bar where the only sounds are of a Mexican janitor sweeping up. *Plus the door's locked.*

The actor walks around and unlocks it for you. Once inside you discern that the two accomplices must be a current girlfriend and publicist. She keeps her head down refusing to make eye contact while the publicist keeps shaking his head and saying *we should really go.* They introduce themselves as Dave, Bill, and Susan. You go along with it as Christian runs around back and grabs you an Amstel Light.

    So why are you here man? He puts his hand on the bar.

    Umm... I live there you point upward

    The all-seeing eye eh? he says disinterested.

    Yeah listening to "Living on a prayer" karaoke style all night long you smile.

    Uh-huh

The actor glances around and starts stuffing beers in all the available pockets on his brown overcoat. The publicist looks even dourer as the girl starts getting insistent with *really Christian, let's get out of here, you coming to my place or not?*

A Crash Course On the Anatomy of Robots

Don't you mean Dave? you say *What are your guys' real names anyhow?* They laugh and keep avoiding eye contact, the guy staring at the actor, the girl staring into the bar as if trying to identify new forms of mold. *Hey look at me for a second* you say to her and she lifts up her gaze. You hold one of those significant exchanges for maybe 3 seconds that feels like a minute before Christian comes behind you to lead out the Calvary.

Alright, later he says and goes for the shake. You can't help yourself and hand him a card and a sticker before they flee out the door and into the night. Looking around the empty bar and you slam your beer before the owner can come out and ask you what the fuck you're doing there.

On an unseasonably warm day last weekend you and Jez, your current Texan girlfriend, head to the West Side to catch an exhibition at the Nomadic Museum. It's aptly named since it consists of a series of giant shipping crates stacked for the duration of the month with makeshift paths and hanging parchments. In front of you in line are a stunning girl in shockingly good shape and a rumpled looking suburbanite with a baseball cap and flannel tied around the waist. When they turn around you realize they are the tabloid couple of the month: Giselle and Leo. You once rode around in a weed delivery van with Leo years ago when he was still relatively unknown and his eye contact bespeaks a clueless sort of remembrance. You decide not to make mention of the drug deal or his fat ass.

After the exhibit you head to the Frying Pan, an old barge turned club where your buddy Lego is installing some new sound gear. Jon Stewart is walking past you along the two-block walk and Jez nearly can't stop herself from shaking his hand.

There are so fucking many of us on the cusp or those who have momentarily grasped the fire. Playing pool with the lesser members of the Wu Tang Clan, sharing smokes with the chick from Roseanne, making eyes with a 70's rock icon's actress daughter - you often think of the guitarist from a one hit wonder band that begged you to come to his show in a bowery shit-hole while his track was still getting top forty play. He looked worse off than you did. Which, as a poet, is difficult.

There was also this guy at an East Village party that comes to mind. You hit it off by the bathroom and talked for hours about the trouble with art and survival and limelight in this town. Everyone is anonymous and simultaneously famous. Near the end of the night you told him not to worry since your times would come and joked about how his foot was already in the door since he looked so much like this one comedian from the recently defunct *The State*. It was with no small measure of mutual embarrassment that he mumbled that he hadn't gotten real work since.

We are all seconds from the flames.

Casual Malevolence

February 2005

It's been a week since the Slater incident and Kienyo has left a card under the expensive assembly-required Swedish-engineered skeleton of your loft. It says "Friends of the Family" and guarantees admission to a swank hidden club in the Meatpacking district. For some reason Santa is on it despite the fact it's the end of February.

I think of Christmas in the Chihuahuan desert just a few months ago when I started smoking again.

With nowhere to go these things start to eat you alive. It'd been more than a decade since you spent the holidays with a complete family. Jez's most nerve-wracking stress-inducing throw-down Texas holiday ever would have ranked as one of your betters even then.

You try and reminisce about the last, years ago in Southwestern Connecticut - but any degree of accuracy is relative, buried in months of Orange Sunshine MOC made good on a week after purchasing the batch. After that it was free acid for everyone, far cheaper than booze.

Before that you were 17 and you just don't recall. Maybe you were drunk, maybe it was hellish, probably both.

There is your father and his pajamas. That's what you can see, probably due to the aid of photography and its instant nostalgia. Ten times too big for you, the wool hangs over everything and is wrapped in parts more like a blanket than anything else. The guitar, a classical, is at least twice your size making your fingers look comical; you, wearing that shit-eating grin while waiting for them to fully get up, the brightness of the day and sound of their slumber still a recent memory.

As it dusted outside on the industrial highways of Texas I was told it is the first fall since '89. I was 14 in that year, a freshman at prep school and already at the end of my illustrious academic career — and shortly, very shortly, pleasant non-tragic family gatherings.

That day, like the snow, it happened again, in a different state, with a different family, but just as cold and just as rare.

I'll be cool again.

When you're tired of the riffraff that make up the world and all the gated communities cannot keep you quite exclusive enough…

When all the stores are closed and your car keeps breaking laws not slowing down for pen-wielding poets — no damn good anyhow…

When the jokes are all inside and you're inside out and the dead just aren't listening to your pleas for please close this cause they never listened anyway and now have an excuse...

When the fast food reality can't move fast enough and the radio host can't take away the sound of the infant screaming and dog barking...

When Dylan quotes Nietzsche and Proust quotes you and all the quotes in the world won't fill up a book and your heart feels like dying and your mind feels like sleeping but you can't get it moving cause psychosomnia and hypochondria are mutually exclusive...

I'll be cool. I'll be cool again.

Δ Δ Δ Δ

Back to Robots

The thing of it is, maybe the uncanny valley has to do with more than just our visual perception. What if that slight imperceptible shift in our viewing of someone or something extends beyond just the appearance of normal or cute, into our interpretation of whom we think they might be – a social valley as it were?

Everyone has interacted with someone on the street or a couple stools away at the bar that looks a bit off and generates mistrust or apprehension. I don't care who you are if you think you haven't you're just shoving those thoughts down to a nice comfortable hiding space in your psyche. It's like discrimination of any sort, just a bit more nebulous.

Conversely we've all met *friendlies* - those people who gain instant trust and openness due to nothing but their warm smiling faces and genetic luck. It is not hard to see how Ted Bundy got away with it for so long and why everyone insisted on continually fucking with Michael Jackson.

But perhaps there is another valley, one that only some of us who are more open to our intuition than others can sense. It is the missing pieces in the vacuous blonde, the odd little bit that is off in the nice old man at the deli, that extra little gap we have to ignore when talking with the stranger that no can figure out whose friend brought.

We sense something *off*. We wouldn't go so far as to say wrong, since that would probably denote some level of judgment or pretension on our part. If the off is enough, we will find ways to avoid them, and if tolerable, we will simply label them eccentric or strange, and do much talking behind their back.

Of course we are not alone in realizing that *they*, or that *we* as it may be are off - that some of our robotic parts have been manufactured. One senses the missing pieces in oneself and tries to compensate. If one is morally groundless one becomes overly religious or spiritual. Not because one is truly faithful or altruistic, rather one realizes that like any mask the mask of normality must be worn at all times. We see the valley in others' eyes. The uncomfortable laughter shared amongst our kind. We see it and it frightens us into normality, into a kind of societal submission. Shielding us from overt attack and snide undercurrents till we believe it ourselves and question the emptiness that dominates and permeates throughout our beings.

And you who have seen my metal limbs and plastic eyes, who have turned in polite disgust, and pretend ignorance – You have the audacity to ask why I hate you boring fucking people?

Δ   Δ   Δ   Δ

The Asian Journal of Damien Wood Part 1 (cont'd)

April 16, 2006 - Southern Thailand
At Pen's Bungalows Yet Again

In Thong Nai Pan you eye someone too young, find yourself too bored, and too tired to write about things you've already done.

It all feels a bit soft, like Mexican shores and words from a girl, who was and is, lost to you ("I like you" in the sand, swaying hammock kisses in the humid swarming evenings to bad reggae, U2 and Manu Negra).

Electronic emails tentacles stab and hurt, once thought to be banished, but only changed and matured: different animals of similar species.

A Crash Course On the Anatomy of Robots

You crave warm dark flesh, and touches that sing, but it appears the effort has been lost in libations, loves, and stories that were once real and stimulating - maddeningly alive and fresh - now barely worth the effort.

An Iranian hustler talks trash in German. A motorcycle refugee smokes spliffs in the sun. A duo of Englishmen scope birds and the one heals from septic leg wounds.

There is no music here, only the sounds of ocean and long-tail boats, frustratingly calm water warm as bath that makes wounds linger longer than they should - the nature of the sea and of the injuries it nurses consuming you.

A cute Scot, young beyond her years rolls in the "world pool" with an Irish hard-drinkin woman who vomited on your feet last night when you left an Israeli beauty to nurse an inebriated friend.

We know nothing of each other really. Only names, towns lived in, places visited, years lived - barely more than could be read on a resume, barely worth the energy to discover more.

There is the desire for affection and company and abandon.

There is the hope for something more but fear of its aftermath.

There is this but there is more.

This is a paradox of simplicity.

May 7, 2006

Your room smells like wet dog and your clothes are covered with small black insects feeding on your body's cast off proteins. Heading to Krabi tomorrow and it couldn't be soon enough – bored and lovely here. You've completely had it with Ivy and her emails. If she needs to believe you were doomed doomed doomed and pine over a CLEARLY doomed drug addict then fuck her. You've said all that you can say and none of it got through her thick skull so the hell with it. *I'm comfortable with being disliked, just another part to replace.*

I'm the six million dollar fuckin man.

Δ   Δ   Δ   Δ

A Crash Course on Destination, Confessional Literature, Poetry, and Prose

Let's talk a little about poetry and confessional literature, shall we?

Don't bother looking up the word poetry. All you'll get is the same old, 'same old' – you know - beautiful, imaginative, elevated thoughts, 'even' prose with poetic qualities; art of rhythmical composition - the whole nine yards.

Damien isn't quite sure about the whole elevated thoughts bit. Nonetheless, he will concede that poetry, at its base, is indeed prose in a metered, or at the very least, versed form. By this logic, prose can be seen as a

type

of poetry

with the spacing

pulled

out.

Confessional Literature is a genre which draws from and presents elements in the author or character(s) that are deeply personal in nature. Whether fictional or contrived (or contrived fiction) these present experience from a tell-all, intimate, conversational and (let's face it) confessional tone. (*See Special Features section for examples*).

For Damien, a confessional writer and poet, his method of delivery varies from narrative fiction to email updates to journal entries and narrative verse, hopefully conveying the range of intimacy meant to reach the reader. A third person narrative may guide you through physical realities, whilst a first person poem puts you in the protagonist's head. Some might describe it as the difference between flying first class or taking a chicken bus - the equivalent of trying to find a shitty hut in Burma, but I digress…they are both examples of methods to reaching a particular literary destination.

For example, if he's talking about flying from LA to Bangkok, he may describe the airports and various modes of transport (crowded, annoying, hot, cold, faux modern, rickshaw, bus, tin can, regurgitated air con). You've all been to an airport or bus terminal and it will take no great leap of imagination to see yourself there.

But perhaps at a certain terminal he sees a girl and they make eye contact. She smiles and walks off while Damien scribbles journals. At this point Damien, the sentimental sap he can be, may start writing an interlude on the possibilities that existed

in

that brief space of time

when they saw each other

and the tea

in the back

of his throat

mixed with cigarette smoke

to remind him

of his mother.

Here you would have what some might describe as a poem, but Damien would prefer to see it as prose (or ahem "literary work") in a more easily consumable form. The words themselves have been slowed down, cut, and metered out as to express a seriousness and harmony and - oh fuck it, *elevated thoughts* - that may be otherwise obscured in a straight forward paragraph. He's laid it all out you see, the pauses, dramatic breaks

you

can read

Without thinking

at

All.

Course the irony is that most people spot breaks in lines and their minds start to wander back to some high school nightmare of Shakespeare or Wordsworth or some such deconstructionist hell where every line was chewed apart and reassembled into some flimsy argument of which characters were gay and how T.S. Eliot was really a fascist and you can see how tiresome this starts to get.

Put simply, if you suddenly notice that a bit of prose abruptly leaps into verse don't panic. Imagine you are watching a film and a voiceover has appeared (annoying plot device I know).

Or just ignore the spaces and read it like the printer really, really fucked up. Or if you must, as it has been included for your convenience, just skip the fucker and read it when you finish the book at the back of the appendix,

or simply

don't read it

at all.

Damien is a fictional character who cannot judge you (though I will harbor feelings of resentment toward you till the end of my days – sorry, shit breaking character).

Speaking of which let's find out a bit more about him, shall we? Something along the lines of:

In the beginning...

Parents (A Crash Course on Death, Family, and Fallout)

"I've been a moonshiner for seventeen long years
I spent all my money on whiskey and beer
I go to some hollow and set up my still
And if whiskey don't kill me I don't know what will"

-Irish Traditional (Dylan Variant)

A Crash Course On the Anatomy of Robots

Origins (Not Like Heroes and Hiro, like umm...Damien)

Joan Wood was born Li-Yun Chen in the Guangzhou Province of China sometime in the late 30's or early 1940's. Damien does not know for sure since the records of his mother's family exodus to the states are littered with inconsistent birth dates and questionable 'relatives' his grandfather brought over from their village (to this day he isn't quite sure who he is related to and who just happened to be good buddies with his '*Gung Gung*' in the homeland). However he does know one detail that narrows the range.

Damien's mother always had an almost irrationally powerful bias against the Japanese. Once, when he had asked her the reason she responded with her first memory. It was in the middle of the night and she clutched to her mother's chest. They ran through a burning field and little Li Yun screamed in her arms whilst bombs dropped all around them. She remembered the stars and fire and the explosions till she died and never got over being freaked out by loud noises.

The second Sino-Japanese war covered roughly the same timeline as the Second World War (1937-45) and amongst a million other infringements over time is why the Japanese are universally hated in Mainland China. You may have seen a little bit about it in the film *The Last Emperor*, where the character played by Joan Chen gets addicted to heroin, and the emperor basically sells the Forbidden City in a yard sale to save his ass. It is with no small irony that

Damien thinks about his mother's choice to change her name to Joan when she arrived in New York City in 1961.

Joan spent the 60's going to school, working at her father's restaurant, learning English, and eventually getting a job at a large pharmaceutical firm doing research. It goes without saying that she studied science and excelled at it, that all of her money went back into the family, that the restaurant was Chinese, and that she lived at home under her parents' thumb till she was on the other side of 30 and met a fellow researcher named Bryan Wood.

Bryan Tomas Wood was born in 1942 of a working class Irish family in South Boston. He had 2 brothers, one of whom would die in Vietnam; the other Bryan would push away for reasons Damien could never know. It is really only worth mentioning this brother as the father of several children including one named Ash. Damien would eventually have a rather uncomfortable conversation in a pub with Ash that would essentially demolish his entire perception of who his parents were - but let's get back to Bryan.

Like many father-hating, self-loathing, lower class social climbers, Bryan would work his way through school away from family and dive into work in pursuit of wealth, happiness, and the American dream. For him, a sensitive man at heart, this would consist of an OK degree, from an OK school, with OK grades. He bankrolled the degree by working considerably Not OK jobs then moving to New York after graduating, and eventually getting in as a research assistant at a big drug company. Years later he would become a peddler for such giant immoral conglomerates, jumping from pharma to pharma, selling millions in questionable raw materials for even more questionable purposes. But that was decades away. For now, he was young and driven, if not a bit insecure, and it was the end of the 60's in New York. He had an OK apartment in the village and was even an OK musician (guitar, of course, the OK instrument of choice). He would eventually move into the R&D section of the company where he worked and where he was considered, as he would be throughout his life, a really swell guy.

It was in this unnamed corporate testing ground that Joan and Bryan would meet on some project most likely involving toxins and small bunnies and it was in this decidedly unromantic setting that they would come to know each other. It was now the early 70's she was a head researcher (almost unheard of for both a woman and foreigner at the time) and he was a mid-level technician.

Joan was polite and respectful, extremely intelligent and to Bryan, amongst many others, incredibly beautiful. He was earnest and sweet in a way she was not accustomed to in Chinese men (persistent as well, but that particular male trait is fairly universal). Still, he was attractive and fit and driven in his own way (even if he drank too much and insisted on doing bad Al Stewart covers in crappy bars). In a way he represented for her a gateway into an America that her parents did not understand, that perhaps even she did not understand; and for him, she was about as far from South Boston as he could imagine. They began to fall in love and soon married.

Joan was then disowned.

You couldn't really blame her parents. That's just how it was then. We won't go into all the details for reasons we'll discuss later, but let's just say this still isn't the fucking *Joy Luck Club* and we're sure you've got the internet. Anyway for marrying a *Gwi-lo* (*white ghost* would be the nicest translation, *soulless devil* is moving toward the more accurate), Joan was left out in the cold. Bryan's small family consisted of a dying mother, lunatic father, and brother who he didn't speak to for reasons even he couldn't admit to himself (but probably have to do with that same damn pub conversation Damien and Ash would have). Relations with her family were virtually nonexistent until the middle of 1974 when Joan announced she was pregnant. There's nothing like grandchildren to squelch the good old disowning thing. The next year Damien Michael Wood arrived, sporting slanty little wacky blue eyes, and wispy blond hair.

Over his lifetime Damien's hair would go from blond to auburn to jet black and finally settle into a mad hodge podge of dark brown and burnt tones that would go the full fall spectrum in the sun (imagine childhood torments of tearing out blond strays to avoid being called gray at 10). His eyes too would grow darker and darker. Most people thought his eyes were anywhere between a light hazel to dark mahogany depending on his mood. He was tall, but not huge, and had a Western build with Asian hair tendencies (head, face, pits, and privates: check. everywhere else: nada).

All of this is to say Damien could be described as a

half breed,

mongrel,

mulatto,

ABC (American Born Chinese),

Banana (Yellow outside, white inside),

Lost Generation,

A Crash Course On the Anatomy of Robots

Eurasian,

One foot in one country,

One foot out,

Chink,

Slant,

Nip,

Ching-Chong,

Kung-fooey fighting,

Math excelling,

Chess killing,

Computer wrecking,

walking stereotype,

or insult receptacle.

And probably has been,

and occasionally still is,

but this

as said

ain't *Heroes*

or the fucking *Joy Luck Club*.

This, dear reader is to assure you of several things that will not happen in this novel, or if they do happen will happen within the realm of the real and not some insane drama-filled Jackie Chan kung fu, Hiro time stopping with a funny accent, Beau Sea histrionic, Margaret Cho LA vomit, racial pandering bullshit.

Damien is half-Chinese and a spoken-word artist and writer. Yes he has written a piece or two about race, but he generally thinks this is weak and easy and burying a potentially groundbreaking new form of poetry which is why you won't see him on Def Jam anytime soon (not till Mos stops all this acting presenting bullshit and gets back to saving hip-hop, and Mr. Simmons stops spending so much time on his clothing line and gets some actual fuckin poets on the show).

Damien will spend more than a bit of time in Asia where there are bound to be endless times someone asks if he is:

Vietnamese

Thai

Cambodian

Burmese

Laotian

Chinese

Pacific

Fucking

Islander

and whatever other ethnicity you can imagine. Of course since this is no different than any other day of his life you too can stop asking since now you know and can desist with all the "but where's he *really* from?" bollocks.

Eulogy for my mother, 7/17/03

It's been about 9 years since I've stood at this podium. At the time I was nineteen and I had not been in Connecticut or this parish in years. I remember I was desperately trying to think of something profound to say. My father had just passed, with some minimal degree of warning, but ultimately suddenly. At the time, I was instantly launched back into my mother and brother's life full force. I did the best I could, which I guess is what we all do when these moments arise, and of course, as we all do, I wish I had done better.

*"Mother" is such a strange word, familiar to us all. She is the foundation in our lives, what we envision when we think of home, of comfort, or love - the idea of a maternal presence, a model of femininity, the human being who means the most — the least artificial or robotic. Joan was, of course, a fantastic woman, much more than that. She was what we all think mothers should be. From my own extremely subjective view, she was **the** perfect mother. Giving, strong, caring, concerned (perhaps a little too much), and always there for us; she was, simply, a beautiful person.*

This is not to say that my mother and I had a "perfect" relationship, far from it. Culture, generation, and outlook all played major roles in what charitably could be described as a communication gap consistently seeking to be closed. My mother was conservative and traditional in many ways. Since my brother and I are both artists, needless to say we disagreed with her on most worldly issues. But she was always there for us, when my brother needed someone to talk to, or I needed a place to stay, and she loved us more than we deserved to be loved, and was quick to express it. She may not have always understood our lives, but she tried, and always supported us, even when she didn't. In ways she never recovered from my father's death, which was totally understandable given their closeness.

Ultimately I guess the question is, "Who does?" We all have those loves in our lives and ideas of our futures or those that have not yet been or have not yet been lost. My mother loved proverbs and sayings and to quote the overused adage, "It is better to have loved..." and you know the rest.

I believe that my parents have now become united - I have to. They were a pair so deeply in love that it is all I can believe and find satisfactory. As I stand here, I realize that there are many obvious things I could say about her now. For example, she was born in China and her heart never left though she never regretted leaving; or that she was a painter and gardener, and a scientist… or a lover of food and phenomenal creator cook; a family woman, traditionally Chinese yet distinctly American, and in the end, despite her constant proclamations of being profoundly unable to understand such words, a poet, if not in words themselves, then in life.

She was and will always be loved. By friends so numerous and diverse it boggles the mind, by a caring family spread across this globe that loved and loves her unconditionally and fully.

She was and is my mother. I loved her. I love her. And always will.

Δ   Δ   Δ   Δ

Re-writing for you with FreeCell and smokes

New York - March 2005

I'm playing solitaire in the dark with the memory of my parents. I start game after game obsessively checking the statistics and cheating my way out of negative scores by signing out before the computer can log the results. Of course it is my refusal to emotionally accept history. Of course it is the repetitive mantra of denial manifest in neurotic acts.

But I did point it out; surely that must count for something.

I killed my girlfriend last night. I'm smoking her Pall Malls, which I always hated. I can never afford to buy the menthols I so infinitely prefer.

I like to say I'm a poet, but I'm really a pusher. That is to say I score emotions and words and appearances from the street. From countless corners and midnight bars, from empty parks, and soulless malls, from choked rush hour overpasses and industrial hot spots – I've got my sources. I take this raw product and refine it into something commercially palatable. I don't got that pure shit, that died with James and Homer and The Dubliners. But I try to cut pleasant, a sentiment here, some pretension there. Mainly I self-deprecate and simmer the mix with some bullshit Yoda style truisms. I cut it all down with Woody Allen's three S's: self-important, sophomoric, and self-indulgent. Whatever those old white men uptown tell you, that literary shit is yesterday's junk and shooting it is like Drano in a Crystal bottle: real pretty death shit. But business is slow these days as all the customers seem to be dying or making their own junk. Pall Malls will have to do.

I got a call from another pusher today who doesn't smoke at all or touch his own product. You should never trust anyone who can't stomach his or her own shit - though I've been told the opposite by that uptown gang. He told me *Damien, I think this is killing me*, and I told him to *stop quoting Billy Joel*. He said *no I'm serious man, I feel like I'm just on the cusp of something big, maybe an agent or advance or some shit*. I quoted Bill the Butcher and told him *if you go on believing that Jack you're on the road to damnation*. But who the fuck am I to talk anyway? He said *I hear you man, I hear you*, though I don't think he did. That's about the gist of it. How this lasted twenty minutes is beyond me.

Sometimes we drift - just kinda float through life cause the alternative is too much. I'm not talking some clichéd unbearable lightness of being which is of course another fucking cliché, and that is of course, another unnecessary revelation, not to mention a cliché, but what I mean surrounds clichés or at the very least stale themes. The human experience is limited. Every story, song, or work of art seems to have the same basic premise. There are only so many riffs you can do on loss and love and hate and the experience or observation or exercise of them that it ultimately simply comes down to style and background. Maybe that's why visual artists can go so much more abstract and not be immediately called amateur. When Joyce wrote Finnegan's Wake the old white men of the day (of whom Harold Bloom is their heir) were quick to point out that he died before he could reach any reasonable conclusion and that he was probably completely off his fucking rocker anyway (the second bit being answer to any contention of the first).

A Crash Course On the Anatomy of Robots

We get to paint pretty pictures and scramble'em all up, whether through our own tired perspectives or gimmicky tricks akin to freak show strategy. We aim for oh's and ah's of a crowd too desperate to invest meaning in a headless chicken. Talk about the death of culture all you want, we were fucked on that horse from the start. If you can tell me the major advance between cave art and *Goodfellas* without using the word complexity I'll give you a dollar. And for what it's worth, a couple of grunts while jerking off and stealing your dead friend's girl after killing your friend, well that's as good as any book I've read. One look out of a window on a boring road on acid can cure you of any illusions you may have about the greatest writers of all time and their attention to detail.

My dad used to take me to the Upper West Side when I was little. From what I have intuited it was a benign yet desperate desire on his part to imprint me with what I could have if I worked hard enough. The smell of the horses and carriages on the park, the rows of brownstones and impeccably composed denizens, the spacious halls at the private club he was a member of, where rows of dark hallways lit monuments of great past athletic events and political deeds - it is only with time that these become as they are to me now, both nostalgic and bitter. The two can be the same if you step back far enough.

By my guess, which is only that, it was in the haze of steam and flaccid old penises that he trolled unaware and found what did him in. Maybe it was some small bathhouse in the village between his gigs as a guitarist, or that fancy athletic club where I last saw him healthy and jerked off to free cable while he lay with his demons. He was so proud to be a member.

I never knew why he hated the city so, why he hated me living there, and why we had become so estranged. When I try to make sense of it my mother's passing and a chat with my cousin on St. Paddies is mostly what comes to mind.

The setting, any Irish pub you can think of. This one was in Providence but you can imagine it the same anywhere. Like Chinese food in ghettos, or brasseries in Paris, you know this place intimately, and if not, a description is akin to a 12-year-old's views on excess and depravity based on reading Miller. It was dark, and there was old wood, and old men, and cigarettes. If you like, imagine that The Pogues were playing and the day had come on.

"I've got something to tell you Damien," he says, this cousin named Ash.

You love me man? I ask, *you wish that we met more often,* I say and throw my free arm around him keeping my balance.

"Well of course that, you're my cuz and the closest I've got which my father thinks is sad but he's from another generation, your father's, his brother's that is."

I know who my father was Ash, how bout another round?

"In a second cuz, in a second, but I want to tell you this first and you can decide if you wanna tell Ronnie but that's not really my business."

Ronnie is my brother and before I continue I must point out that Ash has a lisp, not the kind you're born with but developed from years in New England, the rage of alcohol specific to our Irish bloodline, and a certain proclivity for drama that is jarringly obvious to all but himself. Ash follows up with a statement that either confirms this proclivity or denotes a lack of faith in my ability to observe the glaringly obvious.

"Damien," he says, "I'm gay."

He ends it like that on an operatically theatrical note, loud as fuck with the liquid courage that fuels the ability to yell something like that in a bar like this, you know the kind I'm sure you've got it pictured.

I try to act as if this announcement is neither shocking nor out of the ordinary whilst watching my peripheries for airborne libations aimed in our direction and say, *I know that Ash, I live in New York, lots of my friends are gay, and I'm totally cool with that anyway.*

In the second that passes I try to think of gay friends, or situations in college where I might have been curious, movies I've seen, and conversations I've had – some sort of appropriate filler for a friend or family member coming out that I'm sure I've handled but under a dozen pints am having difficulty pin-pointing.

"It's because of your father."

I stop breathing and at some deep 6th sense level know not only what he's said is true, but that I've somehow always known it as well as what will be coming next.

*"*Your father was a homosexual cuz*"* and drains the end of his beer.

The way he says it is repulsive, drawing the syllables out in a slow New England drawl. To his credit I despise the word. It feels inherently dirty and shameful in the way *hetero* feels clinical and oppressed. Whether this is Catholic school baggage or growing up conservative is anyone's guess, but I've always preferred the calmer *gay* and *straight* terms, though those too are either cloudy or misleading. Gay people aren't exactly all happy and straight people aren't all, well straight. Ash absorbs in my puzzled look as I grapple with linguistics and the inherent prejudice of language for denial or stunned silence then launches into

"Your father was a fag Damien and he spent his whole life trying to be someone else, to hide what he was, to hate what he was. Your mom and you and Ronnie were his way of trying to deny his own urges, and when he died I thought he must be the saddest loneliest man in the world and decided I didn't want to die that way. I wanted to live, I wanted to come out and be who I was and live my damn life and what a sad man your father was" he says and pulls me into a hug.

In moments like these I always find myself consoling the titular consoler. In a way it is the right thing to do because no one consoles anyone else without really wanting to be held and comforted themselves. It was like when I told my girl Jezebel about my mother passing and she broke into tears and *oh-my-gawds* before I could finish and we were at a new bar where I just wanted a drink and instead had to explain to everyone present what the hell had just happened.

After three weeks in a hospital sleeping on the floor outside critical care being repeatedly mistaken for a vagrant and ultimately having to decide to pull the plug it was all I had left to talk about it - let alone project some freak show phantasmagoria for all to gawk at, shrink from, and mouth insincere platitudes to.

Like Meursault, Camus's existentially challenged protagonist, I could not feel her death, only observe its impact. Jez cried because to her my loss was tragic while to me it was fact and that's why I did the *it's alright*'s and *there-there*'s. It was like that.

Ash wasn't trying to tell me about my father, he was trying to tell me about himself, but he needed a lead in and my dad was as good as any. I held my cousin while he wept while aiming preventative hostile glances at any drunken onlookers looking to make comment and the rest I already knew before Ash even said it. As he went on I wondered if *Fairy Tale of New York* was the most beautiful Christmas song ever written.

I knew that my dad had not gone to Canada to vacation but to die. I knew that my mother found out it was AIDS and not hepatitis because Canadian doctors have to tell you shit like that. I knew that she made my uncle promise not to ever tell me but he had gossiped it to my cousins, and knew that after ten years all it would take was one call to my lawyer to procure a death certificate in order to confirm it. I had always somehow known that I had bought in on the denial, and knew however logically I approached it I had lots of resentment and anger in the mail.

All the parties were dead, all the history was written, the guests have left the restaurant, and I'm holding the check.

If you've seen *Barfly* or *Garden State*, read *The Dead* or *Angels in America*, ever listened to Pink Floyd's *The Wall* or The Pogues in the dark – you know what I'm saying. There are only so many themes, insert your own background. I'm selling good junk but you gotta bring your own works.

My mother died of cancer. An alien monster chewing her guts, perhaps brought on by loss and shame. Sometimes I think it's my fault and start playing solitaire again. If I keep logging out before the computer can record a loss, the statistics will say I'm predominantly winning.

The robot has finally, at last, left the building.

Of course I didn't kill my girlfriend. She's just been out for the night and I miss her and sometimes it's easier to think people are already lost to get a head start on not missing them.

But I am smoking her cigarettes, alone in the dark, with the memories of my parents.

Δ   Δ   Δ   Δ

Back to Earth

April 2005

You did a reading yesterday and all the poets were dead.

In their place were a schoolteacher, you, and a gaggle of idiots. The schoolteacher fared best but you got the longest intro. The small ingratiating lady who called you *Mister* told you how honored she was that you deigned to appear, sober you might add, and nervously approached the podium launching into *It is our distinct pleasure to introduce... and he's a star of the... read in such places as... distinguished...* so on and so forth.

You understood Bukowski on a whole new level. It made you shudder to think most of what she said could be construed as true, at least in the Fox News sense of the word.

The lady stepped down as the clapping began, your stomach knotted, and you noticed that her suit screamed control. It was a purple number, not flashy, not cheap, the style that proclaimed authority that comes from delegating responsibility and reading a lot of books, that and the Times on Sundays with European coffee - none of that Starbucks shit, the kind that had to be bought in a store selling $50 olive oil and soft French cheese. This observation came with the knowledge that you were wearing a *Phat Farm* oversized button down, pimped-out black overcoat with a fur collar, *Gucci* shades riding atop your head and a gray scarf falling lazily over your shoulders – this and brown suede shoes. As you walked to the podium you realized you probably looked more like a drug dealer than an author or more aptly, a cliché of a dealer - in a low budget film at that.

You cleared your throat into the microphone, took a breath and said *Look at me. I'm a fuckin caricature and I'm running this joint. Fuck. Are you pathetic losers really my fans? Fuckin hell. I thought I would grow up to be one of those hip wunderkind writers who fucked models and was widely read by punk rock chicks and European DJ's. God this is disappointing.*

At least that's what you wanted to say.

Instead you said *umm… good afternoon. My name is Damien and I had no idea it was national poetry month, or that I was the main attraction for that matter, which I guess makes me a shitty poet and uninformed guest.*

A Crash Course On the Anatomy of Robots

They laughed. Audiences often mistake honesty for wit.

But that was this afternoon. Tonight Lindsey Wagner taunts you between playing cards and jerking off. *What if I'm happy with my insomnia and uncomfortable night's sleep Miss Six Million dollar woman? Can you mail me a mattress for that?*

The *Law and Order* Network is running back-to-back episodes of the *X-Files*. The dad from *That 70's Show* is playing what will surely be a bad guy. Some actors are born with the unfortunate luck of looking like angry customers at a Wal-Mart. They are relegated to the roles of villains or pencil pushing idiots. Or maybe it's the other way around, and cubicle monkeys take their cues from TV.

It's already 5am and your laptop has decided tonight is the night it will actually last. On long flights and dead layovers it maxes no longer than 30 minutes. Go figure. The power supply is at your feet. You told yourself that when your computer battery died or 5am hit you would quit playing solitaire and try to sleep, whichever came last.

Jez has a nickname for you: "Mr. Wiggles." It refers to your physical state in the hours right before the sun rises till you fall into fitful nightmare-racked R.E.M. You imagine you must be hell to sleep next to. *It's tough enough on this end of it.*

You kick back the end of a light beer, part of this whole low-carb craze that has seized the nation and you occasionally indulge in with half a heart. You feel like you must finish this game. Even if it's just more meaningless statistics on an inconsequential screen that doesn't even exist outside of a series of electronic connections and linear thinking geek dreams. Even if it means nothing in itself at least it conveys a sense of time, a sense of even odds.

The power supply is at your feet.

You are not exactly out of shape. In fact, compared with most 30-year-old Americans you would be considered in good shape. Considering you smoke a pack of 'Ports' and drink half a bottle a day you realize why some experts think the life expectancy norm is making a U-turn. The tin-man barely needs oil these days - inertia is our new WD-40. Only in a society this lazy would you be in the healthy group. These are your thoughts as you fall into slumber.

You wake late in the afternoon and it's the first real day of spring. The city feels warm and people are smiling. It won't last but for what it's worth you feel brought up by it along with everyone else. Jezebel is at the gym – the one you've got a free week trial at yet have not stepped in once since you got it last week. She signs a note that sits in the construction site of your Upper East Side pad as *El Bebi*. You think it should be *La Bebi* but maybe it's one of those weird gender rules in Spanish deep-rooted in some sort of long forgotten cultural context, like how regardless of gender Poet is always the feminine *Poeta*, as if to denote some softness in the blunt act of expressing raw emotion.

A Crash Course On the Anatomy of Robots

This neighborhood is not me. I am far more at home in a seedy little corner of the Village or Brooklyn, for that matter an entirely different country altogether, preferably one where most people cannot speak English and Village is far more literal. On the up side you've found you no longer have the need to interact with other human beings other than by phone or ever leave the apartment if you so desire. Cuisines of all cultures are just a speed dial and a delivery tip away. You tried Argentinean pizza today and concluded it's not any different from a low-end *Famous Ray's*, just another gimmick. Go figure.

In six months you'll be in Mexico dying of an intestinal infection with your friend Alex trying to save you; in nine you'll be in Los Angeles battling loneliness and losing Ivy barely recovered from Jez; in a year you'll be in Thailand drinking buckets and sinking into aimless depravity. It'll still be the same. There is no catharsis. *Does it matter? Maybe beyond then, further than can be seen.*

In the cold spells you remember sitting on the top of the stairs in your parents' house waiting for your father to come home.

It was a raised-ranch in a New York border town in Connecticut. You guess it's called a city now; perhaps it was then, but in your youth it was a suburban sprawl layered in New England woods and streets you could still play whiffle and kickball on. You got your longest and first remembered scar in the cul-de-sac your house cornered.

You were five or six, lacking the fear that comes with previous injury. You had taken off your training wheels finally and took a bad turn on that damn dead end. The gravel tore through your arm and you howled till your father came running from inside the house. You felt as if you had been screaming forever as you lay on the asphalt noticing the things that you only notice when you're in amazing pain. The sky was clear and blue with cirrus clouds and the brightness of late afternoon – the kind that's enough to seem terribly bright to a child's eyes, yet has let the sun loose long enough that it can still be stared into.

That sky sticks to your memories like so much archetypal shorthand. The way that when one hears about a neighbor's pissy dog they instantly envision the first dog that ever barked or maybe bit them. That was your sky, and in the same way so this was your night.

I would sit there with my thoughts and wait. It had been many nights that I waited for him to come home. So many nights sitting on that damn green carpet-by-the-foot, its shag long lost, holding onto the shaking black metal railings that in the darkness were the shadows of trees in autumn.

You couldn't begin to guess how many nights you sat there looking through the four square panes of glass on the top of the peeling wooden door for the right car to come. At around ten your brother would be asleep, as would your mother if she wasn't still at work. The streets would be dead by then, only the occasional drunk teenager or lost motorist looking for a shortcut through the main road would break the clarity of your focus. You could almost see your father then, quietly driving down some black highway, playing some pedestrian classical - Beethoven, perhaps Mozart - thinking over the day's events.

He would've been with Pennwalt at this point; you could always tell where he worked by the corporate junk he accumulated. Automatic pencils for *Atotchem*, penknives for *Pfizer*, and in this case small card-shaped rulers, all adorned with the logos. He would have spent the day driving to unknown cities to meet with men like him over expensive lunches and dinners and drinks, eventually transacting millions of dollars worth of raw chemical material transactions, deals based only on a handshake and a smile.

Not all of this is speculation. I know this from when he would take me with him on the road. The long car ride with my father is another one of these combined series of events to me. Groton became the same as Brattleboro, as Albany became Mystic and so on. So much sameness in a world of variation – there is a reason people are so prone to stereotyping. Reasons there are so many robots.

The drives are the same, once more combined into one enormous trek across thoroughfare with your father imparting such fantastic pieces of advice like *never get a girl knocked up* and various versions of *one day all this can be yours*. Save except when you were sixteen and you drove since he had grown too weak from the "hepatitis." The silence was palpable.

These trips with my father, these long drives leading to long meals where I could pretend sophistication and spout mundane trivia at jolly rich men – I imagined when I was only about nine or ten that these old white men were truly impressed by me, truly understood my ideas and were not just humoring me.

Your dad had a talent for embellishing the mundane – for making legends out of acquaintances – significant decisions and events out of trivial occurrences. Even at nine you knew it was horseshit, pure and unadulterated, but you loved him and you loved him telling it and knew as sure as the vodka and menthol that would be on his breath, that he'd have a good one to spin before he put you to bed. Even now there are names that come to you now and then, a town or a salesman long retired for a company long bought-out. They are like whispers calling from those silent dark steps, between the shadows of the railing, under the unseen sky.

I had another dream of hell last night, or rather throughout the night and morning and god if every time I looked at my girl and she mumbled something about my sleep patterns. I was skinned alive over and over, it was reminiscent of the film Hellraiser or at least the woman wearing my skin was. This is all you can think of at 5am sitting in the cubicle under your loft bed that you have the optimism to call an office.

In your nightmares there are a series of reoccurring faces. Often you cannot recognize them but are sure you have met them somewhere before. Perhaps that is the doom of all people we meet briefly; to become extras in our serotonin-addled slumber.

How to form this mess? Disjointed, uneven, unfocused - I've been accused of worse or the same. You read a venomous review of the novel in the Press last week that accused you of being no more than just an over-praised hack. It went as far as to describe you as vile. *I guess there's something to that.*

There was a time you're told when all prose was meticulously constructed works of inspiration and tact leveled with not a bit of control and premeditation. *I wonder if I'm alone in thinking this stupendously lazy or masochistic. Clearly and amazingly they seem to be more in love with themselves than the average, or the opposite I suppose if you take the masochistic bend.* You had to read your first novel more than any other in your lifetime and have come to the dual conclusions that it wasn't all that good and time would only dull your ability to fix it. You are aware that there are people, in fact the majority, who can work the same tedious tasks year after year and find some fulfillment in it. *I guess if I could enter solitaire as an Olympic sport I would be more sympathetic.*

The Boys of Summer… that fucking track.
It is only narcissism and bitter denial than can make us think those who have burned us will want us back or even care if we are doing well. That's why the Don Henley track and its countless variations are so enticing. Remember that big beefy bouncer you've imagined beating the shit out of? The lady who snubbed you in line at the

grocery you plan on cutting off next time? The amazing comeback you have for a nasty co-worker? *Trust me, none of those fuckers have given a thought to your slight.* With a lover it's the same but deeper. If anything it's with pity or uncomprehending regret that they imagine you. If you're amazingly lucky they think of you with equal hate thinking up witty attacks to shrink you down while working out to show you what good shape they're in when they never run into you. More often you're a footnote in the diary of their lives referenced with all the other fuck-ups. Deal with it. Only artists have the penchant for self-flagellation by reliving and re-creating those particular hells. Your best hope is only making that bastard who scorned you more important than they deserve.

It's hard to stop though. That's the bitch of it.

But there's worse of course.

The dead really don't care.

A Momentary Poetic Interlude

October 2005 (Guanajuato Mexico, recovering from breaking up with Jez by drinking oneself into the hospital)

I told Alex I was scared
Those were the exact words

"Alex, I'm scared."

It must have been six — seven
in the morning
on a lazy Guanajuato night
turned dawn.

I remember
after some
particularly heroic
benders
(the kind that take
a good part of a week
multiple partners and successive blackouts)
that vomiting could produce
a little

(just a little)
the lining having worn thin
from cocaine,
puking,
excess…
(See Special Features section for more)

OK, so here's the deal.

Since Damien's agent and editor are dead set against the poetry in his second novel, the publishers thought perhaps we should introduce each one, briefly describe what it's about, maybe share the first stanza or so and then say something like *If you're interested in studying the whole 9 yards please turn to the Special Features at the end…*

It's a cop out that lets Damien keep the poetry, spares the publishers from having to slog through the damn stuff if they don't want to be bothered, and disabuses you of the thankless task of flipping to the end of this lovely book every 20 pages or so. Damien is a fucking poet after all and it's bound to show up now and then if only for the credibility of his character.

If you are however one of those readers in whom the very idea of separating (or dividing or organizing) prose into stanzas causes an inherent and painful allergic reaction (flashbacks of Dante and Yeats and disciplinarian Nuns), we're sure you will be pleased that you can proceed at once to tearing out the last pages of this book and tossing them post-haste into the shredder. Otherwise start flipping. Believe me, Damien most certainly is (pages of course).

on top of the giant

August 2003 (New York remembering Mexico and contemplating Chaos)

There's a National Geographic in the bathroom of Joan's house. It's sitting on top of a Natural History, an AARP (American Association of Retired Persons), and a local art paper. The art rag has half a jazz band on the front and is torn because the toilet paper ran out. The Geographic issue is about Mt. Everest and those who lived and died on it. The man on the cover looks determined and worn in a handsome 1940's sort of way. Dr. Bull, the surgeon who operated on Joan, was the oldest man to scale the mountain until last year when some ancient fellow toppled the record. The periodical has not moved since she died.

There's a school of thought that the world, the universe - all of reality in fact - could be understood if only you had the ability to step back far enough and watch it all happen. This is the idea behind "chaos theory," whose nonsensical fractals become drainpipe centipedes of color and pattern as perspective is increased. The same holds true for Complexity theory, although dispensing with chaos theory's snapshot view also takes into account constant movement and interaction. Death, loss, life – all become moving parts in a defined system. There is the very human tendency to believe that understanding any of this really means anything.

If you could see Jezebel now, she would deck you. The hole she left - yet another to fill with mechanical parts.

You remember when Jez got a slow horse on her birthday. She cried in a cab near *Auditorio* about how she loved you more than anyone before and asked you if you had slept with anyone else. You had to sneak out of Amalia's at 7am and out of *Carcamones* at noon. You went to San Miguel and arm wrestled in a cantina and held her in the streets in Melaque after she lost her journal. You made out in front of the *Iguana* on New Year's morning and sang punk tunes on shrooms and she waited to cover your mouth before you said "step-daddy." There were all the nights at *Barfly* staring out onto the street, talking at the door, kissing at the bar… and that first night at *La Dama* making out on the balcony.

At the hospital they asked you what you wanted done. You spoke out of instinct. *"Peritonitis"* they said, *"What do you want done?"*

When you were 19 your father choked on his own toxins, borne of poison blood, contracted in New York, years before you knew why he hated your city. It was Canada and, thank nationalized medicine, you didn't have the choice to resuscitate him. This was your chance to make things different. To change a past where you could not prove yourself, where regret was un-washable, where part of you still stayed in that cold room of weeping.

It was a mistake. You knew it seconds after they revived her, but there was no other way to live with yourself.

Very slowly we see the picture painted. Its details are unclear. It is apparent that some could be made out with enough time and focus, but never the whole. We know many have spent lifetimes trying just to see the image. Others simply live in the details.

We deny it, interpret like a Rorschach, postulate theories, fall into apocryphal rhetoric - dismiss the simple Gertrude Stein-ness of it. A rose is not a rose we tell ourselves, if it looks like a face, or a word, or a life, or a love.

This house is a memory. It has textures and smells and items that have not moved. It has no substance. You walk through it in haze, an REM state of hangover and denial. There is nothing living here, you do not count.

"Your birthday will be the best ever. I will be healthy for it. It will be your best birthday ever."

After you made the decision to remove the artificial breathing and fluid systems she fought for another 30 hours. You were the only one in the room. It was 6 hours before you turned 28.

The fire that burns in our bellies belies the fact that we drink down furiously fountains of knowledge. Unfathomably thirsty we choke down ideas, thoughts, opinions, and desires – all the while equally desperately avoiding understanding. This hollowness we feel, this lack of true enlightenment, is a self-chosen masochism, an attempt to control flames that are our very nature to indulge in – as important as the fire itself or an opposable thumb, or all as irrelevant as it were.

You remember when Jez told you to sleep on the couch and when you told her you wanted to be together for the first time at the party on the rooftop before she went to Maurauta. There were all the nights at *Ocho*, far from sober days at *Spanglish* and *Truco*, for far too much *chisme*.

There was the dinner for Alex at *Ciao Bella*, all the going away parties, all the welcome backs, barbeques at Alex's and freezing in hammocks out in Palenque.

You recall making love in the room with Ian snoring in Zipolite, Palenque, San Cristobal, Mexico City (no, wait, that was everyone) and talking to her from her parents' phone in Texas, she not even there.

A Crash Course On the Anatomy of Robots

There is a need, which is constant, and there is life. The life of timing and circumstance, things bartered and traded, events experienced and remembered or forgotten, the concept of the past and future and *augenblick* of moments. Often, more often than not, it is the latter we bury ourselves in. Objects, a home, age, sex, anger and all other temporary emotion, drama, desire, and the fear of a chaotic universe where we cannot find stability or structure: automatons playing people, and perhaps the opposite. Then there is the fear of predictability, equally oppressing, the utter meaningless nature of our actions in the construct of the infinite, beyond the detailed ideas of a butterfly flapping its wings to the core of the ultimate relevance and importance of effect. Perhaps our actions and existences are significant, but only in the context of an insignificant reality.

Parties raged at *Embajadoras* with lost cell phones, Norwegian orgies, big old crazy German girls - her, you, crazy German girl, bad girl Brit, and Canadian effort boy in her bed and bi-curious Canadians trying to get you both.

There was Adena and all her bullshit, J and all his bullshit, Kienyo and all his horseshit and you and all of yours.

There was drinking in cantinas, *Why Not?*, and laughing at *Crapitolio* people.

There was showering (and not using conditioner), ecstasy, way too much ecstasy, the tub at Valencia and heating water on the stove.

There was never finding the other *presa*, sneaking into Howard Johnson's to swim, hiking, sitting out on the balcony and listening to music, too many damn games and movies and intimate mornings - those slow crisp intimate Mexican mornings.

You can't remember the last time you had sex – literally.

You know you woke up naked on a living room floor and later in a bedroom you pulled a condom off and out of your pants while mumbling to a girl who you hoped you hadn't slept with. A girl in Seattle keeps sending you distraught emails while another plans to visit with her new boyfriend in a month. One final that made a mark continues to torment you with a flightiness that is either male revenge fantasies fulfilled, or a serious denial of incurable cultural sickness. Then again the idea of fucking makes your stomach turn. You feel out of shape, overweight, unattractive, and full of self-loathing. Vaguely you are aware that it is mostly personality and body dysmorphia. You write off others' advances and attraction to low lighting and the pheromones of damage.

After she died everyone told you how sorry they were, asked about your brother, and informed you that they would *be there* if ever you should need them. You wondered if their regret was a viable currency in paying off karmic debt, if your inability to take care of yourself probably meant you were completely unaware of your brother's state, and if *anything* included taking their car, driving to Mexico, picking up some of your more financially challenged friends and having them crash at their house for a month.

You only said thank you and shook many hands.

They say Asian diets high in salted and cured foods can contribute to stomach cancer. As you sit in the kitchen concocting soup out of leftover dried products you think about the swollen gland in your neck. You wonder if it is coincidence, then you wonder if you really care either way. The pot is large and stainless steel and belongs to the same series of items (a vintage 60's stove missing the front right burner, a cupboard full of empty Chinese pastry tins), which she left you.

You think of cooking with Jez, with or without too much salt, love, fighting on the roof before she had to go to work, nearly breaking up in *Veloche* and breaking up countries apart.

You remember falling apart, tears, laughing, sarcasm, honesty, hope, friendship, and words...

Words...

All these words could not save you.

The breadth of human behavior is limited and therefore to an extent predictable. Its details are ultimately only important to those involved, but this is inherently self-reflexive and cyclical. An experience, however predictable, is often fairly unexpected to those who experience it. Even self-knowledge and awareness of the pattern does not necessarily diminish its probability. In the end, the less likely an event, often the more inevitable becomes its occurrence. Are we really all just bad versions of each other - robots with human parts, mimicking what is expected and never quite getting it right? Yes and no.

After the funeral you traded doctors and priests for lawyers and accountants. Everyone agreed it was a beautiful service. Sitting in her house Ronnie's voice droned on. You thought how blissful it must be to be him. Oh, to obsess about cleaning and futures and friends. Who's popular, who's not, who's fucking who… it made you want to strangle him. Meanwhile the screen stared defiantly back, bills sat in piles screaming for attention, the phone rang then went to call waiting and all the time the cell was going off. So sorry, sorry, they were all so wonderfully sorry. If you could light people on fire with your thoughts the world would be a very different place indeed.

Sir Edmund Hillary.

That was the climber's name, the one who scaled Everest and lived to tell the tale more than 50 years later. Many failed before him and he nearly died several times, but somehow he made it. When asked why he did it he simply replied:

"It was not glory we sought, unless it be the common glory of man's triumph over Nature, and over his own limitations."

Even to a robot, if you step far enough back, it eventually makes sense.

Δ   Δ   Δ   Δ

The Asian Journal of Damien Wood Part 2

June 4, 2006

James the mad ex-navy spec ops says the giggling drunk Swedes "practically have Down syndrome."

You're grabbing a slow bus to Bangkok after a boat ride through Burma, which in a total of 15 minutes you decided was worth a miss.

Phuket was flesh peddling, middle-aged slime, persistent lady-boy, and Nepalese tailor overload.

A perfect t-shirt, English in front, Thai in back, stated simply

> *"NO*
> *I DO NOT WANT*
> *A FUCKING*
> *TUK-TUK*
> *GIRL*
> *MASSAGE*
> *OR SUIT!"*

From all accounts this is Thailand's Delhi: Disneyland meets Sodom, a Thai commentary on what they believe Western sleaze desires.

A Crash Course On the Anatomy of Robots

A terribly nice southern gas station owner, his store blown away into the sea as Katrina hit Mississippi, talks to a girl who continually calls in pigeon-English.

You are growing sick here

Israeli girls travel in packs, talking about you in Hebrew you cannot gauge.

Lingering thoughts still haunt and tear. You feel as if a breakdown is imminent. Like those twats on the "Amazing Race," except you're alone, and there's no fucking prize.

Every time you notice the slow shuffle of someone wanting to sell you something, wanting

Wanting.

You feel besieged.

You fear not having travel insurance and the abyss of Cambodia. You fear daytime mosquitoes and the disease they harbinger. You fear "harmless" reef sharks and always being a loner.

You wanna stop it.

You smoke in spite of it.

But you remain alone.

Marie is engaged and trying to move in to your small Mexican town. Jez is with your best friend. Ivy is back with Orlando, no doubt knocked up.

Soft hypocrites we are.

Living ironies.

Biding time till the end where we will beg ourselves forgiveness for becoming our delusions.

It is a wonder how we do not forget those things

Did a dental cleaning today for about 500 baht, and despite white shiny teeth you are clearly regretting it with every sip and smoke. Note to self: dentists are the same the world over.

Setting: clinically antiseptic white chamber with an Asian man in a face mask and smock, small dabbles of crimson on said smock, Damien reclining uncomfortably strapped to a chair with a sheet covering all of his face except a clamped open mouth. Ominous metal objects plugged into mysterious units operated by fine figured Thai girl also in smock and mask who by her eyes appears to be in permanent state of amusement.

Dentist: *(with thick Thai accent)* How long since you been to dentist Missa Wood?

Damien: *(Struggling back to the sound of whirring drill bits)* Umm.. I think like – Jesus Christ! – a year or two – fuck!

Dentist: *(Pushing bits at impossible angles into bloody mouth)* YOU LIE! How long?

Damien: *(Fingers going into and through arms of the chair)* SHIT! LIKE 5 YEARS MAYBE 6 CHRIST!

Dentist: *(Smugly while presenting rinse cup)* Maybe you come every 3 months and it no hurt so much yes?

You had a fantastic time with Scottish Eilidh last night, definitely one of the nicest compact bodies and rare British beauties you've ever encountered. You woke just before she had to leave and wanted to convince her to stay but her friends had already bought her ticket. You kinda got the feeling you were being a bit too immediately into her. You hung less than 20 hours, slept together 3 times, wandered the city drunk and sober, and talked about what happens on the road. Well, you suppose none and all of it matters. You did love her shudders though….

June 5

You went to the first decent waterfall you've seen in Asia with Canadian kids. Drank an obscene amount of Lao Lao last night and proceeded to run into the fucking Dutch girls again. Gigantic continent your ass. In Luang Prabang the insides of your thighs are absolutely killing you. It's the same shit as Mexico, which leads you to believe that a certain combination of continuous hiking, sex, going commando, trimming hair down below, and just being a sensitive skin pussy are a recipe for misery. Powdered underwear is mildly soothing. The inside of your urethra itches, that can't be good.

June 16

One fucking week of stunning beauty and mishaps in Van Viang… Weird "obsessive" missteps with Irish girl, birthday hammock kisses with too young Canadians, and positively irresponsible hook-ups with Canada come Osaka fashion designers – paradise on the Namsung and mildew stinkin waters, at night we drink Lao Lao with JD and ex-pat English Alex fishing tubers out the river. We Indiana Jones it and destroy organs on giant rope swings. We try not to scratch our thigh and ass and spreading fungal jungle rot. We listen to Tool and Rob Halford. We piss the night away player style with Norwegians from Ghana. We are not pissing fire yet but we must be careful. We find young English in packs at world cup games very much resemble suburban super bowl parties from hell.

We fuck to rainstorms in the jungle. We kiss cousins by the Mekong Delta. We lose ourselves in the sway. Stinking of rice whiskey.
Millionaires in Kip. Compatriots in travel crime.
Lost, not like the show, but like a soccer match, the grail of our lives,
Empty
Looking better and better in spite of it
There is but one world.
One man. One woman. One bar. One beach. One jungle. Desert and plain.
Hot and cold, Sweet and soft
Hard as hell, and coming back for more

June 18

"Ari G'di" is "whatever" in Thai. "More stupid moves on the road" – that should be the title of your new book. Some things should never be done, and certainly not written.

Furious contemplation of your life and nature of it; realizing the past year's laziness and bullshit: jungle rots, women thoughts, feeling childish and immature and like a loser aging playboy. What on earth can one do on a bus with shit films and no reading lights? Was anyone even aware a straight to video *American Pie* about Stifler's brother at band camp even existed… all this and more, the mundane ramblings of the self-important smutty poet. It's a dangerous world you're told, but it always seems to be at arm's length from you. The towers fell at your doorstep. The tsunami trashed the beaches you've lounged on taking entire villages out to sea. The cosmos does its chaotic dance and you, the waltzing automaton, just keep humming to the beat.

A Crash Course On the Anatomy of Robots

Portrait of an Artist as a Not So Young Man (A Crash Course on Survival)

"If you're like me, untangling symbol and allusion seems as irrelevant now as it did in high school... It is difficult to imagine a world without movies, plays, novels and music, but a world without poems doesn't have to be imagined."

-Bruce Wexler, "Poetry Is Dead. Does Anybody Really Care?" 2003

A Crash Course On the Anatomy of Robots

Work and South of the Border

You may have some questions.

"Where does Damien's money come from?"

"How and why does he spend so much time in Mexico?"

Blah, blah, blah…

These are questions Damien receives on an almost daily basis and to which he frequently answers:

I make a living through my writing and music and live between the States, Europe, and Mexico. If this sounds miraculous or unlikely, just remember you too can have this if you starved through all your teens and twenties, sacrificed healthy relationships, and chose to spend most of your time in countries where you can get a pack of smokes and a meal for under a dollar.

But perhaps that is a bit obtuse so why don't we go into some more specifics.

Damien, whilst at University essentially rode in and out of debt to credit cards and student loans desperately trying to balance work, study, and art. Next to the city and church, NYU owns more real estate than anyone else in New York, yet their dorms in '93 ran at roughly a grand a month for a shared room the size of spare bathroom (attached to smaller shared bathrooms) and a single school credit was somewhere around $600 with the expectation of around 16 credits per semester. Even with financial aid and a Draper scholarship Damien had to work full time to make ends barely meet. This era of his life included late night flyering (*go on, if you can find a better price, start your own damn airline*), computer game beta testing (no, it is not as fun as you think, especially playing malfunctioning educational games designed to teach children to think in code day in and day out), and interning for a subsidiary of the drug company his parents met in.

In this particular job he started initially on the assembly line in the pilot plant putting boxes for hair dyes and such together. Within a year he was a technician in the R&D labs making up batches of existing beauty products with cheaper raw materials for dry runs at the pilot plant. By the time he graduated Uni (with a degree in Psychology of all things) he was a full on Chemist in the midtown test facilities formulating entirely new products and testing the results on little old ladies who wanted their hair done for free and knew no better. To his knowledge Damien is still the youngest person without a degree to reach that level (no Asian comments please).

His quick ascension through competence and confidence taught him a valuable lesson about work and determination: anything is possible (just not everything). Damien had discovered that the making of money was something he had a talent for, which was lucky considering he wanted to live as an artist, a vocation that is decidedly devoid of said income. Through his twenties amongst other things he would become a manager for a high-end glassware boutique (through Kienyo), a staff accountant for a famous Italian fashion company (through a temp agency, initially doing data entry for accounts receivable), and eventually a highly paid academic and corporate freelancer consultant writing mind numbing prose to make billionaires and bureaucrats sound intelligible.

A Crash Course On the Anatomy of Robots

This last one was through Jasper, who worked tech in a small Managerial Consulting firm. They hired Damien as a bookkeeper, due to the Italian fashion company, but he very quickly rose from that title to a project coordinator and associate. It's all very long and boring and inspirational. Let's just say that it turns out that a very specific combination of skills and talents inadvertently made Damien the ideal candidate for a junior Organizational Consultant. He excelled at computers and logistics, had a background in Psychology and writing, and the added bonus of experience as a performer and an inherent ability to manage crisis made him a perfect fit, with a whole lot of disposable income.

This is of course not what he would talk about at these various times. Whilst doing account receivables he was also performing nightly in experimental theatre groups. As he ghostwrote bizarre jargon laden opuses on Executive Assimilation he was doing scathing articles on pop figures for literary magazines. And while he figured out the explanation for why hand blown candle holders really were worth $200 a pop, he managed to record poetry with European DJ's whose remixes would rise to the pop charts.

He learned to invest, and after traveling around the perimeter of the US and down to Mexico, he learned how to spend, and that he could spend a whole lot less if he spent more time down south.

However we are not there yet and that's not even this story. Just to satisfy your curiosity let's just say that if you desire you too can flee the metropolitan sprawl for a small town in central Mexico where building a home and opening a pub in a modern colonial will cost you less than a decade worth of rent or a down payment on your house. It is no different than moving to another state except that you should pick up the local language, and travel becomes a bit more of a pain in the ass. There are shitloads of foreigners living there doing the same thing. In fact, that is where Damien met both Jez and Ivy (who will come back up in a bit), and subsequent travel to Texas and LA can be uniformly blamed on them.

So the lesson here is that you too can have your home base in a tranquil city outside New York that has a much nicer standard of living at a third of the cost along with a whole lot of artists doing just what you are and that is exactly what Damien did in 2002 – albeit in Mexico.

Anyway let's get back to New York.

No more questions.

OK?

Δ　　Δ　　Δ　　Δ

Anatomy of a Poet (Part 1)

Surviving as an artist in any city is difficult. In all likelihood you will need a day job, determination bordering on obsession, and a skin tough enough to weather an atomic blast. If you are very lucky you will make enough from your craft to get rid of the day job and will learn to take criticism and bad press in stride. If you are in the right place in the right time you may actually make a decent living at it.

For example, Damien is a *star* of the spoken word scene (his agent has drilled it into his skull to use "star" rather than "fixture" as apparently the latter conjures images of home decorating for most). That this is a contradiction in terms is a point that causes his publicist to frown whenever brought up.

Dammit Dave I'm a poet (not unlike Doctor 'Bones' McCoy) *who happens to perform live shows, and some of those shows happen to be with musicians and well-known DJ's, but I'm still a poet. Christ man my last novel had practically no press and I still sold more copies on the road than most authors do in their lifetimes and I frankly hate all this genre shit.*

Dave is a 54-year-old Jewish guy from Queens. His assistant is his 20-year-old Eastern European wife named Helga who Damien suspects was of the mail order variety. He cares as much about craft as Damien does about baseball but he needs him cause what Dave does care about is money.

"You're a product Damien. Many people come to see a show or buy an album or one of your whiny shock-poetry collections cause you're young and Asian and they think you're trendy and hip. If you were standing on the strength of your prose alone you'd have problems getting a vanity publisher."

This usually is where Damien huffs and puffs, points out that he is carried on poetry curriculums, speaks at multiple reputable forums every year, and generally struggles to name magazines he's in that aren't aimed a 18-25 year old slackers. It is a short rant.

A Crash Course On the Anatomy of Robots

Spoken word is a very particular offshoot of several different subcultures. The most obvious would be poetry. This however is misleading in that it does not encompass just how much of the form is derived from the 'spoken' and not the 'word'. Performance is a major, if not 'the' major component of the craft. An average piece will range from 3 to 7 minutes in the competition form (known as slams) and are rated by three random judges on a scale from 0 to 10. 10 being the greatest piece ever performed, and zero being something a word generator could write and read. The practitioners of this art are actors, comedians, MC's, struggling writers and coffee shop poets, and the poetry is the one element they have in common. The pieces fall into many categories as one would expect, but the ones that tend to score highest can be broken into a few broad themes. Race and gender is the big one as anyone who has watched *Def Jam Poetry* or the film *Slam* can attest to. Think of using branding as a metaphor for racism in the commercial lens of American consumerism (Sarah Jones to give credit where credit is due). Hip-hop has made its clear mark in this realm both in subject and delivery. Scorned or intense love gained or lost would be the other juggernaut. Pieces range from intense description of lovemaking positions, to flightier odes to unrequited infatuation. There is then the folk open mic contribution to the genre, which are pieces that can be put into the "so dark and lost is my life" realm. These make frequent reference to suicide and menstrual cycles. A final category would be the 'spoken word spoken word' pieces, which mostly complain about poetry, poets, and other slam pieces.

A Crash Course On the Anatomy of Robots

Damien is a longhaired Chinese/UK mutt with a fair amount of tragedy in his life between parents and friends dying, a terminally excessive youth, and your average urban over education. He studied some acting, is a competent musician, and is well versed in classical literature as well as more contemporary hip-hop. This all makes him a prime candidate for the genre. Here's a nice easy one. Despite its subject matter being essentially a complaint about all the ethnic pieces in competition, it won the slam that night – at the very club it was parodying no less.

too many nights @ Nuyorican
I guess I should do a piece about being Chinese
and you being white
a woman
or an angry black man.
cause you all look the same to me

so I guess I'm the ultimate
racist and sexist
in the world.

Whether you got melanin
or estrogen
or a belt of sin in your culture's past
you still
all look the same to me

I think we're all just people

A Crash Course On the Anatomy of Robots

and it matters more

who we fuck

or kill

than our parents did,

and we're all responsible

no matter this justification

of Hitler killing Jews

whites killing Indians

women being suppressed

cops targeting Africans

it's all the same.

Society's fucked

And you gotta take your chips and deal.

No one ever said it was fair

(and if they did they lied and you were a fool to believe them.)

Hating the rich and regal

cause they hate you

does not make you better.

You say society holds you down,

that its walls stereotype and confine you

but you can't seem to see that you're the gatekeepers

and I'm your prisoner.

After all I'm white Asian male

and all the good or bad that comes with it,

My clothes and hair

A Crash Course On the Anatomy of Robots

tell you my state
like my scars and my eyes
which tell you my past
and who am I to say
"Motherfucker you don't know me!
Take your shit somewhere else!"
cause I accepted my cage
when I acknowledged you and your ignorant hypocrisy.

So what if I threw off the chains
And told you I was
Black
and Jewish
and a little Swiss Dutch girl?
what if I told you I was
an elephant
or a child
or a comet chewing quasars?

Would you say I was
buggin'?
or nuts?
or deranged?

Would you call me
a poser?
or wannabe?

A Crash Course On the Anatomy of Robots

or flat out mad?

See, I'm not angry my
brothers
sisters
fellow human beings.
I've already played that game
and no one can win.
Bitch and complain
about justice
and race
and rage
and frustration,
it only makes them stronger.

My weakness is my strength,
and my scars
are my knowledge,
and my tears
quench thirst,
and my laughter
heals children,
and I love you
and hate you
and sometimes,
I am you.
But the last thing I am

A Crash Course On the Anatomy of Robots

Is what you expect me to be.

Cause I am everything
and nothing
which is what I see in you,
and you can't touch me
cause you can't see me
cause I've finally
become

clear.

A note on advances and poetry:

As in music contracts, literary contracts often offer an advance to authors based on projected revenue. Poetry is the one genre in both music and writing where you can't expect much of one. It's a big loser: the agent loses money (if you by some miracle have one), the house loses money, stores lose money – even the fucking poet loses money – all in the name of what many, including Damien's agent, believe is a dead or dying art.

There are two exceptions to this rule: celebrities and performers.

Here is the best example he knows. Sometime around 1993 or so the anti-folk singer Jewel (prior to her evolution into a pop star tart) released a poetry collection, which reportedly received the largest poetry advance of its time, about $200,000. Though this may seem not all that large compared to other professions or other genres like fiction or self-help, it was unheard of at the time. Ask yourself, when was the last time you voluntarily bought or read poetry? This is not to mention the fact that the collection was – well let's just say that having a #1 single at the time didn't hurt.

In the same year, an unnamed spoken word artist wrote what can only be described as what the British refer to as a 'piss-take' on the Jewel collection. In the work, he takes the titles of all of the Jewel pieces and writes his own poems. It's funny, but essentially a one trick pony. He is incidentally one of the few other Asian performers Damien knows to break the yellow ceiling of public image – and no Amy Tan and Maxine Hong Kingston and other writers of *respected* work don't count cause only 3 people who read about Asians by Asians have memorized the photos on the book jackets and actually know what they look like. That's part of the problem with popular spoken word; it's like genre writing. People buy it because they know what to expect, you only have to look at the author and you'll have an idea what's coming.

Oh, and at $100,000 guess who purportedly got the second largest poetry advance in history? That's right, Miss Jewel's piss-taker himself. Never underestimate the public's hunger for a novelty or gimmick presented by a hip minority…

A quick bit of history…

Damien first published in a local paper at 12. A move which, though he would never admit it, was entirely driven by a junior high English teacher who informed him that he could not write.

A Crash Course On the Anatomy of Robots

Throughout his teens he proceeded to publish short stories under various pseudonyms (mostly sci-fi and horror zines) and wrote lots of bad rhyming poetry (most which would classified under the 'so dark and lost' or excessively cryptic for the sake of depth category) that would usually end up in the school lit mag,

Towards the end of high school he put out his own private paper without censorship. This was inspired by his expulsion over an article in the school paper on administrative corruption as told through the metaphor of the cafeteria.

In order to be let back in to graduate, Damien wrote a retraction saying how sorry he was to have hurt anyone's feelings and misprinted facts. He did not think that anyone would think a reference to the school *pizza having the same nutritional value as cardboard* would be taken seriously, and this had a lasting effect on his belief in the general public's intelligence and sense of humor.

Damien's writing would make a rather large turn when he turned 17 and entered University. He dropped rhyme for the most part and his stories began to be more about 'normal' people as opposed to demonic computers who think they are Jesus. His writing rapidly matured (if not in subject then certainly in style). After wooing certain professors and fellow wordsmiths he managed to put to together a collection of short stories and poems. To his shock, with the help of some of the aforementioned, several agents and publishers had expressed some real interest in the collection and he was introduced to that magical and elusive word 'advance.'

Damien wished he could say that it all fell into place from there and he was now a well-established member of the literary vanguard. He still daydreamed about how he was lauded as a prodigy, a wunderkind of the highest realm and now at work on his 6th successful and highly lucrative novel. This would however be in denial of a celebratory week he spent in a shitty RX-7 on a road trip through the Northeast popping speed like candy.

After a very reputable press in Greenwich Village had steered him to an agent and dangled the greatest sum he had ever been offered in his life, he and his friends MOC and Kienyo decided to grab MOC's car, load up on crystal, booze, and herb, and go find Maine. He was 17, riding high, and these things happen. At the end of 4 days, once they were down to stopping by roadside pharmacies and asking for diet pills, it was generally decided that enough was enough and they went back to the Village and promptly collapsed in Damien's dilapidated flat. To this very day Damien told himself the book would have been a failure, or worse being a success at such a young age would have ruined his career or, given his habits at the time, resulted in some sort of Jim Morrison type death in the bathtub scenario.

What did happen was two-fold. First MOC, upon arriving at his pad, managed to put his foot through his desktop. In a way this stunning development was emblematic of many of Damien's gifts and weaknesses. A former computer whiz (you can hold off the Asian comments right now thank you very much) he had built his own desktop out of various parts into a powerful workhorse – one that due to laziness and a lack of patience in seeing things through he had neglected to design ergonomically. In other words, no shell would fit on his creation and its parts were exposed without cover and no match for a size 12 boot. He had not yet realized the importance of back-ups and would have panicked right there if not for a hard copy he had saved for his illustrator in Connecticut.

A note on parking on Washington Square Park in the early 90's: prior to the 360 degree cameras, mobile police unit, and lack of Rasta herb dealers that would come with Giuliani's 'quality of life' program, there were few places worse to put your vehicle in Greenwich Village. The combination of lowlifes and constant influx of clueless students practically guaranteed some degree of breaking and entering should you be stupid enough to leave items in your car of any value, let alone all of your clothes you were planning to wash at your folks' house and your only existing copy of an as of yet unpublished manuscript.

Staring at the empty trunk of MOC's ride, Damien proceeded to contact a less than savory acquaintance, acquired a .45 Glock, and wander the streets looking for someone selling his clothes in Alphabet.

If he had found that someone, we might have the story of the young jaded artist who killed a junkie or downtrodden homeless man.

If he had had the balls to go into the publishing house that Monday and face the music or return his agent's phone calls this might even be one of those pulling out the flames type things.

It is neither of those, but it is part of why Damien became a slam poet and met a girl named Marie.

In the months that followed Damien more or less gave up writing. His hard drive had contained not just his novel but everything he had written in his life up to that moment. His grades went to the gutter and his drug intake took on Herculean proportions. Therefore, it was not a bit ironic that the suicide of someone else would be the motivating factor in Damien's literary transformation and rebirth.

Δ   Δ   Δ   Δ

Anatomy of a Poet (Part 2)

New York, 1993

On one cold day in February, 19 years old and 6 months after his father's sudden death, Damien woke up hung over with the smashed bits of his roommate's answering machine cradled in his arms - late for a make-up computer science final that could not possibly save him from failing the course – to the disconcerting sound of someone screaming. This coincided with a flashing blur outside his window and was followed by a tumultuous crash and series of car alarms. Grumbling and more or less falling the meter-and-a-half off his loft bed Damien made for the window overlooking University Place and found himself staring into any empty park and abandoned streets. Clearing his head out and grabbing a Newport, he leaned out and saw the figure of a man rolling and kicking five stories below and a van stopped with severe damage to its front right end. It must have been a weekend, now that he thought about it, since Washington Square was essentially deserted. It was eerily quiet for a Manhattan morning, even in studentville early on a Sunday.

Yanking on some jeans and slippers he dragged ass to the elevator where he ran into Marie Rahm, a sophomore he knew from the floor and had been nursing a crush on all the previous semester. Marie looked flustered and said

"Hey did you see what happened?"

Naw just woke up to the crash, not sure if it's a student or not, think he got nailed by a van

"No he jumped. I just talked to a friend on the 14th floor, they said they heard him start screaming."

Shit, oh man, OK let's see what's happening.

They rolled out the lobby where the security guard (nicknamed shades for the obvious) was watching morning television and sipping a coffee.

Hey shades you call 911?

"Naw Why?"

Some kid jumped from the 14th

"Aw fuck me" he scrambled on the receiver with images of job security and smoking on the job surely flashing. Damien and Marie went out the front and found that they were the only ones out there.

"Oh my god Damien, Jesus Christ he's still moving"

Fuck OK, what should I do? Should I move him? Oh the fucking van

The U-haul he had initially thought struck the jumper had in fact been the only thing between his head and a clear fall to earth. Aside from doing a catastrophic amount of damage, his skull had also left a fair amount of human debris including most of his scalp and lanky black hair. Damien turned Marie away before he could get a better look. She was in full shock babble.

"Shit. Shit. It must be my friend Mark's roommate. He said he was really depressed. Oh my god, where the fuck is Mark? He must have heard something. Where the fuck is everyone? Shit, shit. My dad is visiting me in a like an hour. It's the first time he's been to New York. Oh my god Damien what am I gonna do?"

He held her and felt complete shit for feeling attracted to her in that moment. She had curly red hair and the most deep blue eyes. For the first time in his life he felt the kind of bond that occurs amongst strangers in moments of extreme trauma. He had to physically restrain himself from kissing her.

Hey, it's ok, it's gonna be ok alright Marie? Just calm down, the cops and paramedics will be here in a minute. Don't worry I'm not going anywhere OK?

After the cops arrived the boy in fact turned out to Marie's friend Mark. They smoked and joked over the body, which had stopped involuntary movement by that point, and no one even bothered asking for a statement. That night he wrote a poem about the whole incident and slid it under her door. By the next weekend they were sleeping together and in a month they were living together.

Since he had written the piece to Marie he had started writing again and now was looking for feedback. Damien didn't know much about it, but when Tower Books announced a slam about a month later he went down with a few other wannabe writers and signed up. Maybe it was his lack of experience making him seem new, maybe it was his age or the power of the piece, but he ended up winning over several dozen more experienced authors and spoken word artists.

From this point on Damien wrote furiously and went to every mic and competition he could find. Kienyo was DJ'ing a lot and he soon found himself filling in at shows and subsequently asked to record with various musicians looking for something different to add to their mixes. By the time he turned 20 Damien found he had embarked on a new career. At the time he felt he was on the cutting edge of the new underground, a fusion of all musical styles whether they be rock or rap, electro or folk, with the new wave of poetry's future (one that actually paid) right at the center.

It's a strange career in truth, and you're mostly on its sidelines – the equivalent of a professional cello player: never short on work if you're looking, but never quite the star. It is one of selling personal pain for scores and album appearances, bartering death for radio interviews, and tragedy for gimmicky book deals. That's what he says these days anyhow. All cause of a kid named Mark who he never knew, a girl named Marie who changed his twenties, and a poem named "The boy she said" that he can't find or even remember.

Damien likes to distill his principal detractors down to two gross stereotypes, one for each scene. From the establishment, he pictured a 60-year-old Lit Professor, and for the performance scene world a 19-year-old undergrad goth girl. Both of these characters, incidentally, were actual people who had confronted Damien at some point or another with the intention of telling him just how bad he was (in the case of the undergrad the insults had a particularly personal edge to them).

The Goth girl was at an after-party of a rather heavy day in Vermont. He had begun the morning by attending a poetry elective class at Burlington High School where his last book was on the curriculum. It was fairly harrowing (just think what you would have done to some of your least enjoyed required writers at that age). In general Damien preferred University appearances where all he had to do was talk a bit, read something, and field a couple questions. Sitting in a room of 16 and 17 year olds forced not only to read a book but then forced to deal with the author on a Friday afternoon was about the last thing he wanted to deal with. The school however bought at least 20 copies of the book per semester and offered him a $200 stipend for every appearance. For one hour of work every 6 months it was not something he was likely to refuse, plus although the kids generally scared the shit out of him, it felt pretty good to think he was encouraging them to write. Once more at the insistence of the powers that be (i.e. Damien's agent who forcefully claims poetry doesn't sell), you'll find the first piece he read them at the back, in the Special Features section.

Because they were high school students the fact that he used 'fuck' instantly gave him credibility, and the fact his delivery was in the rapid-fire manner of an MC made it accessible. What Damien viewed as a smart juxtaposition of a Biggie Smalls a la Che Guevara shirt with a Tommy Hilfiger sport coat and jeans and the fact the piece had been recorded as a trip-hop track with moderate success on

European radio (a fact he credited more to the well known DJ who remixed it than his own skill), eventually won over the room.

After he left the high school he went to speak at Burlington College which was far easier and mostly consisted of eager 'how can I get published' inquiries. After that he went to lunch with some of the college's professors who were suitably left-wing ex-hippy for his taste. He had not noticed the Goth girl at the BC reading and did not make the connection when he saw her later that night while playing at Nectar's, the town's main performance venue. Due to unforeseen equipment problems the show had been an unexpectedly intimate one. Rather than wait for a soundman to show up, Damien asked the entire audience to sit on and around the stage and proceeded to do an acoustic set with volunteers and no mic. It had gone off so informally and pleasantly that he told himself he would do another show like it as soon as possible.

Some of the kids at the show were fans Damien had met before and when they asked if he wanted to go to an after-party he joined up merrily, feeling that the day had been an unequivocal success. It was several drinks and a few joints later on a college outdoor porch that Damien felt eyes boring into his head and soon a voice to match from a girl dressed in all black and glaring at him from a patio chair.

"Hey, can I ask you something" she said pulling Damien out of a conversation with the hosts.

Sure, what's up? He said expecting something light along the lines of 'I really liked your show' or 'where are you originally from'. Instead he got

"How do you manage to get published? I mean I found your work to be pretty vulgar and to be honest really immature" her stare Damien realized was one of pure hatred.

Umm... I'm sorry; my name is Damien how are you? He walked over and extended his hand, which she begrudgingly accepted.

"Sarah, and you didn't answer my question"

Well that's because I'm not really sure how. Luck I suppose, years of writing and performing, countless rejections and pressing on through mental and financial ruin beyond common sense. Pick one. Damien was determined not to let her wind him up.

"Yeah well I think it's a shame that there are real hard-working talented writers un-published out there and a hack like you gets a book deal."

Uh-huh, let me guess, you're an artist of some kind, a poet I'm guessing, and you're in your second year of Uni. Wanna drink? Damien snubbed out a Newport and opened the screen door beckoning her to follow.

About an hour later they had plowed through about a dozen shots of Montezuma (possibly the worst tequila available in the states) and Sarah was unabashedly hitting on him. His current girlfriend Jez had been in a particularly bad mood and lately his drunken temptation was coming out as heavy flirting, but he managed to pull back and decided to give her the 'Obi-Wan' speech.

OK, Sarah, so look, I want you to understand something. We are alone, as writers, poets, artists – whatever. We have chosen crafts that require us to be solitary much of the time. We don't play well. No one is as catty as a group of authors towards someone they think doesn't deserve to be a peer. And forget about the public, most of them view you as living a blessed lifestyle and getting overpaid to write cute little stories. Unless you're Salman Rushdie they think you are living off a glorified hobby. I'm telling you this because in the end we only have each other. No matter how bad a writer is I try to encourage them. I will go to readings and buy books by authors whose work I can't stand because we're friends and I want to support them. In a way I'm really just a big fan of art in general. I support these people because someone has to. We're all alone and underpaid. Major publications like the New York Times still pay 10 cents a word and haven't changed their pay scale since the 70's. Random House buys more books than any other publisher, like over a hundred a year, but dumps its marketing funds into less than a dozen titles. The others have to make it on their own or become tax write-offs. This is what we're up against, and we can spend our time tearing each other down or we can help lift each other up. I prefer the latter.

She nodded, turned to the side and began to vomit in a potted plant.

Damien felt this point was an appropriate commentary on his advice and right about the time to flee. Her initial comments however plagued him for months. He suspected the same insecure part of him that believed all negative criticism is what drove him to talk with people who he fundamentally disliked or disagreed with. In the end, he supposed he just wanted people to like him and thought if only he could talk to them, whether through words or speech, they would see what a nice talented fellow he was.

Extroversion as a means of seeing the world – hearing your inner doubts spoken out loud by those you feel the least akin to, and by default are painfully the most similar – it's a real bitch sometimes.

Anatomy of a Poet (Part 3)

There is of course the question of what actually constitutes success for people like Damien. The masochistic nature of baring your intimacies and weaknesses to a critical public may suggest that the question itself is moot. After all, in traditional success there is a certain amount of stability and satisfaction, financial social and otherwise, that contradicts the very nature of performance poetry. Spoken word is confessional, memoir-esque, and not a bit reliant on personal woe and injustice. If one were to be successful in the manner most people defined it, there might not be a whole lot to write about. This thought plagues Damien more than most, since most other slam poets are too busy focusing on refining their three winning pieces over and over again to think about what they would do next if there reached the national or international stage.

These events tend to be held once a week. Nuyorican Poets Café and Bowery Poetry Club are good examples. They will hold a mid-week slam for the course of the year and poets who repeatedly make it to the finals will eventually be put on Friday or Saturday night. Here you face all the other mid-week winners. Winners of these will be ranked and given solo nights. Win enough of these and you will be in line for each venues slam team. The teams, varying in number but usually around 10 with alternates, compete against other teams around the country and the world. Though various countries and states provide interesting variety (such as the Cowboy Poets from down south) it is worth noting that coastal US cities have almost always won (New York in particular).

Slam and performance poetry is not a very mass media art form. If you are incredibly popular you will be given a tour, probably a book deal, and maybe an album if you fit the right criteria. More likely you will be stuck on a string of 'special guest' appearances. This will cover every medium from film to commercials to the end of hip-hop albums. Your job becomes one of adding credibility. This gangster rap group must be socially conscious if they have Sara Jones at the end of their album. This film most surely be hip to have put Saul Williams in it. Isn't HBO cutting edge to have Floetry narrate an ad for the coming season? Then there is the slew of one-man/woman acts - low budget plays that let a slam poet rant for two hours.

Damien is a renaissance robot. He has had bit parts in low budget film and television as a sleazy Asian drug dealer or whimsical poet buddy, has appeared on several dozen hip-hop and experimental techno albums, has played every venue imaginable from stadiums to dive bars, and had his last book picked up by an alternative publisher and distributed in about a dozen countries. You still would probably not recognize him.

Aside from other authors, who can't even comprehend how he is published and funded, most other artists view him as a friendly sort of jack-of-all-trades but master of none. Maybe if you ever needed an ethnic minority to act, write, produce, and do a voiceover all at once Damien would be your man – but that's what specialists are for. Damien's most popular role is as an interesting fellow you meet on the road, tells you some stories and feeds you some verse. You'll probably order his book, might download some tracks off the web, and maybe even check his blog from time to time; but it is doubtful he is likely to become your favorite artist to recommend or follow over time.

So what is success to Damien? Well, if we're talking financial he's got it covered. Between all the royalties on miscellaneous projects (book, albums), the occasional academic or corporate gig (ghostwriting autobiographies for illiterate millionaires), a good head for investment (with cash from the former), a lack of debt, the occasional gig, and a penchant for traveling and living in third world countries, he is fairly well off. To those who envy his lifestyle Damien is quick to point out that starving throughout his teens and twenties and having traded any opportunity for a stable family or long-term relationship for a nomadic lifestyle is not exactly unattainable or even that difficult if that is what they really want.

Here's a simple math equation. Damien owns his home in Mexico. He bought right after Joan passed in '03, practically 9 years to the day after Bryan died, for those keeping count. It was $15,000 for the property, which used to be a Volkswagen shop. Over 4 years he's dumped maybe another 40K into building it and now it's a three level home with a courtyard and Jacuzzi. His total electricity and property tax for the year is less than a hundred dollars. He is the co-owner of the only Mezcal bar in town, which covers its own costs as well as his considerable drinking habits. Damien is paid to perform and sells copies of his book everywhere he goes, and even when he's not working his investments keep him out of debt. Personal travel tends to be in more exotic (i.e. cheap) locales. The trip he is planning right now involves 6 months through Southeast Asia to clear his head. It was a trip he had planned on taking after touring his last book for six months, one that he had wanted to take several years ago with Marie but had been sacked by the towers, a long distance break-up, and general catastrophic depression. The plus was that it was the impetus to live in Mexico and he regrets the situation not. But back on point – after Joan passed he had to cancel his tour and after 6 months of dealing with his parents' lives spent the next 2 years piecing together a rag-tag tour across North America and Europe that provided more relief from estate matters than the desired commercial effect.

Here's the money situation: a round the world ticket that goes from Los Angeles to Hong Kong, Hong Kong to Bangkok (Thailand), Bangkok to Siem Reap (Cambodia), Siem Reap to Phnom Penh (also Cambodia), Phnom Penh to Ho Chi Min (Vietnam and better known as Saigon), Saigon to Hong Kong, and Hong Kong back to Los Angeles is $1,450 after taxes. You read that correctly. The dates are all flexible as long as they occur within a year. This is how Australians travel (since it is too expensive to do it any other way if you are in the middle of the ocean). It is the same exact amount as his Upper East Side pad per month when he's not subletting it out. Southeast Asia including accommodation, food, and a reasonable amount of drink or tourist stuff is between $10 and $20 a day, depending just how frugal you are. That means on a reasonable budget your total cost for six months of living and seeing the world including ticket will be between $3,500 and $6,000. That's a high end of $1,000 a month, now what did you say your current living expenses were again? Keep in mind; wherever he calls home, Damien gets paid the same.

Although this equation may provide the answer to some people's idea of future retirement, joy ride lifestyle, or dream vacation, it did not necessarily equal one of success for Damien. It was simply a means of survival, albeit an interesting one, but survival nonetheless. What Damien wanted was something far more normal and ultimately elusive.

He didn't want to be obsessed with mortality - to continually be haunted by the awareness of just how fragile and dangerous the world really was.

Automaton tendencies aside, Damien wanted to be happy.

In this his vision of success was very much like any anyone else's. Even with artificial parts you can vow to be renaissance. His home might have brick walls in the Mexican Central Highlands rather than a white picket fence. His office might be the wanderlust world. His day job might be a complicated balancing act of gigs, author appearances, recordings and publications; and his retirement fund might be entirely due to a 401k from having been a staff accountant for Prada (2 years, temp job turned cubicle hell, long story, just accept it) and an Asian kid with a head for investment – but ultimately he is much like all of us, and like all of us he is looking for love and appreciation. The difference is Damien wants both from everyone, and that is of course his downfall.

Δ   Δ   Δ   Δ

The Asian Journal of Damien Wood Part 3

Chiang Mai, Pai, and too much Samson
Saturday, June 03, 2006

Current mood: ☺contemplative

So I got to Chiang Mai about a week and a half ago and found it to be the coolest, therefore most troublesome, city I've yet to find in Thailand. The vibes here are so much more open and mellow than the south, and the city itself is way less hectic than Bangkok. I got in at an ungodly hour to what would turn out to be an all-Israeli guesthouse on the edge of town where my buddy Van Gogh who I know from Stamford and haven't seen in 2 years was mysteriously staying. Proceeded to go on wild partying spree ending with very crazy Dutch girls, billiards, and general drunken madness. Steve had to do massage classes at 9am each day and I can only say that he has proven himself to be a saint and a trooper.

I've met some pretty damn cool people, two smokin Thai girls who run a wacky bar called double sixes that is next to a Thai boxing ring, Deb very awesome Brazilian currently lovin it up with VG, and an assorted cast of rotating others. It was in this climate of fun and debauchery that I made a very questionable decision last weekend and, guard down, decided to flee CM Saturday afternoon to meet a Canadian in Pai. Disaster! I went from what was a fairly magical 24 hours in CM to a hungover hell ride up North to the Jungle hippy land.

A Crash Course On the Anatomy of Robots

Within a few minutes of arrival I felt something not quite right but dismissed it as general traveler angst. I proceeded to buy a local map, rent a motorbike, and drive what seemed like forever out of town in the pitch darkness, repeatedly stopping and trying to find the bungalows I was supposedly staying at. Some very kind monks eventually pointed me down a dark muddy dirt path where about a klick down I located a deserted looking set of huts. In fantastic, fucked up fashion I then managed to ride up to the door and dump my bike right into the reception. No damage, but mounds of laughter.

The next 24 hours was a particular study of how things can go very wrong very quickly when you're staying in a remote jungle village with no one there but a girl you'd rather not be seeing and her very young friends. That and a puppy dog Polish guy with a name like a superhero failingly attempting to get with one of said friends. By my second night she said she wanted to stay in her friend's room and I said fine I'm going into town to get wasted. Stupid...

Anyway, next day move into town and met some very cool people and Van Gogh arrived to save me. This of course was a wonderful relief but did not stop me from pulling one final act of utter foolishness. Said Canadian of course shows up at bar with said friends and me, glutton for punishment, convinces her to stay since I can give her a ride later (on my bike). Insert drunken making out with Dutch girl, opening mouth and inserting boot, loss of sandals, and then unwisely getting on said bike. Insert not noticing enormous gap in bridge, insert front tire in said gap, insert full on crash with Canadian in tow. Insert bleeding rather profusely from smashed right arm, poorly apologizing, having everyone in bar run to my aid, Canadian storming off, embarrassment, stupid, stupid, stupid...
This week however has improved greatly since.

Spent a lovely day in Pai out in the mountains and waterfalls. Daytrippin with VG and going to parties, meeting good people and having Australians take the piss out of me. Left to go back to CM, not exactly sure why except that VG wanted to get back to Deb and I wanted a change of scenery. Meet awesome Scot Eilidh. Not enough time before she dipped to Bangkok. My dear Eilidh, maybe see ya in Cambodia.

Now battling to decide what to do. Just ran into some Canadian girls I know from Phuket who are flying to Laos. Want to go but part of me keeps thinking of my hellish ride to Burma and that I've still got 10 days on my visa and why waste em. Still Rob is up there and everyone keeps telling me how fantastic it is and I've just stocked up on Cipro and Doxycycline so....

That's as much as I can muster, write more from Laos or Pai or wherever the road takes me next.

Laos, Canadians and Lao Lao...
Saturday, June 10, 2006

Current mood: 🙂mellow

So I decided to be spontaneous and flee Thailand. I went to Luang Prabang last week via a somewhat questionable plane ride (I'm not used to propellers) and have been chillin since. Hooked up with a group of wacky young Canadian kids.

Luang Prabang was a charming little French colonial village and a good intro to Laos. It is illegal to be on the streets after midnight, and unless you are married, physical contact with locals will land you in jail then thrown out of the country. Of course none of this is particularly enforced and I spent many a night out till dawn. Anyhow, ridiculous waterfalls, tuk-tuks from hell and Vietnam bar are gonna be what sticks.

We all just got to Vang Viang two nights ago. It is truly spectacular here, misty limestone mountains and jungle and beer Lao and Lao Lao (rice wine) in omnipresence. Spent all day yesterday tubing down the Namsong and stopping at river bars with zip lines and giant rope swings - one of which I landed particularly wrong and did a 5 meter belly flop. All I could think was fuck these kids for pulling the rope so high, Laos has abysmal medicine, and surely I've done internal damage to myself. No harm no foul. I have been battling the desire to rent a motorbike here on

121

account of completely shit roads and my track record as of late. Hooking up with Rob, who I got lost and dumped motorbikes with in Krabi, has only been a reminder.

So anyhow, just a quick update. Anything more interesting would be unfit to print. Peace

Leaving Laos, Bangkok again, off to Cambodia...
Tuesday, June 20, 2006

Current mood: 😵 drained

I'm exhausted and back in fucking Bangkok. I've got two days before I fly to Siem Reap in Cambodia to witness what will be the greatest collection of Wats (Buddhist temples) on earth at Angkor and meet up with my friend Eilidh. But right now I just wish I was anywhere but here. So Laos... After climbing to a series of off the beaten path natural pools and jungle to the local waterfalls (complete with sad eyed caged bears and Asian tigers you could feed buffalo on a stick to), I begun to grow weary of Luang Prabang. As the days progressed more and more people I knew from Northern Thailand begun to pour in and my anonymity was feeling a bit shattered. A couple nights in the amazing yet eerily quiet Night Market (Lao Lao with snakes and scorpions and millipedes in the bottles, questionable food vendors (I think I ate dog there by accident), throw rugs, weavings, trinkets and beer Lao shirts), and later nights at the towns only speakeasy (Vietnam Bar where they literally remove the door to let you in), I was ready to go. Hence I, and crew, hit the road for Viang Vien. For a week we hung and mostly tubed down the river, swam in the Namsong (which is refreshing but afterwards makes everything reek of mildew), biked out to caves on stream strewn dirt roads (very adventure sporty), watched too much Simpsons (preferable to the ever present "Friends" bars), and hung out at night at Jaidees (possibly the best bartender on earth) and the Island cafe (quite appropriately across the ricketiest bridge I have ever repeatedly crossed). I had met up with Rob from Kendall earlier and after 7 days we decided to high tail it to Vientiane, which was miserable. For some reasons all the guidebooks list it as a "charming" mix of old Asia meets new. For me it was like the most boring part of a factory wasteland combined with the hassles of Mexico City. That we stayed on the river helped a bit. Rob's friend Alice was also an amazing comfort in that she had a room with AC to stay in. Other than that it was baking in the day while looking for things to do, and trolling for clubs at night that were expensive and awful (I was groped for the first time in Asia by a middle aged Laotian man whilst on the back of his motorcycle taxi). One notable exception was going bowling with Rob and Alice and a bunch of Canadians, only colored by the fact that I am frankly growing sick of Canadians. To my Canadian friends reading this, it of course excludes you. I've already got one email today calling my blogs tasteless. That following the hate mail from a non-fan, calling my writing a combination of "mountainous self-importance and childish smut" (which I actually kinda agree with, but that's the point you fucking loser), I am not really in the mood to defend myself civilly. Ahem. So Rob and I got across the border with little hassle and showed up in Bangkok at 5am. Ian and Georgia were none too pleased that we rolled in unannounced at that godly hour and I am learning to expect that I must send email much further in advance. This afternoon I got money and medical supplies and set my flight for Thursday. I've discovered getting the visas will be cheaper and easier in Cambodia as well as less restricting. So that's the story for now. If you're in Asia next month write me. I'm trying to get something together for my b-day, probably on the beach in Southern Cambodia. Peace, love and all that shit

A Quick Guide on the Art of Traveling

There is a difference between a traveler and a tourist that will never be fully understood by the latter, and within the two there are subdivisions that almost no one understands. Damien is a live abroad, part-time expat (though he will cheerily point out you can't be an ex if you were never a patriot in the first place). To understand what this means let us view the two major types:

Tourists and travelers as broad terms differ in one main area and this is time spent abroad. The determination of this time is subjective and changeable; usually by the parties described (i.e. more ambitious tourists would like to be thought of as travelers). Travelers like to think that they come to a place to 'get native,' in other words live like the locals, eat the food, pick up the language, and make local friends, that sort of thing. They think of tourists as rich people who attempt to cram as many sights and countries in as short of a time as humanly possible in the least efficient economic ways. Tourists conversely think of many travelers as dirty hippies and aimless young people who spend more time drinking than learning about a place, or aimless drifters unable to live stable lives. As in all things there is truth to all of this so let us get down to the subdivisions.

- At the bottom of the food chain are *Package tourists* and they are just what they sound like. They purchase all-inclusive tours that cover hotel, airfare (or cruise or bus or what have you) and some meals. These tend to be either of the whirlwind (see all of Africa in 2 weeks) or exclusive variety (enjoy the beautiful beaches and cuisine of the Caribbean without having to actually meet any locals). They receive the ire of locals, travelers, and even other tourists.

- *Vacationers* and *families on holiday*, just like it sounds, all of us have been there.

- *Rich folks slumming it.* If you ever end up in the third world and meet a nice middle aged couple who have somehow managed to spend more on their daily budget than you would for a month yet can't stop remarking just how cheap everything is you've met one of this type. They range from very nice and likely to buy you a meal, to condescending fucks that will demand you put out your cigarette. They tend to be fascinated with the traveler type.

- *Market hunters* are professional tourists and to be fair they come in both tourist and traveler variety. In the former they supplement their income and furnish elaborate homes, and in the latter it's totally a matter of income. They essentially run back and forth from impoverished countries buying up as much inexpensive local wares as humanly possible, usually with the intention of selling those same wares for about 1000 percent their value in their country of origin. Go to any market in Asia and Latin America and you will find them lugging dozens of suitcases around while their husbands or partners sit in local cafes reading English language papers.

- *Solo travelers* are just what they sound like. Students on a off year, artists with time off, and general travel junkies with hoarded time off – they come in many varieties but their commonality is the need to travel on their own schedule as single entities (though they will often link up for short periods of time with other solo travelers, without strings of course). Damien falls most closely into this sub-grouping.

- *Trustafarians*, rich kids on tour, usually financially aided by said trust fund, often accompanied by ill-suited dread locks. Ill-suited as they are almost always of European descent. Catch signs are an over abundance of local or beachwear and too much time in India studying at an Ashram. They tend to have a philosophy which though ill defined is generally harmless.

- *Chavelers*, derived from the British slang for Ghetto or lower class (Chav), these are the frat-boys and sorority girls of the traveler nation. They tend to be loud and young (though immaturity knows no age boundaries) and have come to paradise for a good time, quick lays, and cheap drinks. They are given to fighting in public, arguing with natives, and generally complaining about temperature and local conditions ("What do you mean there's no hot water?"). They often refer to their time abroad as 'holiday,' tend to be in admirable physical condition (as much of their time is spent tanning and playing), and are OK for a drink as long as you don't talk about football.

- *Terminal cases*, a leftover from the 60's but also in younger varieties, these are the people that are never off the road. Though a certain amount of credibility is shared among travelers in time on the road (i.e. 1 month = amateur, 1 year = cool) there comes a point where it becomes incredulity. Often these people have been traveling for decades and can speak several languages with an unspecified knowledge base, which makes them wicked trivial pursuit players. Unfortunately the long-term effects of drug use and local moonshines dull some of their abilities to form continuous thoughts and often the conversation will linger on how good a certain type of hash was, let's say in the 80's in Central America. Mostly harmless and good company, but due to the nature of time spent an unfortunate amount are permanent grifters and must be watched out for.

- *Gurus,* beware of this type as they may come disguised as any of the former types. They have gone everywhere, done everything, and will be more than happy to give you advice and stories perpetually ending with the lamentation of how shit/built up/no longer cool/no longer real that place has become. Nothing you can say will impress them as they've done it before, probably before you were born, and it wasn't even that good then anyhow. Most prominent in the trustafarian and terminal traveler strains.

- Those that defy conventional labels: The Americans, Israelis, and other anomalies.

  o Israelis are by far the most notorious of the traveler nation. Invariably they travel in packs of 4 to a dozen and have all just finished mandatory military experience. They stick to themselves, converse in

Hebrew, and usually refuse to learn or conform to local culture. Though this makes them wicked bargainers and fairly competent in many natural settings, it does make them a bit of a pain in the ass to be around and when not being antisocial conversations will often be in the form of vigorous political debate. They smoke insane amounts of hashish and tend to be afflicted with the same afflictions as any small insular group of young people.

o Americans are the flavor of the moment in the easy target realm. Not a little influenced by the war on terror and international policy, they are the low end of the traveler totem pole. With less than 10 percent of the whole country holding passports and a rampantly jingoistic nature they are instantly looked down upon as a group. These assumptions however, like those toward Israelis, fly out the window in the case of most solo travelers. The most common remark a solo American may receive after being delivered a lecture on Iraq and Bush as Hitler is 'but you're nothing like that.' Further inquiry will lead to the discovery that they may be the first American the other has encountered and fully interacted with, probably systemic of the passport issue.

o Expatriates, though not really necessarily tourists or travelers, tend to be both. They are the permanent residents of countries not born in. Usually motivated by financial (retirement, cheaper living), nationalistic (heritage, dislike of one's own country of birth), and personal (fell in love and never left). They are both local and foreign at the same time. Though they will never fully be accepted in the surrogate society they are as close as a tourist or traveler will ever come to getting truly native. Damien is also one of these.

o The PAID Traveler or Tourist is in a way what all travel junkies aspire to. It is the next step up from a paid businessman who moonlights as the international wanderer on the corporate account. It is the businessman whose business is travel itself. These include professional travel writers, international diplomats, translators, and Cable television special commentators (think David Attenborough and that Insomniac guy). The ghetto version would be the guy or gal who bar tends and runs hostels at every town he or she stops in.

You are now armed and ready to understand the groups around you and where you fit in them. There are many combinations and degrees of these types as well as some interesting sub-types you are sure to find (think a Canadian businessman who opened a bar in Bangkok and now travels around Laos in his spare time writing articles for *Conde Nast*).

When you do hit the road do your country and generation proud by not being a twat. Tip well and try to learn at least a little about the local culture, history, and language. Certainly don't expect to know anything cause you watch the *Travel Channel* or read the fucking *Beach*. You certainly wouldn't think you could perform surgery cause you watch lots of *ER* (at least one hopes you would not, you're not American are you?)

And if you happen to be somewhere hot and remote and find yourself unreasonably bored and you happen to see Damien scribbling in a bar or reciting spoken word to a bunch of Canadian girls, buy him a drink.

Don't worry. He gets generous after a couple

Δ   Δ   Δ   Δ

The Asian Journal of Damien Wood Part 3 (Continued)

June 23, 2006

In Siem Reap with Eilidh, Rob's got Typhoid, Ian's back to Newcastle, your pack weighs a ton, spending American making it tough to track budget, the mosquitoes got you stealth on the river today.

Ms. McLeod what are you doing to my judgment?

A Crash Course On the Anatomy of Robots

Battambang with Eilidh

On a bamboo train amongst rice paddies

And smiling children who scream "hello!"

I felt the heat of my motorbike

Against my back

And the curve of your hip

In my side.

As the sun set I thought silly things

And remembered last night

And that sometimes bourbon

Makes me more

American

Than usual

That is to say

I don't know when to let

Emotions stay silent

Or practical

Or acknowledge the specifics

Of time's passing

(See Special Features section for more…)

July 4, 2006

Independence Day, foolish emails, no brauts or beer quite yet. You've just sent an email to Eilidh, doomed you're sure. You're both traveling alone, short on time and sure to meet others. Still, that part of you that longs completion still needs closure or (*breathe idiot*) continuation of this. You are more and more aware of your shortcomings and weakness, more craving to come clean to yourself and those around you. Your thoughts of past friends and lovers and loved ones fill you with dread and shame of combined actions, those with mal-intent and not, but mostly the thoughtlessness of a selfish species.

Like Joan, when you die, you want to be loved and remembered and all those things that we never receive in life. But unlike her and Bryan, and this is key, it will be without regret – perhaps for others or even times with them, but never yourself and what you have done

You have eaten Kangaroo and frog here in Cambodia, and once maybe dog in a night market in Laos; licked the insides of thighs on several young ladies; and smoked and drank like a combustible engine. But the taste of redemption has somehow escaped you, the vintage of freedom just out of reach – as landmine victims grasping with phantom limbs, or childhood ambition in the bottom of a wine glass. Like the memory of lips as they wet upon yours, like the speed of light known but unreachable, you are reaching for stars.

July 16, 2006

Eilidh gets in in an hour and a half and you're waiting in an airport in PP after sharing a cab with Chris from Liverpool and his newlywed Irish Annette. Scaled a barbwire gate and woke up Ben to get your key last night in the not so blissful guesthouse that Angela runs. Anger over two nights ago faded though agitation remains. Fucking Danish arrogance, why open a guesthouse in Asia if you don't like travelers?

Figure you and Eilidh will spend a night then head back to Kampot. Check out Bokor and Kep, maybe a night each, and see what Kampot has to offer (Rabbit Island and such.)

Queasy, not sure why, perhaps you're feeling lost, maybe generalized depression. Maybe it's as simple as just being tired of being alone all the time, bumping and drifting into peoples' lives, re-envisioning yourself and life to make a coherent story rather than the aimless chaos that seems more likely.

August 1, 2006

Eilidh's in Bangkok. You've been sitting in the airport for over four hours and you've got more to go. You felt like crying last night and couldn't sleep. Apparently Eilidh did the same after you left Battambang. Fuck, you love her. How fucking rare and impossible, how lucky and unlucky.

Oh shut up you twat...

A Crash Course On the Anatomy of Robots

Escape from New York (A Crash Course on the Anatomy of Relationships)

"Amor de lejos es amor de pendejos"

Literal translation: "Love of afar is the love of fools"

-Mexican colloquialism

A Crash Course On the Anatomy of Robots

Test Drives

New York, Los Angeles and Mexico
January – April 2006

Here's a cruel equation. Everyone you meet has a shelf life.

The hot girl behind the bar, that buff guy with the perfect teeth, your secretary at the office – in the back of your mind there is the inherent understanding that if you were ever to be lucky or stupid enough to work your way into some unimaginably torrid affair that it would end pretty quickly and most likely in disaster. This does not just apply to relationships but is inevitably exacerbated by them.

You see with friendships there is always the safety valve of space. Perhaps your good buddy at work is a 2-hour per week kinda pal. Maybe your shopping girl is an all day Sunday partner. You call to get your weekly or monthly fix and that's that. The death of most roommates and travel companions comes at the lack of understanding this fundamental ratio. Some very irrational correlation develops in one's mind completely out of the context, let alone time constraints, of the relationship. You start to believe that having a laugh at the pub every day after work will make your drinking buddy a good flatmate or back-up in a third world country. By the time you've started brushing the toilet with their toothbrush or pricing out professional hits in Argentina it's a mystery to all involved as to why one thought it was a good idea in the first place.

That of course is the trap of intimate relationships. By definition you must spend lots of time together, adjust and compromise to each others' habits and schedules, and most likely live in the same domicile at some point or another (if you are in a major city for no other reason than the financial sense of it, which of course will not factor in later therapy sessions, lost sleep, and pet settlement).

This logically brings us to Damien's current unhealthy (and not at all unfamiliar) existential crisis. Though he is aware of all the pitfalls of the prior conditions (most especially due to unreliable roommates, travel partners, and not a few ill-advised girls behind the bar - in one case a secretary) the unique parameters of his life in the city and abroad have guaranteed a certain amount of a slight variation if not combination of the prior conditions. In short, living in the city and on the road eliminates the shelf life equation.

When everyone you meet can be ditched for the next destination of the road (and to be fair can just as easily ditch you), and every event you attend while living in a city of 15 million promises dozens of one-time encounters, there is a lack of consequence to hooking up. More aptly, as consequence might to be too moral of a way to approach this, there is a degree of safety and appreciating and seeing people for who they are. You may be fully aware that a cute affectation a woman exhibits might drive you positively suicidal after a week, or that the way the handsome boy talks to wait staff would eventually make you slap him – but – for a night or two you might find it cute, what's more you can tell yourself that they would change eventually without actually having to be around to find out how disappointed you would be.

It's like cars, to use an unbelievably crude and cruel metaphor. You can appreciate a Corvette though you'd never buy it. It's too flashy and Guido for your taste, and completely impractical for your lifestyle and the city – BUT – you wouldn't mind taking one for a test drive, and hell maybe when that mid-life crisis blindsides you, you might even consider leasing it. Partners on the road are like leased cars; as soon as you're dissatisfied you can trade up. This might sound heartless but it is the imperfection of the metaphor. After all, you are being leased just as much as you are leasing.

The problem for Damien is that sometimes at the end of the lease you decide to buy a model. It's like shipping a giant antique wooden table from Malaysia that when you saw it you couldn't imagine anything more beautiful in the world. When it arrives you realize it's three times too big for your apartment and not as nice as it looked in a smoky Ashram just outside Chennai. It is far tougher when you are dealing with people.

And of course a robot like Damien loves cars.

Fucking bored and censored in the city of lost angels

Los Angeles, February 2006

Los Angeles is a lot like New Jersey with a bit more rep and a lot more palm trees. The concept of walking to get around here is just that, with a 20-mile drive considered to be just around the corner and someone an hour away to still be considered to live in your same town. Combine that with highways that never get any better than your last 10 miles on the Van Wyck to JFK – except for a hundred miles – and you've got some idea of what awaits you on the 405. The fact that every freeway must be prefaced with "the" gives you some scope of the epic nature of automotive navigation here.

It was then with little surprise but quite a bit of agitation that Damien found himself driving a rental through Tujunga the first week he had arrived. In true stereotypical fashion he had managed to get t-boned by some 17-year-old Middle Eastern valet kid in Santa Monica within 24 hours of his arrival thus near totaling his car and reminding him of his dislike of Southern California. That and his inability to vocalize this due to the sensitivity of the city's inhabitants, most especially to New Yorkers, left him with a low-level continuous road rage and general malaise at the inability to walk to a local drinking hole.

He was currently staying at the far off the beaten path home of the childhood friend of Ivy, his daytime amour. Tujunga incidentally was the setting for the film Memento. Apparently it used to be the meth capital of LA and quite a white power trailer bike spot. Now it was more or less a moderate upscale strip mall in the middle of nowhere with fairly nice views, tons of fast food, and somewhat shitty paved roads that were all but recently shitty dirt roads. If you can remember the Travel Inn that Guy Pierce holed up in you can imagine that Damien was up the hill behind it about a half mile. Damien however, unlike the retrograde amnesiac protagonist of that film was stricken with the unfortunate ability to remember everything.

For example, the night he and MOC arrived from their grueling fifty some odd hour drive from Manhattan, was frighteningly clear in his head. Stinking of road and menthols and not enough baby powder he had rolled up to the nondescript ranch on the hill feeling delirious and needing some rest but more or less overjoyed to see Ivy. At first there were kisses and awkward shifts into comfort that come with separation and exhaustion and remembering someone's taste and touch. But all this was too brief before repeated glasses of vodka were shoved into their hands which he may not have minded except that it was through necessity not festivity and that his last ex Jezebel drank tons of the eastern European firewater and he did not need a reminder of what he had just fled.

Jenny, the girl who owned said house on the hill, is dying of a liver disorder. She has lost much of the use of her legs as well as quite a bit of weight since her degenerative condition onset several months ago and has basically gone from the kind of girl you would make multiple proposals to on any given night to someone who would make Calista Flockhart feel fat. She is sweet but perhaps a bit damaged and loopy and most definitely cabin fever socially out of it. She is also still a raging alcoholic. Therefore as Damien rolled out of his car, stinking and dizzy and smiling all the same, Ivy ran up and told him Jenny was downing Vodka in the name of being a gracious host, despite the fact dying on them would probably be somewhat rude, and that they as friends must dump and drink the handle of Kettle One before she had a chance to make another cocktail.

They did the deed played some very shitty pool and then stumbled off to a decrepit couch to do what Damien surmised would be very bad sex, but instead found himself lying in a puddle of cold vomit from a passed out Ivy in a freezing guest room that smelled of cat piss.

The week has not improved much since.

Δ   Δ   Δ   Δ

The daytime lover

At this moment Damien thinks Ivy is quite possibly the love of his life. She is from California and not very adept at holding her vodka. She is beautiful and voluptuous in a Betty Page meets Shirley Manson sort of way, has multiple sexy tattoos, used to be a punk rocker and is currently a women's rights advocate. For all these reasons and more Damien, in Mexico, made some very wrongheaded assumptions about her. For example, when they first met outside a local pub in his expatriate colonial town, he was drunk waxing prolix about the nature of art with some classical musicians as he is sometimes predisposed to do when having had enough tequila. In his mind he comes across as wise and humble and not a bit experienced. The truth is easier to see in the eyes of a red-haired stranger or rather the rolling of said orbitals and mutterings of "egotistical moron" under said breath. For this reason, which Damien could not help continually observing out of his peripheral vision, he surmised that this girl who did not know him, instantly disliked him, and saw him clearer than any of the art fag fashion snobs around him. In these two cases he was probably right. However, upon their next subsequent meeting at a house party he mysteriously found himself accompanying her home and beginning to like her and making several, inaccurate, assumptions about her. These were grave misperceptions indeed, which would later haunt him (or more like nag him) on a daily basis.

The first of these assumptions was that Ivy was a night person. Since she was a former LA punk rocker who worked seemingly ludicrous night shifts in women's shelters and seemed like rock and roll embodied in a nonplussed smirk, Damien simply assumed she was a fellow nocturnal creature. They had met in a bar, become acquainted at a party, and for most of their following courtship hung out at night. He also, due to gross stereotyping of tattoos and red hair, assumed she was both a smoker and a drinker. The fact was that she was allergic to smoke, and you already heard the bit about the vodka and – well you can see where this is going. Damien was an unrepentant lifer when it came to smoking, drinking, and adapting his insomnia into an active nightlife. He wrote in bars and clubs, slept like a Vampire in the late hours of the afternoon, and generally felt that excess was far preferable to the omnipresent threat of boredom. Damien was unfortunately fairly accommodating as well, which he might attribute to the sort of company he had to put up with on a nightly basis, and it soon became clear that of the two of them, it would be he that would be waking up at intolerable hours, smoking in frigid nether regions of his own home, and cutting back his partying to a very weekend warrior sort of level. All of this was at first a welcome breeze in the not so healthy yet balmy glide of his current existence. Of course after a while one misses the creature comforts of familiarity.

The other big misassumption, and this one is a whopper, was that Ivy was being open to him because she was looking for a romp in the sack and not a whole lot more. His female understanding seemed to have plummeted as of late, a fact that he blamed on his recent break-up and being out of practice. The town in Mexico they called home was also notorious for travelers and temporary students and residents, who as a whole tend to be a promiscuous low consequence bunch. In his mind, Damien saw that a girl who so clearly found him arrogant and disagreeable must simply want him around for physical reasons, either that or a male revenge fantasy masochism he did not care to contemplate. For himself, despite a growing feeling of what he would alarmingly and clumsily describe as "really like," he'd convinced himself that some friendly or not so friendly copulation would be harmless and possibly snap him out of his depressive rut.

A Crash Course On the Anatomy of Robots

Of course he was again wrong. Ivy as it turned out had never been out of a relationship for most of her adult life and was lastingly serially faithful with an aversion to most of Damien's casually debauched tendencies. For the first time in his life, which may of course be a comment on his taste, Damien found himself with someone who had actually slept with fewer people that he had. That plus anything less than full on vaginal intercourse counted as a zero on his list of experiences which brought him with Ivy to the uncomfortable number 13 (her favorite number by the way), digits he found only a bit less unnerving than the number 6.

Despite their extreme differences in matters of daily life and routine, Damien and Ivy concentrated on the commonalities, moved in together, talked about forever, and were relatively content with one another. All of which is to say that by late September due to an unforeseen loophole of misperception Damien had convinced his mechanical self he was deeply in love with someone who could actually love him back till he received a call on a sunny Sunday afternoon.

They had planned to take a break from Mexico for a bit to check out Asia. Damien needed to travel to clear his head. Ivy had some free time to prepare before her latest Mexican outreach project was launched and they figured now was the perfect time to focus on one another and ride off into the sunset. She would go up to LA and save cash, he would go to New York, empty his apartment and finish off the last shreds of logistical bullshit with his parents' estate and house in Connecticut. By the time he left the east coast to drive to Cali with his friend MOC their lives would be in respective order and they'd be ready to hit the road. What exact delusions made Damien think that these already suspect and complicated plans would go off without a hitch seems like pure nonsense to him now.

But when he thinks of what started the whole mess that followed: the unbelievable convergence of circumstance, fraud, poor judgment, and simple bad luck - it was unequivocally the one event.

The phone call got shit rolling.

$$\Delta \quad \Delta \quad \Delta \quad \Delta$$

The call from J

Central Mexico, January 2006

"Damien? That you?"

The voice was delayed and the reception was bad and Damien's hangover was brutal. He had spent all morning running from butchers and vegetable stands attempting to avoid an unpleasant ride to *Commercial Mexicana* in the center of town. Now, amidst questionable meat marinating in equally questionable sauces he picked up his cell phone to an unavailable number with a recognizable voice speaking in English. It was all a bit surreal.

Holy shit! J is that you?! Damien said through his haze as he thought how less and less of his friends made the effort every year to make the holiday shout out.

"Yeah big D, what up kid?"

Jesus Jasper you're the last person I was expecting to hear from, whatcha doin brother?

"Nothing kid, nothing, how's life down south treating you?"

Dope man, I'm just about to do this going away fiesta for Ivy. She's goin to LA for a minute to make some dough."

"Cool man, then you guys are off to Thailand or some shit right?"

Yeah man, lounging on the beach, smoking some opium, getting trashed on Thai whiskey, you know me.

"Right, right."

But check it kid, I've got like 40 people showin up in the next hour and I gotta start the grill and shit and clean up around here, but I wanted to tell you that I'll be back in the city in like a week or two to get some of my stuff from the apartment and tie up shit with my folks' place in Stamford.

"Yeah I heard about that. That's kinda why I was callin."

Well word kid, we should definitely get up. Hopefully my cell's gonna be workin again in the states and I think I still got your number…

"Word, yeah we should do that. But…"

What?

"Well I heard you were coming back and I wanted to be the first to tell you."

His voice was hesitant, not like the *guess what I'm engaged* or *I just got signed to Sony* kinda hesitant, it was more like the *do you remember so-and-so? Well they got hit by a bus* kinda hesitant.

Tell me what man?
"Well..."
What man? Is something wrong?
"I'm kinda seeing Jez."
OK...

It had been almost six months since she had broken up with him on his birthday/2 year anniversary of his mother's passing. Six months with intermittent contact ranging from drunken messages in the middle of the night (*fuck you, you fucking cock-sucking piece of shit motherfucker*) to somewhat polite email exchanges (*I'm doing better and started dating again and trying not to be so angry with you all the time*). He had dealt with voluntary exile, nearly drank himself to death with his buddy Alex, met and fell in love with Ivy, and was finally heading to Asia – a trip he had planned with Marie before it all went to shit and Joan had passed almost three years ago. When he thought of Jez now he mostly just hoped she was happy.

Which is why he found it somewhat strange when he heard a hollow somewhat toneless voice emerge from his throat saying:

I'm not quite sure how to respond to that.

"Yeah well I just wanted to be the one to tell you. I mean I heard you were coming back and all and Lego and MOC have been pressuring me to call you."

So you called me cause you heard I was coming back and are trying to avoid a beating?

"Naw man, it's not like that."

You can't call me to say hi and how am I doing you just called me to tell me you're sleeping with my ex?

"Naw man, of course I want to say hi and hear from you. I just heard you were coming and wanted you to know. I mean are we cool?"

With Herculean effort:

I mean... yeah man... I mean that's crazy, that shit is... how long... no wait. I don't wanna know... shit man that's nuts – ok, fuck. I'm really hung over right now... Yeah look dude, it's cool I guess congratulations and I hope you're happy.

"She's a really cool girl man."

Yeah, I know (and pretty good in the sack right buddy?)

"I mean we were fighting it for a hot minute man. I really had to convince her my motives were noble you know."

Uh-huh.

"I mean we're really happy."

Yeah.

"I'm so glad you're cool with this man. I knew you would be. Adena flipped, and everyone's kinda been crazy about this whole thing."

You don't say.

"But you're cool with it?"

Yeah man.

"That's great. I told Jez you'd understand, she thought you might freak cause she made such a big deal about making you promise you'd never see any of her friends, let alone close pals"

Uh-huh, well I'm crazy hung-over and I gotta start cooking.

"I guess it's better I got you now before you got drunk right?"

Right. Cause if it was later I might just tell you I was on my way to the airport to come get you.

(Laughing) "Yeah right so I'm glad I got you early."

Right. Well I gotta go.

"Alright kid, I'll see ya in a minute."

Uh-huh

"Love you man."

Yeah

Damien hung up the phone and went from a slow chuckle to a despairingly uncontrollable series of laughter-like sounds that could also be mistaken for schizophrenic tics. He was in the process of muttering curses to an unresponsive lime tree when Ivy came up and asked him what was going on.

I'm blindly fucking crudo and the house is a mess. My best friend is fucking my ex and called me cause he heard I was on my way. I told him I was cool with it. I think I'm going to kill someone.

He spent the afternoon getting alcohol poisoned and pissing Ivy off with being so bothered about the Jasper thing. A week later she was in LA and he was in Manhattan.

Back in fucking New York

January 2006

From the moment he left his friend Julie's bar in downtown Guanajuato to get on a plane to Miami then Jersey, Damien had the unshakable feeling of dread. It was always a bit unnerving getting on a plane inebriated and exhausted having to look forward to a slew of annoying custom questions. Of course it was preferable to actually being sober and awake. Also, thanks to the wonderfully inept Bush administration he could look forward to yet another round of inane inquiry from Homeland Security, which Damien felt sounded a bit too much like Motherland, with bored agents who didn't do much to dispel the fascist parallel.

All in all however, his trip was fairly smooth and agitation-free. He read yet another Continental magazine and Sky-mall brochure, saw some horrible Queen Latifah flick without sound, and more or less arrived in Newark unscathed. His friend Lego, to whom he had lent his late 90's sedan, picked him up on time without incident and had even managed to fix his side view mirror and replace the spare in his absence. As they rode through the ghostly Holland tunnel under the Hudson River and into Tribeca he had the fleeting thought that perhaps it would be nice to be back in the northeast and say goodbye to his hometown properly before becoming a permanent expatriate.

This thought did not last.

He was back in the Upper East Side for approximately twenty seconds when the temperature hit him. Wearing an Adidas jump top over a t-shirt suddenly seemed like a profoundly bad idea. The bar on the corner was in full frat-boy karaoke swing and a gaggle of morons was currently arguing with a homeless Knicks fan in his doorway, having long forgotten the reason they had exited the bar to smoke in the first place. Wrestling with his luggage and keys Damien managed to almost step on his neighbors' freakishly small dog (or freakishly large rodent) before tripping over his own backpack and stumbling into the stairs. Muttering and stinking once more, Damien made his way up the pad.

Once inside he was greeted by Kienyo, G (a frequent Baile Funk partner white guy DJ subletter), and G's girl. Damien unpacked into the living room and promptly collapsed into the couch with a double scotch neat. We could theoretically start here with the onslaught of rumor and opinion and expectation making he was subjected to throughout the next endless 10 days. We could detail how G and his girl whom Damien had never met began right off the back to talk about how fucked the whole situation between Jez and J was while Kienyo tried as hard as he could to make everyone pretend that nothing was happening at all. We could even describe how Damien went from simply very tired and agreeable to consenting and hospitable while internally growing very dark indeed – but the thing is that all that will become apparent soon enough.

What is more relevant to his subsequent descent toward the ninth circle is a one-bedroom turned two above a shitty bar on 92nd and 3rd in Yorkville, the home of Gracie Mansion, Carl Schultz, and a very lost Damien come home.

Δ   Δ   Δ   Δ

The apartment, Penny, and unpaid bills

In lieu of the actual owner, Penny is Damien and Kienyo's landlady. She is an unseen all-seeing agent for a management company somewhere in Long Island City, which despite its name is actually in Queens. She is manic and loud and given both to yelling at you as if you were family and blaming you for whatever problems she has. She is dogged and uncompromising, refuses to yield on the most minor concessions, and given to pithy remarks designed to make you feel incompetent and wrong. Damien has never actually met Penny, but he intrinsically despises her.

From the moment the three of them moved in (this was when Jez was still around, in the apartment anyhow) Penny had been a continual and constant source of frustration. If she was fined for garbage on the street it must be their fault. Having a potted plant on the fire escape was a massive violation to be scolded for at once. The Con-Ed bill going to some mysterious address because of the former tenant - ditto. The neighbor's tub flooding their bathroom - clearly they were to blame and needed to talk with the plumber. Going out of the country, god-fucking-forbid, who's in the apartment? Having Damien's name only on the lease was its own set of endless harassing phone calls about subletting and other such horseshit. That and somehow the woman couldn't tell who was who since she repeatedly talked to Damien in the third person. But with prices being what they are in New York, and the fact that he traveled all the time, Damien had thought that after awhile things would calm down, the finder's fee would balance out, and it would eventually all be worth it.

It was the wall that ended up being the camel's back breaker.

They had gotten the apartment with the assumption it could be converted into a two bedroom. The rent had seemed almost reasonable given this fact and the realtor and super both assured them it was OK. Even later in a meeting with the owner (who later denied any such event) it was understood that a wall could be erected if it was removed when they left. The three of them, that is Damien, Kienyo and Jez, decided that despite a lack of construction or sheet rocking skills that they as resourceful young intelligent people would be able to build such a barrier. Therefore it is understandable that after hundreds of dollars each and countless curse-filled nail-torn spackle-ruined hours none of them anticipated having to remove the thing for a good many years when they would eventually vacate the overpriced shithole. This was so critical to both the daily living situations (not having to experience each others' sex lives in 3D for example) and practical future of the apartment (subletting while Damien and K were on tour DJ'ing, reading, or whatever), that it was simply a given. It even seemed that when Damien had spoken with Penny and subsequently the owner, that there was a very clear understanding of "as long as we don't have to hear about it" from both parties.

It was therefore, not without a bit of terror and alarm, that Damien learned of the current living situation that could be summarized in one simple word: illegal. Some time before he had arrived it appeared that Penny had discovered the wall and demanded that it be torn down, at which point the super and owner spontaneously experienced amnesia as to stating any such wall was authorized to begin with. This posed several problems in that for one that they had barely figured out how to put the damn thing up in the first place and two, G, the current sub-letter, was currently living in the second room surely with the expectation of privacy. Damien's disbelief at Penny's announcement was made even worse by the following realizations:

- K had failed to come up with rent for several months and was writing checks out on Damien's bankbook.

- G had never contributed to any utility bills since he was never asked which led to the discovery that none of them had been paid.

- All of Damien's belongings had been hammered into a bathroom closet that now very closely resembled both in appearance and functionality a very large *Jenga* puzzle.

- Jez had fled the apartment with everything she cared for that did not make it into said puzzle. Including, Damien suspected, his prize iPod, the only gift of substance she had ever deigned to give him.

- In lieu of renewing the lease in December, Kienyo had decided that the situation had become unmanageable and they were more or less living as squatters under Damien's rental agreement which neither G nor Damien had known until that moment as Kienyo had convinced himself he would remedy the situation before either was the wiser.

And the final of course, in perfect time – Damien had till the end of the week to find a home for his possessions and somehow clean up this mess which included taking down the wall, covering hopelessly overdue bills and shipping everything down to Mexico along with his stuff from his parents' house in Connecticut which had incidentally sold the week before and he now also had only till the end of the week to accomplish.

All of this came to Damien's attention and profound dismay the first 3 days of his homecoming. He remembered it between heavy drinking, desperate calls to Ivy, and the omnipresent input of the peanut gallery on how he should be reacting to the whole Jez and Jasper thing. So without further ado we'll simply say that for 3 days Damien was not so happy to be back and more than a bit stressed about what to do with all of his life's possessions and how to salvage his credit and all the while desperately wanting to be in sunny California with his Ivy. It was on this third day of what he planned to be a week that Damien, waking up on his couch and contemplating a quick dive from a tall building, heard his phone ring and groggily answered without checking the caller ID.

"Howdy stranger," the voice said and *Hi Jez* he said and quite irrationally within the hour he found himself sitting across from her in an Irish spot drinking coffee and forcing down food to pretend he still had an appetite and smile to show he wasn't really hurt while listening attentively to show he wasn't actually mad while sitting composed choking on the comedy of it all.

Δ   Δ   Δ   Δ

A casual drink to destroy all self-worth

As one gets older one's tendency toward self-destruction becomes all the more evident. Damien could think of no other logical reason that he not only agreed but also suggested that he and Jez grab a coffee that Sunday afternoon. In his mind he told himself he simply wanted to wish her and Jasper well, make sure she was doing OK and achieve some closure that he chronically sought. He was leaving on Thursday for Los Angeles, and the time in between would be a frantic scramble to move all of his belongings into a storage space his brother had rented for him in Stamford, compulsively take inventory of the items to clear Mexican customs, and then have the shippers he contracted a year ago pick it all up and send on its merry way. He saw little sleep let alone free time beyond those tasks and any beyond that would surely be spent dealing with lawyers and accountants over his parents' estate, getting his car tuned up for the long drive, and trying to smooth over any lingering real estate problems with Penny. Therefore Damien went to the Kinsdale Tavern quite confident it would be the last time he and Jez would see each other and quite possibly even speak for a very long time, if ever again.

It was in this frame of mind that Damien arrived at the local pub on a Sunday afternoon clad in an old winter jacket he'd inherited from his father by default (his brother was much too big for it) and armed with the determination to be cool with whatever happened. He spotted Jez immediately and was seated by a polite mid-thirties Irish server after the customary ceremonial kiss and hug so specific to exes feigning ease.

"You look great" Jez said with a big smile and for a moment he believed it.

You too. How have you been? He scanned through the menu remembering how distinctly unpleasant eye contact could be with someone you didn't want to be able to see inside you.

"Great. Great. I'm so glad to see you. J told me about your talk. I'm so happy you guys are cool. There's been so much drama here with all our supposed friends. I'm sure it's the last thing you want to hear about."

Trust me I've been hearing it. He wondered what he could possibly stomach at this moment and decided upon crab cakes with carrot hash and potato mash.

A Crash Course On the Anatomy of Robots

"You have no idea what it's like here. You've only been around for like a few days. Trust me I've been getting shit for a long time now."

She proceeded to order a wheat beer of some kind. He didn't actually hear the name but the yellow stein appeared with a lemon in it and he was quite confident in the ability for an Irishman to discern the proper garnish. They chatted sparingly surface for about 15 minutes till his food arrived. She talked about how she had finally gotten her work and living situation together though it was still pretty financially rough and that she was living in Spanish Harlem, which wasn't a whole lot different from central Mexico. She and Jasper were happy if socially exiled as everyone found their relationship to be in extremely bad taste (including Damien). He mentioned his Asia travel plans and how he was very happy in his current love and how pleased he was that Jez had seemed to be really together and satisfied in her life. None of these remarks were a lie per se. Damien was happy for her and as a friend had always hoped for her well-being. However, right about the time his food arrived something sour had started to twist in his gut and he promptly switched from coffee to a Yeungling.

It was right as an odd plate with 6 perfectly round bumps arrived (2 crab, 2 hash, 2 mash) that he suddenly became possessed of the image of his first guitar. He had bought it when he was 15 at a mega-outlet in Torrington. It had taken him months of saving up his pathetic salary at the local library (the only legal part-time work he could get before he turned 16) and it was a beauty - that is to say, it looked beautiful. The 1989 BC Rich Warlock was in fact an unwieldy showy piece of shit. With red and black marble crackling and a wicked X-shaped body, the thing practically screamed metal and rock-n-roll. It was one of those axes you'd see Marty Friedman or Steve Vai or whatever virtuoso of the moment wailing on through some music-geeks bootleg video. The problem was, if you weren't Joe Satrioni or Andre Segovia, the thing simply played like shit. The action, the height of the strings from the neck, was obscene. You'd have calluses like a 70-year-old bass player after trying to practice for a week. The thing weighed a thousand pounds and constantly went out of tune. The fine precision pegs on the bottom designed to balance the whammy simply fucked the whole thing up, and on top of it all it was made in Mexico which basically reduced all street cred to anyone who knew well enough. It was also, of course, very expensive. So it was with little regret that in the summer of 92 Damien decided to sell the damn thing. It just happened that his friend Chris was interested in learning to play, so after a few free lessons, Damien offered it to him at an amazing price. In the end Chris got his old guitar and Damien ended up with a much nicer, more dependable Fender that he loved to this day.

The thing was though, Damien was suddenly recalling the last week he had the thing. Through two high school bands and several years of torment he had trucked this hunk to and fro the tri-state. It was only natural that he had developed some attachment to it, and therefore wanted to make sure it found a good home.

Therefore Damien proceeded to modify the bridge so Chris wouldn't have to deal with the same shit he did. He began to fine-tune the assembly and realized how far he had progressed in his knowledge of guitar electronics. What began as just trying to balance out the bridge turned into a complete overhaul of the pick-up system, neck, roller nut, and whammy bar unit. He even ended up sanding and glossing the chips. After he had done everything in his knowledge base Damien tried the instrument.

For years he had slaved with the fucking thing and now, as he was about to hand over the Warlock to someone who had never owned a guitar, it played fucking beautifully. The action was perfect, the tuning steady, and even the sound and quality had drastically improved. It would do things now that it could never have done while he had it - and he was practically giving it away!

The one thought that went repeatedly through Damien's head then and was rapidly developing in his mind now was simple. He hadn't wanted to keep the Warlock back then either; the Fender was vastly superior in every way. But he did keep asking himself the question that simply wouldn't go away about his friend and new owner:

*Why the fuck doesn't he (*then his buddy Chris, now his buddy J*) have to deal with all the fucking bullshit?*

By the time Damien had force-fed himself both crab cakes and what-ever-the-fuck the carrot mash was constructed of he had made it through two pints and was quite possibly considering a tall glass of brown liquor. Jez had continued to speak the whole time about all the things she had gotten over and how happy she was while Damien responded with a gentle smile and well-timed spoonfuls of speech blocking mush. More and more it dawned on him that she had picked not only one of his best friends to become blithely in love with but one that mirrored him so closely in mannerisms, behavior and most especially relationships that a well-oiled shorthand had been all they ever needed to communicate volumes on their respective love lives. It also seemed to be becoming more apparent that all the things she had recently gotten over were what had sunk their very relationship and made the last 6 months together a virtual living hell. By the time they had moved through the restaurant to the bar where she proceeded to regale him with her version of righteousness over trying to be cool with J's ex-girlfriend/her best confidant and his baby's mother – both of which were mysteriously furious and disapproving despite her best attempts at maintaining friendship – Damien had moved safely into a happy place far from there where all he had to do was count back and forward to a hundred for all eternity. It was with no small measure of Oscar level skill that after a bit more approval he said that sure he would love to walk her home to meet Jasper and why the hell couldn't they be friends, after all they were getting along so well.

It was right before they got to her street that they decided to part ways since he was sure he could see Jasper at another time and don'tcha know it was kinda bothering him that she didn't call to warn him of the situation he was walking into coming back but hey that's cool and why should she ask him so whatever do you feel like one more drink, yes why not. They went into a small cantina that truly was a slice of down south and ordered a beer and that was right about when she told him about how she was always open to a threesome and why didn't they do that with this one particular girl in

Mexico and by the way that she slept with one of Damien's exes over Christmas with a strap on and here's some more details but you don't mind, do ya Damien?

He gave her a hug and a kiss and wished her well and thanked God that he was leaving in 4 days. He told himself he could last 4 days without saying anything, without causing a scene. He would bury himself in works and task and all the bullshit that must be done. If he saw Jasper it would be brief and he definitely would not see Jez again. Four days he could handle. He truly believed it even though he knew it would be tough, and in the end he was right. He could handle four days.

Unfortunately four days was not how long he got stuck in New York.

Δ   Δ   Δ   Δ

Dinner with J and the concept of sharing

In what can only be considered as attempting to tie up all emotional loose ends in one decisive shot, Damien agreed to go have dinner with Jasper late Monday afternoon. He had spent the day loading his Camry with loose items deconstructed from the *Jenga* closet, as well as a few smaller pieces of furniture and lamps he planned on driving to the storage space on Tuesday. Still, he found he had far more shit than he remembered, and what's more the stuff he did remember had grown exponentially in his absence. It was a pricing issue he would be sure to discuss with his shipping company since he had somehow accumulated far more than he'd initially estimated.

It was in all this plus the nagging suspicion he'd best be getting to the Mexican Consulate to apply for his moving permits fast, that Damien hopped into his ride and headed for the Queensboro Bridge. Jasper had been helping Lego move and set up sound systems all day and the two of them were currently decompressing in Lego's digs in Sunnyside, a neighborhood known for its proximity to all the major highways and Irish pubs in Queens, despite an apparent lack of visible entry and exit ramps.

Upon arriving at Lego's, Damien once more had that sinking feeling he always got when he thought back on when he and Jez had been together. He and J had not spoken since the phone call after Christmas that got all the shit rolling, and had not seen each other since he had last been in the city in October. But Damien was mostly fixated upon last summer which had been a marathon of him and Jez hanging out with J and Adena, which was all so much drama-filled horseshit at the moment. Reconciling the idea of dropping Ecstasy together as best friends in the Hamptons was not quite fitting with his image of back-stabbing prick. Just this afternoon he took down photos of the two of them barbequing out in Long Island, an image surely taken and put up by Jez on the only painting of his mother's no less (even if it was just above the toilet). Reminiscences of the last decade mingled with a somewhat violent fantasy he tried to dispel with smoke as he crossed Lego's lawn and proceeded from the porch to the second floor apartment. It occurred to him that only in Queens could you have a patio and backyard but still have to put change in the fucking meter (this was clearly before he had gotten to LA).

"You reek like stale smoke," Jasper greeted him, and despite the fact that Damien did, he found himself gratuitously aggravated and defensive.

Yeah well I'm gonna quit in Asia

This was not necessarily a lie, more a case of wishful thinking. He consoled himself with the fact that his only previous attempt to stop smoking had succeeded (if only for six months and with a kick start of nearly dying from a massive intestinal infection and alcohol poisoning in his friend Alex's flat in Mexico).

"How are things down there? You getting all local? Drinking fire water and getting a tan?"

Actually I live in the Northern Central Highlands J. The water is nowhere near me so the only tan I'd be getting would be from my patio and I usually keep the blinds closed till late afternoon. Damien neglected to add that if Jasper had actually been any further south than Miami in his whole fucking life he would know Mexico was a whole country, and a large one at that, and that it was not all in fact fucking Tijuana or Cancun.

"Right, Jez was telling me it was more like the mountains and desert and shit."

(Please cue the stupid cowboy question)

"So you been like riding horses out into the desert and shit?"

(Goddamn it, this was worse than being asked if he could do martial arts or was good at math, which quite aggravatingly he did and was)

Yeah bro. I took Jez riding on her birthday last year. She got a slow horse and was cursing me the whole time for it. I don't ride as much as I'd like lately... he trailed off not quite knowing how to move forward this line of conversation. Damien might as well have been talking about flying to the moon.

"Uh-huh, well Lego's in the can, you hungry?" Jasper absentmindedly pulled a Dutch roach out of the ashtray and sparked it.

Could be. You thinking somewhere on the boulevard? Damien foresaw more bad Irish pub fare in his immediate future.

"Yeah. Let's see what Lego thinks, he's a meat and potatoes sorta cat. But you know me and steak." J placed knowing emphasis on this last remark. Of course Damien positively loved a good cut of porterhouse, the bloodier the better, and J, who was very much a man's man and what's more from Long Island, should practically have been required to down pounds of the stuff by birthright. But J hated steak, and for that matter any rare form of beef. It had surely been the source of more than a few painful childhood Island cookouts and there was always a bit of apology in his voice when the subject came up, as if this one inconsistency had moved him into the realm of modern male.

"Sup kid"

Lego's lanky figure emerged from a terminally fucked bathroom into the 'living' room. The whole place had in fact been missing anything livable (i.e. furniture) ever since a scabies and bed lice infestation well over six months ago. Lego wore a low rocked cap and his usual neat yet urban windbreaker. Customary dap was exchanged as Damien felt for Lego who had being cornered into tagging along to this potentially nightmarish meal. The three of them had been close for over a decade, ever since they were derelict raver kids and DJ's back in early 90's Chelsea and Harlem. But recent events had forced them to take sides and Damien felt much like the young'un in a custody battle having to avoid any previously unannounced social collision with J or Jez.

Several blocks and several pints later he ordered a Shepherds Pie and his third Bass. Jasper was flip-flopping between a burger (well done) and some sort of chicken thing (Damien never ordered chicken, anywhere, unless it was the ghetto or rotisserie kind and he was in the sort of headspace where White Castle might seem like a good idea).

"Shit man I can't decide, your pie sounds good wanna share?" Jasper peered over his menu with an ingratiatingly sincere look that about a year ago Damien would have welcomed. Now it made him wish he were the kind of guy to simply punch J in the face, get down to blows and be done with it. As it was he could not help the response that rolled out of *I'm not really the sharing type J* followed by an uncomfortably shared silence.

Not much more was said at dinner, or rather a hell of lot was said without actually being said and when Damien left to go meet Kienyo in the city insincere hugs were given all around with cynical well-wishing and the smiles of sharks. Damien would see Jasper once more though he didn't expect to at the time. When he did, he would have wished that he had the prudence to stick to pints, which of course he didn't.

Adena and Kienyo and stalking an Ex

Grumbling and growling Damien ambled up the street in Chinatown looking for Kienyo's studio. Right around the time he reached Grand he realized that Ludlow had not in fact moved 5 avenues east in his absence and had to turn around again.

Living in New York is not in principle so different from living in caves. Unless you are independently wealthy or a trustafarian child of affluence the square footage of your flat will most likely be akin to that of any urban compatriot's closet. Tokyo perhaps aside, it is the only major city to consistently place in the world's top 5 most expensive cities where even the rich must suffer pre-war conditions in the name of location. Though "pre-war" is now a term of realtor endearment in the same way that the rugged outlands of the South Bronx have now attained the cutesy misnomer of "SoBro."

You live in caves and work in larger caves, whether they are narrow service industry dinge or mini-cave within cavern cubicles. Like Shakespeare monkeys and bridgeless trolls we wander through cramped spaces and shuffle through the megapolis commenting how happy we are to not be living in suburbia. As with artists starving in hopes of recognition, we justify and deny making it bearable.

It was with these thoughts that Damien proceeded down Ludlow and eventually stamped on the service door in the middle of the block till its metal walls opened to the dark staircase below. If you were a denizen of any other city you would assume that small china men stored away fish or batteries there or those cheap toys that break within hours of their purchase. Damien however knew better and gave Kienyo a warm embrace upon entering the hot windowless den of junk and recording equipment that was Kienyo's own personal and literal Neanderthal realm.

Damien had the night to kill. Kienyo was his bro, and despite his utter refusals to acknowledge his current woes whatsoever, was still his closest confidant. K refused to take any of Damien's break-up mania seriously and his knowledge of the downtown night scene made Damien confident the evening could be salvaged with a bit of drinks and damnation.

As usual, late would have to evolve into early morning before any sort of motivating moves were to be made. Kienyo would forever delay getting ready by obsessing on a particularly obscure flaw in a Cuebase track, and Damien would fight comment till it tore him apart, knowing that any sort of advice or technical suggestion would lead to an even longer delay in leaving the studio. Insert any number of appearances by various musicians, funkeras and sycophants of the day and it would be a wonder if their evening did not simply entail emerging into sun light and having brunch in the park.

On this particular Monday night however different forms of entertainment would be taking up Damien's time. The first is named Adena, Jasper's most recent ex and the apparent flavor of the month for K. Adena is Jewish, from Queens, and lives on the Upper West Side. If you are not immediately straddled with an unbreakable image, think a younger version of "The Nanny" mixed with some "Sex in the City" nonsense and embodied in a six foot tall white girl with Big Bird style blond hair, a penchant for West Indian DJ's and former bad boys, and a propensity to leap upon not poorly built unsuspecting Asian writers who nearly collapse into traffic under their weight. She is the kind of girl he was both happy and extremely nervous to see. Nervous since she represents drama, and happy because – well who doesn't like Big Bird?

"Oh my GAWD! DAMIEN where have you been? I thought you were still in Mexico, how is it, you don't look so tan, I hear you got a new girl, Kienyo says she's white again, from LA this time? You're growing your hair out, SEXY! My GAWD baby it's so good to see you. I'm sure you've been hearing all about you know what… my gawd D, I was going to kill that girl, I swear to god I cornered her in a bathroom and Jasper was trying to be all diplomatic and shit… but I'm sure you're sick of that, so Asia right? D, I've always wanted to go to Thailand. Are you driving where we goin?"

Damien blinked several times a la Homer Simpson while adjusting his stance so as not to fall over with the large demanding blond appendage that was now threatening to take him down. He muttered into her hair hoping it sounded like agreement and joy and concern and whatever else eased her to the ground where she affectionately launched herself at Kienyo.

"You know Jez has been reading your email D?"

Somewhere around Avenue B Damien found himself cursing aloud at the state of parking and knew he had settled quite against his will back into a New York state of mind - which sociologists will gleefully point out as bearing all the characteristics of extreme neurosis in any other part of the planet: sweating, accelerated pulse rate, jabbering and growling to oneself whilst making demands upon physical objects and cultural limitations that uniformly choose to ignore you.

About an hour and many expletives later they found themselves in Pianos, a cute club in the LES that catered to Indy rock bands and the occasional East Village Karaoke denizen. Damien learned that his old buddy Jasper was working the promotions and quite thoroughly did not want to see him again. In his absence, on top of everything else, Jasper had developed an obsession with Marie (of Damien's college suicide, first love, 9-11, break-up in India, reason he now lived part time in Mexico fame) and subsequently told her that Damien was a twat and a bastard and he had grown out of his company. This would be only the first of several flashback traumas that Damien had in store. It was revealed only seconds later that Marie herself, whom he hadn't spoken with since storming out of her apartment with the words *I never want to speak to you again* (only to be broken minutes later when he called her cell to ask for directions out of Jersey), worked at the French wine bar across the street. Damien sorely wished this piece of trivia hadn't been mentioned since dinner with Jasper and everything else had already put him in a fragile mood. He knew though that with enough time he would find himself casually guiding his friends to the unnamed establishment, quite unable to control the direction of his heart and feet. That was, if he could actually pry them apart.

"Are we making you uncomfortable Damien?" Adena asked in a manner that said if they weren't she was surely doing something wrong.

Course not guys, it's not like you're acting as a visual aid to my sneaking suspicion that we're all part of some grand incest. Carry on while I get smashed.

"Oh D, in a week you'll be in LA with Ivy and all of this will be behind you. You sold your parents' house, you're giving up your apartment, and you're headed to Asia – my gawd, Asia D!" Adena leaned further into Kienyo who gave a *whatever* look and started chuckling.

Fuck you motherfucka

"What?" he feigned incomprehension and hurt.

Fuck you.

"Come on little guy what will make you happy right now?" K arched his eyebrows in a conspiratorial manner.

Nothing. I'll tell you what why don't we go across the street where I pretend I'm thrilled and shocked to see Marie, maybe I can knock Jasper out on my way out the door. Then after I can call Jez over and we can all have one giant fist fucking orgy. Sound good?

Adena temporarily reverted to JAP queens and her jaw nearly hit the ground while Kienyo buried his head in her chest in a fit of giggles.

You would think this is funny motherfucker.

"It's a bad idea D, didn't you say you were never gonna speak to her again?"

Love, fuck it.

It is a miracle that the wine bar is closing on last call - one only matched by the fact that Marie has the night off.

Fraudulent shippers, Jeepers Creepers trucks and storage space shittiness

It was Wednesday. In the ideal world Damien would be heading to Stamford to grab some stuff for the road, swinging by his buddy MOC's garage for an oil change and check up, then flying off into the horizon bidding the east a not so fond farewell. Since this is not the case let us rewind about 20 or so hours to mid-afternoon Tuesday.

Monday night's uncomfortable dinner and subsequent wacky antics at Marie's wine bar had not worn off. The deeper Damien's burn, the less he felt he could combat it. It was in this defeatist state of mind that he purchases a $10 one-way ticket from Grand Central to Stamford, suburban home to his now deceased parents, and occasional refuge for his still lingering adolescent angst.

Ever the believer in progress and practicality, Damien had reserved movers for his worldly possessions over a year before through a company he had found on the Internet. Sporting a reputable site and glowing references they seemed to be just the sort of job-specific boutique that would relieve him of handling unnecessary paperwork and headache-inducing logistics that the fresh death of his mother and subsequent reliving of break-up wounds with Marie left him incapacitated and unprepared for. He arrived in Stamford, the "city that works" (*what the fuck does that mean?*) around 2pm or so. At the station his brother Ronnie rolled up in a 98 Saturn courtesy of their mother. At 4' 11" it had seemed go cart-ish for her diminutive stature, and with Ronnie, clear over 6' 2" and nearly 16 stone, it was positively farcical.

"Hi D, how was Mexico?"

Great Ron, wish I was there, I've had a pretty fucked up week.

"Oh, well we don't have to talk about it. I know how you are when you first get back to the states."

I'm not back I'm just here to clean up.

"Oh, OK. Have you thought about what you want for your birthday?"

That's over 4 months from now Ron; I'll probably be in Hong Kong.

"Oh, OK. I guess you don't know about October for my birthday yet then."

Without the context of two and a half decades this might seem to be the most banal of exchanges. Without the sandwich filling of Joan's corporeal presence it may perhaps seem even more so. Surely, casual observers have professed curious bewilderment at how such benign conversations have devolved into frustrated screaming matches and fistfights (a particular specialty of the Wood nuclear family). Suffice to say Ron was the last living person who could make Damien lose a decade of growth and patience within minutes and revert to an exasperated adolescent version of himself. This is not to say that Damien did not have the converse effect on Ron, only that their reversions were incompatible.

It was not so much that Ron wasn't listening to what people said, so much as he listened, nodded, then completely disregarded others' input in favor of his own conversation which he continuously seemed to be having with himself.

No Ron can't say I do. So what's the story with the house and the storage space? We have to have everything out by Friday right? You said your friend Mark has a truck we can use right?

"Yeah I got this place on the East Side but they're only open till 6pm every day. We have to get everything in by Friday. Mark works with his landscaping business all day but he says he can help us around 5 or 5:30 today and tomorrow."

Damien was not only surprised to have an actual answer to each of his three enquiries but how completely unsatisfactory those answers were.

Wait! 6pm? How the fuck am I supposed to organize and itemize my stuff if I only have till 6 every day? And how the hell are we supposed to move everything in mom and dad's house into a storage unit with only half an hour with a truck for 2 days? Jesus Ron there weren't any 24-hour storage places?

"I thought this one was better for security"

So much better we can't even get in the fucking thing!

"I'm sorry; you told me this at the last minute. You know I have a life too."

As they pulled up on the raised ranch Damien thought better of putting his head through the dashboard and instead marched across the unwatered front lawn into the near-empty house. Most everything that had not been given or thrown away now resided in the garage, randomly stored if at all and hopelessly unlabelled. In one particular stack he found the paperwork for one ShippingInternational.com with a receipt for 1000-buck deposit and several contact numbers. With the intention of explaining that after a year of idling they'd have to be ready to pick and grab within 24 hours Damien dialed all 3 contacts and each time reached a messaging service. Chalking it up to high call volume he left 3 what he hoped didn't sound desperate requests for someone to get back to him ASAP and proceeded to try and sort his parents' lives.

Around 4pm Damien's good buddy MOC showed up and they started to sort through and trash whatever couldn't be labeled. After emptying 2 dumpsters (one 60 ft, one 80), about 20 assorted trips with packed cars to Goodwill and the Salvation Army, furnishing 2 friends' houses as well as his own UES apartment and Kienyo's studio in the city, and one particularly miserable garage sale, Damien no longer needed any gut wrenching soul searching every time a knick-knack was headed for the refuse. If anything, the last 2 years had taught him to be coldly pragmatic about material possessions (and their hoarding and straddling your children with their care).

Can you drive stick?

This innocuous question was the one Damien had asked MOC over the phone when Ronnie informed him that Mark's truck was standard (embarrassingly it was a skill that neither Damien nor his brother had ever mastered). Damien watched the physical change come over MOC's face as the "truck" pulled into – barely pulled into the driveway.

"You got to be fucking kidding me. That's no moon; it's a motherfucking space station."

Indeed Vader would be proud of the monstrosity that pulled up. Straight out of the film "Jeepers Creepers" - sharp scary tools, rust, and all – pulled up something that looked like a cross between a third world hostage transport and the garbage truck of the dark lord. Mark hopped out apologetically, snatched keys from Ronnie and ran off to his last appointment of the day. Mark's parting sympathetic expression did little to ease Damien's already fried nerves and the three of them began to get to it. The only thing he was certain of was that should they be able to maneuver the damn thing, two trips would be unnecessary.

Two hours later, after arguing with the lady at the front desk of the storage company and having been locked out 3 times, they had pulled off the impossible and emptied the entire contents of the garage into the death mobile, out onto the dock, and into the storage space. This fact had somewhat lessened the impact of the awful discovery made about an hour before when Damien made the mistake of checking his email records for other contact info for his shipper. Not only was the website down, but a subsequent web search brought on what seemed like endless pages of warnings from ripped off or extorted customers and eventually a series of legal documents on indictment for fraud. Page after page detailed the exploits of the company and it now seemed they were better off with just $1000 of his money rather than all of his parents' life held in some anonymous warehouse for ransom. Still Damien was out a grand and a shipper, though he did begin to feel the rumbling beginnings of the kind of laughing fit that is often the precursor to a complete nervous breakdown.

An incoming call sounded on his phone as Damien lit a celebratory smoke for actually accomplishing something today and directed MOC out the gate. It was to be another moment in a growing list when he wished he had checked caller ID.

"Hey you whatcha doin?" Jez' voice sounded bright and happy and almost next to him.

House shit, general nightmare moving hell.

"Yeah, is it going alright?"

As well as can be expected, it's all a little much for me right now.

"Well after this you can put it all behind you"

Yeah I suppose.

"Well look I just wanted to say that I was really glad we got together a few nights ago and I heard you and J had dinner and I'm glad you're getting along"

Uh-huh.

"He really loves you"

Uh-huh.

"You alright?"

Later, and not much later mind you, he would regret ever having let himself lose composure. Much later, when he put it all in perspective and saw it for what it was: a spectacular culmination of bad luck, karmic debt, the death of a previous relationship, and catalyst for the destruction of a new one – well a moment like this would seem trite, even trivial. But now it was all that he needed to launch the next world war.

No I am not fucking alright.

By the time he was finished everything had changed, and it wasn't even Friday yet - which brings us to this moment in Harlem, late Wednesday night or Thursday morning, lying down sober with a drunken girl across him, staring at the iPod he lost in the material custody battle.

Δ   Δ   Δ   Δ

Chasing demons in Harlem and why Damien should have just kept his mouth shut

Damien's in Spanish Harlem and feels very uncomfortable. He can speak Spanish semi-fluently and has from time to time lived in some of the worst ghettos in the world. He is not a huge man but he can definitely hold his own, and right now he's scared shitless.

Let's get some background. It's an artist café. The owner, a fairly friendly looking Puerto Rican man, as well as the waitress, a small black girl, and a cluster of local thugs and street dealers are currently surrounding him. The gist of what they're all wondering and what the bartender succinctly asks is "she's really upset, you hurt her man, why'd you hurt her?"
Jez is the "her" and has become a beloved local white girl who can speak Spanish fluently and the why is due to her running out of the café drunk and in tears.
Look man, she's my ex-novia, it's a bit complicated, sabes?
They look unconvinced.
We were just talking, you saw right? Then she drank a little too much and – hey man don't touch me – and she stormed off and – look God I'm serious you don't know what's up – and I'm calling her right now but she won't pick up and –

yeah well maybe I'm a pendejo but that's my biz — anyway I'm gonna find her now OK?

Damien moves with purpose ever aware that a blow from behind could come at any moment to further aggravate the evening's progression, but aside from a litany of half-mumbled Nuyorican insults and shoulder checks, manages to clear the small crowd. Incidentally, he was not lying and had been repeatedly trying to call her to no avail.

Sometime after he arrived at the café and apologized for a torrent of venom unleashed on the phone from the storage yard yesterday, he proceeded to get right back into it and lambaste her for carelessness, cruelty, hypocrisy, and any other number of conditions ending in the letter Y. This was absolutely not his intention at first but emotion has a way of grabbing hold of you when it's least convenient. Already more than a few mojitos down Jez had moved into the "hold me — no fuck you I want you out of my life" flip flop that he had become so familiar with in 3 on and off years and as many continents together. It was the latter of these commands that he took seriously and proceeded to march down Lexington filled with righteous indignation and moral superiority that began to fade somewhere around 98th street and proceeded to nosedive as he neared 92nd and the safety of home. A series of missed phone calls and one cut off sobbing message about being lost were really all it took to backtrack to 106th and greet the most un-cheery crowd that had gathered in front of the café.

So here he was wandering through Harlem with only the vaguest idea of where Jez currently resided going between picking up slammed down phone calls and making unsuccessful ones. It was only after about 45 minutes of project wandering and stoop waiting that he decided he had done as much as humanly and more than reasonably possible and turned to go home. This is of course right when she called drunk and locked out asking him to meet her on 109th and 3rd. Dutifully dreading the immediate future, Damien made his way east and north toward inevitability and found Jez mashing the buzzers to her entire apartment building and hollering up for all to hear her pleas for passage. On a Wednesday night at 3 in the morning in an ethnic minority working class neighborhood the sight of a white girl from Texas hollering to the heavens – well it is truly something to behold – from a distance.

Babe, I'm sure someone heard you. I can hear them shouting quite clearly from here. Can't you call J?

"He's working till 5 and staying on the island tonight – HEY PLEASE LET ME IN I LIVE HERE – my roommate's home I know it, that fucking Jew hates me – HEY JOHNNY COME ON OPEN THE FUCKING DOOR – he's probably gonna hate me even more"

Hey easy with the Jewish shit.

Jez is from Ft. Worth where the Hebrew population is the same as the Martian population. When she arrived in the city she became fascinated with all things Jewish. She would ask Damien questions and remark upon their friends who practiced as if it was all some new exciting species. It did not take long for her to catch some of the bizarre gentile-Jew mutual condescension that New Yorkers are such great practitioners of (that and every other racial ethnic pettiness expressed as humor). It was at that moment that Damien imagined she had gone as far as to get a Jewish roommate to advance her understanding, only a little bit later (i.e. 5 minutes when a very agitated son of Abraham came to the door in a bathrobe) he realized her roommate was in fact Israeli, a distinction between race and religion she had not yet learned to make. As poor Johnny lead them up the stairs Damien managed to give an apologetic shrug and pantomime some sort of approximation of his current situation to every awakened neighbor on the way to the sixth floor. Johnny, who had not deigned to return Damien's handshake, quite understandably given the circumstance, stormed into his room and slammed and locked the door.

OK so you're home now kid. You need to sleep this off. I'll talk to you later.

"Where are you going? Wait have a drink."

Look, Jez, I shouldn't even be here and if you were sober you'd know that.

"Just one drink, you want wine – no wait you drink whiskey"

Look – oh OK fine, thanks.

He diligently tried to fire down the Scotch slower than a shot but not by much. His stance on the couch was the approximation of one that a paratrooper would strike moments before jumping from a plane into battle.

"Stay with me tonight"

What – no – look I'm gonna get going. I have to see customs in the morning to authorize all my stuff going to Mexico plus I need to find a new shipper to deal with all of it. That's like 3 hours from now I gotta get going.

"I just wanna feel you close to me. We can stay right here, we don't have to do anything"

Look kid, that sounds great and like a terrible idea all around so —

Before he could continue protest he found that she had already passed out in an impossible position across him. He had the very same feeling as when he woke up drunk in Uni at his friend Laura and Jim's place to find a half dozen kittens had burrowed under his shirt in the middle of the night. Not wanting to disturb them but desperately uncomfortable he had sat motionless for hours till the sun was clear up. Resigned in this same manner, Damien attempted to lean back and closed his eyes after the last mouthful of Scotch. This lasted about 5 seconds before his eyes flashed open and fixated on an object across the room. His iPod sat plugged into Jez's computer, cheerfully charging away.

Sometimes lost is really lost.

Δ   Δ   Δ   Δ

Amorous custom guys named Oscar

So there's this guy who seems like a saint in the hell that is New York's Mexican consulate. It's on 52nd street in midtown and you can identify it by exorbitant parking rates and the large seemingly unordered crowd gathered around the door trying to push in.

Anyhow, this supposed saint, Oscar, takes one look at Damien's customs form and starts shaking his head and furiously editing the document with a red pen like a high school history professor gone wild.

"I shouldn't be doing this. I'll get in a lot of trouble if they see me doing this"

The extent of his corrections both grammatical and content reveal that yes, Oscar is probably being far more helpful than required or allowed, and that Damien's Spanish has taken quite a downward slip in the last few days. Damien muttered a series of grateful mumbles and stared at Oscar's wildly crossing hands. When he was done Damien bolted to Kinko's to make the necessary changes armed with a disc and Oscar's promise that he would not have to wait in line. He was on a deadline. Today was the day he would flee this fucking city and get to his baby in LA. In two days all of this would seem, cliché as it sounded, like a really bad dream. In addition, the lovely Mexican consulate was only open till noon, another bit of bureaucratic irony and nuisance.

It was just under that timeline that Damien traversed the angry mob outside and came back to Oscar triumphantly convinced he was done and ready to go. He had the detailed and now properly edited inventory. He had paid the proper fines and registries. He had the right visa and the right attitude and was quite done with New fuckin York. His first hint of upcoming problems appeared at first to be a simple conversation question from his officer.

"So Mexico Damien, what do you do there?"

Ummmm… I'm a writer and a performer

"What kind of performance?"

Mostly poetry with Jazz and trip-hop, you know DJ's live musicians that kind of thing

"Really, you play here in New York?"

Yeah quite a bit, not this time obviously since I'm taking off

"Wow. That's great; you should stay so I can see you play."

Yeah, well next time (forced laugh)

"Really you should stay so I can take you to dinner"

(Even more forced) Well you get this paper work through and maybe we'll do that.

"What are you Damien? Asian?"

Umm… I'm half-Cantonese half Northern Irish.

"So beautiful, you really are beautiful"

It was at this point that Damien realized both why Oscar had been so nice and that there was no way he was leaving New York today. Even worse, it being Friday, he saw no leaving till at least Monday. He couldn't take three more days.

Umm… thanks Oscar… that's really sweet, you're an attractive man yourself, but the fact is I have to leave, preferably today. You see I contracted a shipper this morning, a frightfully expensive one I might add, and they're coming to pick up my stuff this afternoon. Now that's really not gonna help me if they get my stuff to the border and have to hold it there for untold months and dollars. So anything we can do to move this along…

"So beautiful"

OSCAR

"Oh yes, sorry Mister Wood, I'm afraid it's impossible. You'll have to come in Monday morning for the rest of the papers. Maybe we can meet up this week-end before then, yes?"

Umm… afraid I've got a million things to do, moving and shaking and all that, but I'll see you Monday yes. OK take care Oscar – oh a hug yes very nice to meet

you as well – a kiss oh so friendly in these Latin American – whoa whoa buddy,
yeah, got to meet ya see ya on Monday, hasta nos vemos.

Monday, how much worse could it get?

Δ   Δ   Δ   Δ

An unexpected email and the problems with drinking alone on a pier

"I am so sorry for everything that happened between us"
That was the first line of the email.
The second was "I'm engaged."
The email is from Marie. You must remember that Marie was the first greatest love of Damien's life. As recently as this week Damien has woken up to alternating dreams and nightmares in which they are still together and happy or broken apart and fighting. That this relationship spanned numerous states and several countries over most of his twenties gives you the gist. I'm sure you yourself have a Marie or Damien in your life.

  The last time they spoke Damien was suicidal and desperately needing a friend. It was a month or so after his mother had died and despite his clear gut instinct had let Marie back in his life. At his mother's wake Marie sat next to him holding his hand in everyone's clear view, only feet away from the casket. He remembered telling her he was far too fragile to refuse her kindness and that if she didn't plan on sticking around for some rough shit she best get out now. She reassured him that wasn't the case even though he knew it was an outright lie if not to him then to herself, but love can do funny things. Within a week they had slept together again and within a month he found himself in some shithole in Jersey where she cornered him screaming about herself and he told her he never wanted to speak to her again. It had started with something so pathetic and mundane as asking to please sleep in the same bed with him since he felt so goddamn alone and ended with the equally pathetic but moderately more comic phone call he made from the road minutes after saying he never wanted to speak to her again. The short gist was that he was lost and needed directions to get back to the city.

So it was not without a bit of sinking that Damien found himself staring at these words almost two years later on the screen of his computer in what soon would no longer be his apartment solidifying his desire for a drink, or two, or several dozen. He called Ivy, his daytime lover, and looked for words or comfort, finding a few but also the rather disturbing sense that she could give a fuck about his past interpersonal problems and a growing annoyance at the world not revolving around her.

It should be said that Damien did not ordinarily drink alone which might have been his only saving grace in not becoming a total alcoholic. Then again, Damien considered anyone in a room drinking with him whether he knew them or not, to not be drinking alone. It was with this logic that he headed off to the Frying Pan, an abandoned barge dredged up from New Orleans that currently housed a weekly party next to Chelsea Pier. He told himself the air and space would do him good. On the cab ride over he called Marie, whose number was easy to remember since it had been his until about three years ago. That was when he left for Mexico in a fury upon her return from India and many shall we say hurtful choices on her part in that Asian land. By the time he had entered the club he had not only agreed to meet for brunch the next day but also convinced himself he was not at all hurt or wounded or the least bit wanting to cry his eyes out.

It is even less surprising then, that once he had knocked back about a dozen Jack and Diets, Jez called him to tell him she was on her way with Jasper. He greeted the call jovially, perhaps masochistically and said sure he would love to see them and won't you hurry since I'm alone sober as a clam waiting your arrival. That bare acquaintances had expressed general concern for him all night, including a DJ's girlfriend who trailed him like suicide watch, seemed to sink in little. Damien's path to the achievement of total pathos was well in motion.

J and Jez arrived right on time in that horrible land where Damien was just on the cusp of black-out drunk, but still appearing sober and lucid to all but the most trained of eyes. It was in this state that Damien said his most honest things, that is to say the least thought out and likely most cruel and sad words that would find their way to his alien tongue and mouth.

At first there were hugs and explanations and understandings and such. These are always the types of things uncomfortable people say to one another before what's really on their minds, before the requisite 'but's. Damien once heard, everything said to you before that particular word is more or less complete bullshit to justify what comes after. He believed this to be total and absolute fact after first hearing it and now found himself making those same soft white lies to brace the torrent of righteous finger pointing and anger Mr. Jack Daniels had convinced him to release.

Have you been reading my email?

"Hey D maybe you guys need like a minute to..." J scoped possible exits.

You just sit down and shut up bro. You of all people should know better.

"Hey this is about us right? I thought we had talked – "Jez made a valiantly sober effort to diffuse what was entirely lost on Damien as he felt the rumblings behind his eyes.

We talked before I spent the night chasing you drunk around Harlem then had a morning of being hit on by a gay Mexican man who will probably have my shit put in quarantine if I don't go out on a date with him. You are guys are so stunningly fuckin inconsiderate. Did you even think how this would affect me? And now if it isn't bad enough that I'm stuck in this fucking city and my girl thinks I'm losing my mind every time I call LA, I've got brunch with Marie tomorrow to discuss how happy I am that she's sorted her shit and getting married. Do any of you people consider getting over your petty fucking hang-ups and demons WHILE you are with me or is that just asking too fucking much?

"Marie? What? I mean..."

J shut the fuck up, no wait. Here's a twenty, go get us some fucking drinks. He didn't need to be asked twice.

"Look D I think you're a bit drunk and this whole thing with Marie and your parents has..."

Don't tell me about Marie and my fuckin parents Jez, you two have done nothing to help the situation either. I've got everyone and their mother telling me I'm either over or under reacting or pretending nothing is happening at all while treating me like the kid in some fucking custody battle. I do not need to spend my time dealing with this bullshit. If you had only called to tell me rather than J calling only cause he heard I was coming –

"He thought it would be better if he called and frankly it's none of your business..."

When you steal my whole social circle and start going out with a carbon copy of me after getting over all the shit that sank us I find it pretty fucking hard to swallow

"Look this clearly isn't about us, you clearly – "

Oh for fuck's sake where is J and that drink?

Jez sighed as Damien looked frantically around and nearly took his chair round with him. Barely retaining his balance, he turned to face Jez's resolute stare, the benefit of being sober and able to recover from initial sneak attack shock, and found himself lacking in words.

"What is your problem?" she glared.

An imperceptible change had occurred in the span of several seconds and as Jasper returned with whiskey in hand Damien knew he was not only on the defensive but had lost the battle.

Are you reading my email or what?

The unnecessary brunch to move suicide up the options

"You look good" she said. "You look the same."
Damien moved his eggs Benedict around the plate in the same manner as a naval captain might position ships on a battle map.

He had woken muddled and full of regret for words he could barely remember from the night before. It was irresponsible and poorly thought through. The realization of this afternoon's meal made him even all the more aware of his poorly planned moves in the last week.

They met at Sidewalk in the East Village, a haunt they had frequented together but he doubted, and for that matter knew in his case that neither of them had frequented since. He wondered as they exchanged pleasantries to break the ice a similar thought that would be yelled at him by the daytime lover some days in the future in LA, whether or not this was some sort of miserable ex-girlfriend trip he was making – a futile effort to tie up loose ends in a hopelessly cluttered life.

Marie had also appeared to look good and the same but Damien simply said *I like your hair*. Though this was probably not the truest thing he could have said it seemed to be the nicest. He found himself not angry with her, as he would have expected, but more accepting. In front of him sat someone he had envisioned having children with, who he had slept with more times and in more places than anyone else in his life, who he had first spoke words of forever to and been betrayed more thoroughly than he could even express – and the simple fact was he felt practically nothing other than the fact he was sitting across from her now.

You utterly and totally changed the course of my life, he thought, *all that I have become, all that has been unleashed – dozens of sexual nothings, a handful of pitiful relationships doomed to comparison, my very belief in love itself – you buried me in India and didn't have the courtesy to leave the crime scene.*

When his mother had passed almost two years ago she had fled to his side. Undeterred by pleas to let him be, she made promises her heart could never keep. At the wake she sat in the position of honor holding his hand and looking sympathetic for the crowd. It had been the first time in months they had seen each other. He had returned from Mexico for a second time triumphant and sane, a new book on the way, a tour lined up – nothing to hold him down.

After Joan's death all of that changed. The book was no longer a priority and the tour delayed over the next 2 diluted years. What had been independent strength had become terminal loneliness and the dependence of others like his brother Ronnie and any number of face-saving relatives. When he found out about his father's past their reaction was to bury it. You have to love the Chinese and their denial of denial. His uncle took the only heirloom of value in Damien's parents' house, a multifaceted depiction of a village carved in ivory. Damien would've gladly given it, but like a sneak thief in the night the uncle had waited till he was away at an appearance and only Ronnie was home - Ronnie who couldn't say no if the world's survival depended on it. Damien supposed that he thought it was his right as an elder. Just as it was Damien's to turn his back on him.

In this mess Marie showed up once more and found him weak and vulnerable. She begged her way back in as a confidante and within a month one suicidal weekend in Jersey lifted him out of depression and into pure rage. All the usual things of never wanting to be seen again were said (which to his bitter amusement she later seemed to believe she had initiated) and he stormed out the door not to see her again till now.

I still love you, he thought, *it would be funny if it weren't so undeniably and miserably true. Even now you alter my life. I am catching up on a journey to Southeast Asia meant to be with you 3 years ago, before you destroyed me, before I self-destructed across Latin America, before she died and I was left alone picking up the pieces, only Jez and Ronnie around to suffer my rage. I am starting again as if none of this happened; only now I am without you and a home to return to.*

"I was nervous about seeing you." She moved a slice of tomato across her plate, thought better of it and stabbed some alien greens.

Me too he lied. He had not been nervous, more like determined in the way a man on death row might be.

"Sometimes I think it's good I decided to cut off contact"

(HA!) *Yeah* (Yeah right more like it) he stifled an outburst at this bit of revisionist history knowing it would only lead to an entire train of thought and conversation about how she occasionally chose to remember things in a way that lessened her responsibility. A particularly bitter memory of one Thanksgiving phone call and the interpretation of "seeing other people" came to mind.

"I'm sorry about what happened. I was selfish. I don't know if that means anything now but it's heartfelt"

(NO NO NO) *Of course it means something* (couldn't he at least have his fucking dignity? God, was that actual pity in her voice? Why now?)

"How are things with Jezebel?"

Over

"I'm sorry"

It's OK, she's with J now

"Oh Jesus I'm sorry. We sure know how to pick you."

Yeah, no shit. Well I'm with this girl named Ivy from LA now anyway. She's great, really bright. She does battery counseling… what? Don't give me that look.

"At least you're sticking to type"

What type? I have a type?

"Well idealistic and culturally naïve though very intelligent – i.e. an optimist to play against your unfailing pessimism and cynicism, generally blond but dyes their hair – usually red, European descent, humble yet exposed background…"

Wait. OK she's white. So what? And yeah she has red hair but I didn't know it wasn't natural – well I mean I didn't know it was naturally blond, and – I'm not such a cold-hearted cynic. I mean I'm moderately charming and witty no?

"You're charming in a real burnt out beatnik sorta way, and your humor is pretty dark babe, I mean sometimes it's too dark to be even funny"

Well this is disappointing; there goes my gig at the mortuary.

"See, not funny especially considering why you're back here; pretending bitterness is humor, keeping everyone at arm's length so they can grow frustrated and leave you so you can have something to write about..."

OK, I get it. I remember this conservation with crystal clarity OK.

For a moment he shifted into one of his better tricks of misdirection and leveled a lingering stare at her. When they had first met he hadn't been able to maintain eye contact with anyone for any extended period of time. He would later confide in her that it was because he felt that he could read people far too easily, probably an aberrant by-product of too much acid, and that the gateway to this was watching one's eyes. By this logic he feared one day he would run into someone else with the same talent and they would be able to see through his fragile veneer like wax paper.

So why am I back here? He fixed his gaze directly into her clear blue mirrors of the soul and imagined himself lifting the secret veil in front of his own eyes.

"Only you can know that baby. Only you can know"

Δ   Δ   Δ   Δ

"They keep pulling me back in" and off we go

The shippers had picked up all his stuff and the storage space had been closed. Jez had written a hateful email and Marie was off to a blissful future. Oscar had not tried to kiss him and the paperwork was off. His parents' house had been sold at a profit and the apartment was ready to close. Ivy was waiting for him in LA and MOC was ready to be his wingman; first stop Albuquerque, then the beyond. His leftover knick-knacks could kiss his ass or become part of Kienyo's dungeon. Damien was ready for anything.

But the city had one last gift for him. As he and Kienyo walked to his car to say goodbye he discovered that there was no car to find.

Umm… we did park here last night yeah?

Last night was the first in what seemed an eternity that was not fraught with peril and drama. Aside from the hateful email that he had saved for later, Damien's evening had been incredibly uneventful, opting for some quiet drinks in Alphabet with Adena and Kienyo before heading back to the bomb shelter for some late night diner delivery.

"Shit dog, what time is it?" Kienyo pointed to one of the ubiquitous and complex multi-layered parking signs where Damien's car had been laid to rest.

Of course

About four signs down, below "metered parking 9am-7pm," "no parking Tuesday and Thursday 12pm to 1:30pm," and "no parking 12am-4am," was the almost negligibly small sign declaring "No parking except commercial vehicles 7:30am-9am." Despite the belief he had woken early enough to get a fresh start on the day, Damien's cell phone clearly told him otherwise since it was 7:47am and sometime in the last 17 minutes the D.O.T. had decided to relieve him of transport.

Shit, we gotta go to the impound

If you've never been towed in the city of Manhattan those words lack the severity that they carry for most tri-state residents and the unlucky few tourists driving through. Aside from finding *which* impound your vehicle has been spirited away to, there are half a dozen items that must be tackled to start with.

First, you must go down to John Street to the Department of Transportation. In downtown financial dead zone you take the subway to the near end of the line, emerging around the former World Trade Center, tourists, and suits. Once there you find your car on the computer system and must pay ALL violations that exist on it. It is statistically more likely that you have developed a unifying theory of physics over breakfast than have remembered every parking infraction since you started navigating New York's streets. The litany of late night stops and 5-minute double parks on the screen in front of them will astonish most when itemized with prices in neat chronological order.

Once you've paid, if in fact you have enough on a card to pay and don't have to wait in the merciless line to hand over cash, you must head to the 3rd floor where a number, a la supermarket deli, is given to you. Typically it will be something like 764, and the display in front of you will say "now serving 57." Despite dozens of windows inexplicably there will be only 2 tellers working, one of which is talking to a guard and processing angry citizens at a rate of about one every 20 minutes.

When you are finally met, agitated and having gone through airport-like security checkpoints several dozen times for cigarettes and cell phone calls (neither allowed in the waiting area), they will invariably have misplaced your car or found multiple entries. Though further headaches ensue at the very least you are happy to be dealing with a human being.

When the state employee has sorted your forms and bills and handed you the proper paperwork you will then be sent to the appropriate lot, most likely the pound on the West Side Highway. This depot is of course nowhere near any subway line, let alone one near the D.O.T. You will then either spend a whole lot of time walking and transferring, or biting the bullet on an expensive taxi that will most likely get stuck in traffic as by now it will be early afternoon.

The impound itself bears more than a passing resemblance to a welfare office. The "office" itself is in fact a beat up trailer attached to several others that eventually lead to a massive garage. It is staffed entirely by NYPD making one wonder what particular fuck up has landed them there. For example a major screw up may end you up working toll bridges, which by comparison seems like a dream job.

In this trailer, once more given a number, you face walls of most wanted posters and amateur graffiti by past patrons, i.e. "I've been waiting in the fucking room since Thursday, escape while you can." Also, a list of required items to rescue your car sits on the wall reminding you of everything you forgot to bring. As you are in the middle of nowhere you simply pray that they will overlook these discrepancies or you can charm your way through it. Numerous posters about the illegality of bribes and closed-circuit cameras make any other options clearly unlikely.

Should you get through this last hurdle, you will pay yet another fee for towing and, if very unlucky, time in the lot. A full day of your life and several hundred dollars later you are set free to vent and curse the city.

Damien and Kienyo's day essentially followed this route. The unique details were minor though additionally annoying. After discovering his car's absence, Damien had called maybe 4 or so automated servers before he spoke with a human and learned he must go through the whole John Street song and dance. Unadvisedly he called Lego who furnished him with a bogus location the car might be in holding. It turned out to be a bus terminal. Several hours down the tube he got to John Street and paid a couple hundred dollars in forgotten parking violations. Damien and Kienyo then passed out in the waiting lounge and by 3 or 4 in the afternoon met with a representative and were sent off to the impound. He had forgotten his registration but the lady at the counter fortunately did not ask for it and he paid a couple hundred more dollars. The car drove out fine and by the time they made it back to 92nd street it was only 12 hours and about $600 since he had intended to leave in the first place. Double parking and daring the cops to ticket him Damien loaded the car and bid Kienyo farewell. He then headed to CT, grabbed MOC and sailed westward toward the horizon, LA, and ever-looming future.

Leaving LA

Insomnia, low on smokes, city of angels - fuck.
Wednesday, March 15, 2006

Current mood: 😵*awake*

It's 3 in the morning in lovely Los Angeles and you're trolling Myspace for meaning and long-lost friends. You are aware of how fucking contrived that sounds so piss off.

You managed to kick out another page or so on the new opus before you started building up steam and did what you normally do, which is of course open up solitaire, set it to Vegas rules, and refuse to quit till you broke even again. This pattern repeatedly asserts itself throughout most nights here.

You have begun to exhibit physical and mental breakdown; physical in that you're developing a paunch and psychosomatic hypochondria lung cancer. Mental in that your literary and verbal skills have reduced to trite quips and bitter grumblings accentuated by the occasional tragic bit of truth you call humor.

For example: you just found one of your dead friends online. You suppose his partner is keeping the profile going. He's only got 7 friends and the comments are thin. You didn't bother adding him. Somehow it seemed wrong or maybe you're worthless. When you die you want people to read your shit and listen to your music and have a few drinks on you. For God's sake don't write comments to your ex and expect to be heard. Name a kid after you or something you'd find ironic.

You've been thinking about the past and present and ever-dreaded future and its relation to this electronic medium. We are moving faster and faster to a planet populated by metal boxes with intravenous tubes feeding slack, limbless bodies nutrients with images and sound pumped right into the cerebral cortex. By the time the sun swallows us no one will give a fuck or even notice; that or nirvana, depending how optimistic you are.

You suppose you should try that writing thing again now.

Ivy is stressing out about her new project and ever-threatening instability. You are straight bugging about hitting the road longing for jungle, Thai whiskey and somewhere to disappear. We are a million miles from K-1 representing the nation.

To all you friends and relatives and lovers, dreamers and haters and friends' ex-lovers, insomniac twins and electro-highway vampires - good night and good luck.

Δ Δ Δ Δ

Bikers and the Battle of Lost Angeles

Los Angeles, March 2006

Life is brief - unbearably short and unlikely at that. In all the possible permutations of God or godless realities in an infinite or finite universe, somehow you—a gangly seemingly unrealistic combination of complex cells which are in themselves made up of extremely silly molecules and ridiculous atoms—have somehow come together to form this utterly ludicrous thing called a consciousness in the laughable shell of a being, experiencing the highly unreasonable thing we call life.

So what do we do with this rare, in fact, absurdly rare chance at existence? We watch television. We sit and get fat and work meaningless jobs complaining about how we don't have more time to relax and sit around some more waiting till we're old and fearing death and the great unknown and mostly bitching about how we should've traveled or done something with our lives when we were younger, appreciated people while we had them, etc, etc, etc.

Damien didn't have to get a near-fatal disease or be 90 and fucking senile to know he had had it with no sex, no drinking, no partying, and no goddamn fun at all. Maybe the average Joe or Jane had balled themselves into a neat secure little gas chamber of security and false stability but to quote the inimitable Cypress Hill, Damien was not, "going out like that."

It had been 5 weeks in the urban sprawling wasteland called Los Angeles. Five weeks of unmoving traffic, clique hipsters, fusion macrobiotic biodegradable abominations of cuisine, shallow sycophants feigning superiority, and all-around frustration – with nice weather – that had reduced Damien to some joke version of himself. Damien found himself not talking to people in this bizarre land out of social anxiety that had been bred up after dozens of shit outings. The suck-faced losers he encountered everywhere suddenly intimidated him, since at least they had each other to talk to and Damien had no one, worse even a girl who hated to go out with him and made no attempt to disguise her sheer contempt for his attempts to go out and be a part of the human race together. Unlike Jez who had a shifting moral compass to what she desired, Ivy simply had a stone-clad concept of what was right and wrong. Inevitably he found himself on the end of wrong and despite any parallels he could draw between his own supposed slips in judgment from her invariably correct decisions, her insistence on infuriating detail made it impossible to compare anything without eliciting some long-winded response on how those things were quite simply completely unrelated. Why? Because she said so.

So it was here, undersexed, under-stimulated, overweight, and overwrought, that Damien decided that he had had it.

It is St. Paddy's day, the ornery festival of the patron saint of alcoholics, brawling, derelicts and various other members of Irish descent. It has been two years since Damien's cousin divulged his family's illustrious questionable past. A year since Damien's obsessive-compulsive gay editor proclaimed, somewhat intrigued *everyone in your family is closeted homosexuals*. Were it so simple and easy, Damien thought, and came to the same conclusion as usual. Sounds like a good idea, not a fan of the dick.

Ivy has just discovered that her ex, the former and apparently current drug abuser, has just got nailed in Utah for a felony drug possession. However lenient they may be about polygamy and gambling and an odd proclivity to punk rock, drug tolerance laws are not that state's specialty. Damien currently sits in the house while she is out in the garage on a phone call to the ex, as it appears he may be out of commission for a decade or so. Damien, with his own, let's say "colorful" past, gives the best advice he can: the ex should sell the house claiming the need for liquidity for legal fees and jump bail fleeing the Mormon haven as fast as his legs will allow him. Life, once more, is not so simple, but it's a nice idea.

A Crash Course On the Anatomy of Robots

It might do to describe the last month here in LA since Damien's heroic flight from New York, towers, exes, landlords and all. The ride has been, shall we say… difficult. That he, Damien fuckin Wood, was sitting here alone in a living room bringing in the dead of his past while sipping on an iced Bailey's and questioning his paunch on the goddamn pagan festival of his patron half-breed drinking idol – well there's no question that something was off. Of course something had been off some time now, probably starting with that damn phone call from Jasper starting this whole shit. Things had in fact progressed quite sensibly to this point as they would further progress in all likelihood to where he feared most. Damien had never suffered from a lack of intuitional observation, in fact quite the opposite. When Damien heard the words psychic and clairvoyants he did not think of immediate frauds and con-men, though there were undeniably those – rather of a highly evolved form of instinct that was neither magical or all that special, simply highly underdeveloped and underrated in a society that specializes in being as dulled and apathetic as humanly possible to the horrors and travesties around us.

Therefore it did not come as any particular surprise that Ivy's ex had been caught, or caught in an intolerant state for that matter, or that it had been a somewhat questionable quantity he had been caught with – i.e. *Damien, exactly how much cocaine is 500 grams?* (At about 28 grams per ounce, 16 ounces per pound and 2 pounds per kilo – well you do the math).

Strangely at this moment all Damien could think of was an aging biker he'd just spent the whole afternoon watching in a roadside Denny's. The man was one of those 60's leftover Hell's Angels, now rotting teeth, gray-bearded, and probably still able to start some shit if necessary, but suspect as to his ability to finish it. He wore his leathers like a lost vampire awoken from hundreds of years of sleep left only to find himself a stranger in a strange land, a potent but meaningless relic of an age that had passed by without bothering to have the courtesy to let him know. All afternoon he had gotten up and fed quarters into the claw machine. You are familiar with this device from any late-night diner or church street fair/roadside carnival. There is a box filled with stuffed animals and do-dads of the lowest manufacture and quality. A metal claw with limited movement is controlled by joystick and reaches down like God for the Moonies on judgment day to pull the souvenirs out of their box to freedom for you. But the claw is a flimsy thing, a fickle savant's toy, unable to grasp firmly; its digits are like a crushed soldier's, gnawing at the bit, no gums, no pull. This in itself does not repel the errant eye as it is only a quarter and seemingly simple and it obviously had not stopped this aged warrior.

Sitting with a cold plate of what may have been the Denny's equivalent of IHOP's rooty-tooty (etc, etc) the man had amassed a mountain of *ganga* (the Mexican slang for junk at an amazing price, if you care to know). A dozen assorted multicolored creatures of cotton and polyester populated the table. Half-moon yellow beans, mid-sized small bears, the barely commercially disguised items of the day: whether they be M & Ms or bud cans, always adorned with smiley faces and aberrant tags. They were all on call and at attention, sitting amongst faded tattoos and a penetrating gaze into the brown faux-wood Formica that is custom in the chain. Occasionally a small or not so small child would pass the deteriorating giant of a man, who would extend one of these to the tot in question, not with some creepy smile or odd proposition, but with the weary resignation of a gatekeeper to some lost burned city no one should bother entering anyhow. The parents would invariably pull the offspring close and mutter warnings about strangers and strange men which would lead the weary warrior to stare deeper into the table as if looking for some lost explanation for all that now surrounded him.

What had brought him there, Damien thought? What horrible chain of events, or slow subtle death had broken this man, a man he could imagine dominating debates over broads and beer and scuffles and authority. What had reduced him to this state? Was it a lost child? Perhaps some unplanned result of a less than protected night suddenly turned to a thing of light in an ashen life? Was it a progeny and pupil with words of 'daddy I love you' somehow tragically cut on an American freeway? So romantic were his ideas, so thorough were his mind's wandering. Whether it was of this severity or just the need to score with ordinary boredom, he felt this man and mourned, inside as always, and severe as ever.

He felt sure that the biker longed for the small fingers of a child's grasp as the kid spoke his name, and all the fabricated items of the natural world in a diner at the end of deadened road could not save him. Even if Damien knew why these thoughts haunted him now, even a gun would never force him to admit it.

Dead in central Mexico

April 9, 2006

It is the sound and vacuum of skill and trepidation, which can bring about this catharsis; the feel of keys, the lack of noise - in itself deafening - which changes the form of things.

There was the girl. There was the country. There was the awful reconciliation of the two. And of course there was this too – the separation that knew no bounds, the words that held no speech, the brevity that was eternal in its shallows, its unrepentant knowing of things.

Damien sat. And he sat, and sat, and more of the same.

And the girl, and the country, had politely feigned ignorance.

What is this procrastination, this delay that brings such delight that in the wee hours of the morning listening to Ivy's snoring and flashing to midnight bars on the borders of suburban hells brings such completion?

Seconds baby, seconds from the flames.

So Damien's sitting outside his favorite gringo bar in Guanajuato and a trio of German tourists has decided to use him as an oral Lonely Planet. Ivy, in a final act of stubborn defiance and refusal to compromise in the smallest way, has run off to Guadalajara for a free Manu Chau concert and refuses to call him, preferring to torment with nonsensical, fragmented text messages, which she knows he despises. His forms of least enjoyed communication range from in-person talks and back from there. In back he means group conversation, teleconference, telephone, email, and finally and most definitely least – text messages.

It's been, as you would say, one of those weeks – one of those fucking weeks in fact.

Ivy and her "Eskimo" had driven with him from LA and driven him batshit. The unnamed twat had done no favors to their lightning break-up, and in all likelihood had fueled it. She was a physical manifestation of all that Damien found despicable about LA and other American born half-breeds whom he may have been if he only had the sense to rebel a little more or completely give in and become a lawyer or accountant. All the way from fucking LA to their doorstop in Mexico had been a battle. He had spent 30 unforgiving hours straight in his '97 Camry watching his relationship completely disintegrate and his cockless replacement weasel his way into his house and his bed. The Eskimo wouldn't even leave the bedroom as he and Ivy put the final nails in the coffin. Then the ensuing two weeks of damage and letters and speeches and disbelief. He had gone from "so supportive" to a complete twat in the space of days and the change in his perception was jarring at best. Ivy was nothing if not absolute, especially with a little birdie on the shoulder acting as a malicious cheering squad.

They could have each other and stay in his house as long as it took. He still loved Ivy, and the option would be to stick around and try to tidy this disaster. He had done that once with Marie when she came back from India and he'd always regretted it.

So fuck it. He had a week till he'd be back in LA and then off to Bangkok alone, a week to make sense of this – what a difference a fucking week makes.

Δ   Δ   Δ   Δ

Chippendales we are not

Thursday Night

"So I have something to ask you but I think we should be drunk first"

Alex looked at Damien with that specific sort of grin that inspired him to simultaneously want to run the hell out of the bar and say yes before even hearing the proposal at the same time.

OK, sure, what we drinkin?

"Mescal of course." He turned to the petite Mexican bargirl and said "pardoname, me da una boteilla de *Gusano Roja*, y dos vasos, por fa?"

They grabbed a table and the waitress brought over two rock glasses. A slim clear bottle with a cartoon caricature of a sombrero wearing maguey worm smirking and kicking back against a cactus followed this.

A Crash Course On the Anatomy of Robots

God I hate this stuff

As Alex poured two heavy measures out Damien started thinking about *Cinnamon Toast Crunch*, a fantastic junk cereal full of miniature French toast.

When he was 12, Damien spent weeks on end eating it for breakfast and after school with ice-cold milk. About a month in, little Damien started to notice a particular flavor in the cereal milk orgy that was neither cinnamon, nor milk, nor toast, nor crunch. This *other* element seemed to only grow in dominance as he consumed more and eventually was all he could taste. To this day he can't eat the stuff.

Gusano Roja literally means "red worm," and is indeed made with and contains a maguey worm, which bears a remarkable resemblance to a large maggot. Should this not be enough to put you off, the bottle comes along with a flavor pouch composed almost entirely of dried crushed worm powder and salt. Once you have drunk enough mescals with worms in them, it is also the first and eventually only thing you taste. Unlike *Cinnamon Toast Crunch,* however, you have the unpleasant luxury of knowing exactly what the overpowering *other* is.

"Salud" said Alex with a pinch of red powder in his fingers and the bottom of his glass, and *Salud* said Damien, trying to pass the liquid straight from the glass to his throat avoiding all taste buds entirely.

This went on for about half an hour and half a liter between gossiping about local girls and the usual I can't believe we live in Mexico rap till Alex said

"So you know that it's one of the Norwegian's 20th this weekend right?"

Every September and January, the colonial town of Guanajuato, along with Americans, Canadians, Japanese, and Latin Americans of all sorts, receives a truckload of Norwegian exchange students, almost all women between 18 and 22, and almost all uniformly blond. The locals have so thoroughly adapted to this biannual invasion that many can speak a bit of Norwegian (especially the under 30 male segment of the population), and discos provide a discount if you can prove you are among their ilk. They roam in packs of five to twenty, strutting down central Mexico's alleys like supermodels on catwalks and securing 5-month leased Latin lovers who will incorrectly harbor the belief they are shortly moving to Europe. This January had been no exception.

Alex, his Mexican Dutch (don't ask) buddy had been his unlikeliest savior two years back. Damien had fled from New York and the fallout of his parents to drink himself into a stupor, which he effectively did, and moreover into a massive intestinal infestation which had him vomiting copious amounts of blood in Alex's downtown flat. Against all odds his partying, philandering, oldest-adolescent-in-town drinking buddy turned out to be not only reliable but also extremely attentive in his subsequent recovery. That is of course until Jez flew down in a panic (probably having something to do with a near-unconscious phone call where he said *I just wanted you to know I love you and don't worry about coming down you probably won't make it anyway*). Obviously Damien did make it, as did Jez - though they, as it were, didn't. Anyhow, anything involving Alex, Norwegians, and some sort of favor couldn't possibly be good, but after 7 shots of mescal Damien said

Birthday eh? Which one?

"Martina, the little brunette" Alex winked

Right, she's kinda cute. It is worth mentioning that her hair color and not her name identified Martina. The fact was, aside from the Queen bee named Nina, all the blond ones sorta blended together.

"Well they were saying they wanted to get a stripper for her and I was telling them how shit the Mexican strippers are"

Yeah fuck, I remember when we got that crew of rejects for Jez's birthday a couple years ago.

"She made one of them put his shirt back on right?"

Fuck, I even threw some pesos on the bar I felt so bad for em

"Right, exactly, which is why I told Nina that if they were going to do it right they might as well ask someone they knew to do it. You know, someone they thought was hot and fun and wouldn't mind getting down for some free drinks"

Sounds good to me.

"Yeah, I figured you'd see it that way - which is why when they asked about you I told them yes"

Damien's laugh faded as he saw Alex was serious and said *Are you fucking kidding me? No way.*

"Why not man? They're hot, they're young, they're horny"

Jesus you sound like the trailer for the new Girls Gone Wild, if it's so great why don't you do it? Anyway you know how shit everything has gone with Ivy and me. She and that fucking Eskimo are still staying at my house. How the hell do you think a European birthday orgy is going to go down on keeping up civil relations?

"Come on man, shit's over between you two. You take off to Asia in like a week anyway, and what do you think she'll make of your inevitable tell-all blogs about fucking across the continent. She'll probably pull you off her Myspace friends"

Not that Alex could have known, but this would come to pass, not that it made any difference cause Damien's response still was *Look man if you wanna do it more power to you, hell I'll come and encourage you.*

"I can't do that, it'll look like I set it up all along! Hell, you need another shot"

Another turned into another 6, which turned into some vaguely 'bromantic' babbling, which evolved further into blackout.

Friday Afternoon

Damien woke on his couch and had one of those Dorothy moments where it was possible he was still with Jez, liver intact, waiting on an annoying call from Joan about how he needed to come back to the states and get his act together. Instead, the gears started grinding and he was suddenly quite sure he had broken down and agreed to the madness from the night before. As his eyes pulled into focus Ivy was standing above him, nonplussed look and all with the Eskimo hanging several feet back in an oh so hip LA Asian brat stance saying "Drunk again last night Damien? So surprising, you would think with your guys' relationship going to hell you might call"

Fuck you, get the fuck out of my house you fucking Maggie Cho wannabe.

"If she goes, I go Damien. Not that you give a shit." Ivy stared disapprovingly long enough to realize that Damien was not actually looking at but through her.

"Whatever, later" she traipsed off with Eskimo in tow, finger flying high. He thought to himself if she just stuck her tongue out the cinematic stereotype would be complete. Just as he was coming up with a really good line to holler out the door his phone rang and the voice on the other end said

"I think I've figured out our outfits for tonight"

Hello Alex.

"Cowboy and Indian carnal. Que piensas?"

I think it's too fucking early. I'll catch a cab and be over in a minute. Que hora son?

"It's five bro"

Fuck.

Alex had a nice little hacienda on the other end of town that he'd inherited from his Mexican grandmother. Over the course of a decade he had shipped, smuggled, driven, and carried all manner of useless crap from various corners of the earth and his life. Board games no one alive had heard of, beta videos boxes unending, and in this late afternoon's case: a bull whip made from cow testicles, leather chaps, and a cowboy hat. Exhibit A here was Alex's interpretation of the makings for a Cowboy outfit.

"So whaddya think man?"

I think you're fucking insane and I can't believe I agreed to this.

What he had agreed to, even in a drunken stupor, was that there was no way he would do it unless Alex joined him - a miscalculation on his part as to whether Alex's sense of embarrassment would outweigh Damien's, which it did not.

"Come on bro, you get the war paint" the age-old tin of *Kiwi* brand shoe polish was less than comforting.

About an hour later, Damien had secured the leather chaps, some wacky Indian hair wrap (as in India, not Sitting Bull), and a plastic child's hatchet in addition to the tin of black. Alex was in boxers with a leather vest, cowboy boots, a Stetson, twin plastic colts, and a shit-eating grin.

"So?"

I look ridiculous and you look gay as hell. Let's go.

Saturday Morning (wee hours)

They had gotten to Martina's, the birthday girl, flat and proceeded to get steaming almost immediately. Nina, the queen bee, playfully egged on Alex for placing himself in center stage while he half-heartedly protested that his presence was merely for Damien's benefit. By the time the 3-bedroom was overflowing with Norwegians and Mexican boyfriend hopefuls, neither Alex nor Damien was feeling much pain, and after a clumsy battle for outfit components in their changing room (i.e. closet) they proceeded to launch into a now cheap strobe flashing living room with James Brown blaring (*Sex Machine* of course). Damien threw down his best white boy chicken dance stumbling out of chaps with his shirt around the girl's neck while an equally wasted crowd proceeded to whoop and holler in Mexo-Norwega-Inglais. He had half convinced himself that he didn't totally look ridiculous when he felt a large hand land on his shoulder and send him flying. Despite protests of modesty and intent, Alex had managed to get down to his skivvies in the time it took for Damien to gain his balance and have a bottle of *Los Dorados* shoved into his hand. Alex then ripped said boxers off and performed a full monty in Martina's shocked drunk hysterically laughing face.

That was about the last thing Damien remembered till he woke, presumably several hours later, still naked in the living room but now on a couch. Martina was passed out and snoring on top of him and the party at this point was in full swing. Damien realized that he and Martina's state had become so thoroughly taken for granted that they were being treated more or less as furniture (jackets spread across their legs and all). Stumbling to a standing position he scoped out the room for his clothing which had spread the way of the four winds. Out on the balcony Alex, still naked though considerably more pissed, was making some sort of manly display involving a scorpion. At the door, stood Ivy and Inuit.

Uh, hi guys, how long you been here? I was, uh…

"Goodbye Damien" Ivy said and walked out.

Wait, but, aw fuck it, whateva.

The Eskimo didn't even have words for it; she just shook her head disapprovingly and followed her out. It was short, but it would be the last conversation they would ever have (*so much for redheads*).

"Hey man, look what rises from the dead" Alex threw his arm around him while Nina crept up from behind and handed him his jeans.

"Thought you might need these" she said "Your friend isn't looking so well" she whispered her breath hot and fumed "He just ate a scorpion, we told him not to but he made this big machismo show of crushing it with a beer bottle then swallowing it. But we didn't tell him that we killed it this afternoon with half a bottle of Raid"

Ahh…, got it. We'll head toward the bathroom.

"So fucking Thailand" Alex was already starting to look a bit green as Damien guided him to the toilet and put on his jeans.

Yeah man, fucking Asia, it seemed a million miles away.

"Hot Chinese chicks"

They all remind me of my mother.

"That's fucked up" Alex said falling to his knees.

But the booze is cheap.

"I hear that" the lid was now open.

Some of it contains like fifteen ingredients, illegal in spirits everywhere else in the civilized world.

"Not that Bangkok is too civilized, eh carnal?" he was rocking back and forth ready for launch.

Yeah I hear that, Damien took a couple steps back in case Alex's aim was off.

"Hey Dame?" he took a deep breath.

Yeah bro?

"Don't do me any more favors" Alex proceeded to give the bowl all that he had, cheap tequila, scorpion, bile and all.

I hear that.

Back in LA, off to Bangkok, feeling quite aftermathy...

Sunday, April 16, 2006

Current mood: 😖nauseated

No one bothered to tell you it's Easter and you've got a billion things to do. You're in Los Angeles again staying at your buddies' Carl and Jordan's place, running around to places that have painful recent memories, stressed and sad and heading off to Asia alone for God knows how long, and nobody had the decency to tell you it was a holiday. Jeez...

Three years ago today, you Kienyo, MOC, J, and your brother gave homage to the Easter Bunny with your mom in CT. You had lamb and lo mein and the usual odd mix ma dukes had the quirkiness to serve on American festivals. It was pleasant, fairly chill, and the last holiday you celebrated with her before she died two months later - 6 hours before you turned 28.

At the time your last book was scheduled to come out in June (right about when she discovered she had stomach cancer), and your plan was to tour for about 6 months then head off to travel the world. Needless to say, after she passed away the tour was postponed and global romps were the least of your worries or options. It has taken you three years to get back to today and you find yourself in the same lost space.

You have left Mexico and someone you deeply care for, have a new book with an uncertain future, and are frankly scared shitless about taking off alone to Bangkok tomorrow where you have no idea what the fuck you're doing.

You think sometimes that we are doomed to repeat the mistakes of the past in endless variation, plugging holes in the dike like the little Dutch boy, unseeing of the greater wall. That most people view you as impervious to shit like this only deepens the irony.

A Crash Course On the Anatomy of Robots

You are sure Asia will be fantastic and new - that you will have plenty of great stories and amazing adventures and all that shit everyone loves so much. You are only feeling a bit sad that you are not sharing it with someone in particular, and more than a bit miffed at your own inability to not get fucked up by the past - recent or otherwise.

OK...

That's your suicidal rant. No doubt a couple hours of merciful sleep may help alleviate it. Just call it a desperate scream into the electronic darkness. One can hope for catharsis. Call it nerves.

A Crash Course On the Anatomy of Robots

Southeast Asia on a Shoestring (A Crash Course on Travel)

"You have to realize that you are just a traveler; you are not home. You need the people you meet. You need their protection. You need their good will...there are some amazingly arrogant people who think that because they are American, for example, they can collect hospitality... If you're smart, you'll be very polite, you'll develop good manners."

--Paul Theroux

A Crash Course On the Anatomy of Robots

Blogging, Journals, and Poetry

What the fuck are they on about?

If you are among the post-30 or so age set that think they are still young (it is after all the "new 20s"), this is a question you may be asking yourself. *New York Magazine* states in a recent issue that a generational gap now exists between the 'MySpace' generation and – well the rest of us – that hasn't been seen since Elvis started shaking those momma boy hips and the Fab Four invaded the hell out of the states with those wacky mops. As they see it, it is a desire to expose oneself to the masses with journals, pictures, poetry, video, etc. of the most personal nature that later generations are quite frankly puzzled and embarrassed by, and of which they are completely uncomprehending.

As a performer for most of his life Damien is quite familiar with this state of mind and begrudgingly has aligned himself, as usual, with neither camp.

That said, by nature he writes lots of poetry and journals, opened a dreaded MySpace account before hitting the road, and realizing how annoying group emails are on the receiving end, has opted to start blogging—an electronic journal in cyberspace that can be viewed by anyone. An alarming number of people have subscribed to and read it voraciously in a way that would cause most professional novelists to decry the future of mankind, as would Damien if not for the fact he's getting such a kick out of it. MySpace is incidentally a web forum that allows people to post personal information, photos, music, and what have you in a public format where one can add friends, cyber-stalk and be stalked, subscribe to blogs and updates, serve as a secondary email account, and generally consume a hell of a lot of time searching for bands and bullies and crushes from when you were five to see what's become of them now. After 2 months, Damien is totally addicted and dependent on it.

If you have no idea what we're talking about, and think MySpace is for teenagers and pedophiles, think that journals belong in diaries, and have the sorely misguided view that American verse is mountain with Whitman sitting on top – well you might as well skip the next 40 pages or so. If not, add Damien, send him a nice note, and he might just consider putting you in his Top Eight.

Δ   Δ   Δ   Δ

Thailand

Bangkok blues and back with the traveler nation
Tuesday, April 25, 2006

Current mood: 😖Sunburned

Well Bangkok is all that you would expect from a big nasty beautiful contradiction of a city. There are motorcycle taxis and commuting via rivers and skyways, small village huts with skyscrapers in the background, odd organized sex industry madness, and more backpackers from England, Australia and Israel than you can shake a stick at.

I arrived last week and have been staying at my buddy Ian and Georgia's place. Ian is still a mad Newcastle traveler now transplanted Thai whiskey drinker. Georgia is a lovely Thai woman of Chinese descent who sings in a local (and excellent) blues and jazz band. Their friends were extremely welcoming and kind and made my transition all that much easier (even if I could have done without the sex show night with a couple dozen lady-boys humping to the sounds of Mayan techno and some very talented ladies firing projectile items at us from questionable places). Thank you.

I am now on an island beach/jungle off the coast called Ko Phangan, which I am sure I am spelling wrong. My Thai is limited but I've got the polite basics - sort of. The northeast end of the island is full of couples and babies, which is soothing but I'll probably be making my way towards Hat Rin or some of the more party-based areas after this week. This is the land of the fabled full-moon parties (and now I have gathered the black moon and half-moon parties so I guess it's just a pretty lunar place).
So that's about it, trying to describe more would be fruitless, plus Internet is crap round here. Love ya all. More to come…

Leaving Ko Phagnan, in a cave in Crabi…
Tuesday, May 09, 2006

Current mood: 🙂 devious
Why oh why are Thai names so impossible to pronounce and spell?

I just left Thong Nai Pan on the northeast corner of the island of Ko Phagnan. If you've read *The Beach*, or seen the bad Leonardo Dicaprio film of it, that's close to where it's set (the true honors go to Ko Phi Phi, where I'm headin to as well). It's stunning but the waters are too calm and there are too many goddamn Phrang around (foreigners, like ummm, me).

Arrived from Bangkok to couples and babies and more couples and babies. But after a week managed to find a sick ass crew of solo lunatics. Olly and Simon, mad Londoners just come from South America.

A Crash Course On the Anatomy of Robots

Vic and Victor, Finnish and German respectively, mad Elvis-looking drinker and continuously stoned sweetheart. Hamid, Iranian-German master of ceremonies, Harriet, Dave and Jack, sweet English kids. Stefan, prerequisite German model gypsy shuffler thrilled we are leaving so he can get to working out and picking up women. Greg, insane mumbling South African, incredibly nice bloke if you can understand him, since he primarily communicates in gesture and whistles. Ally, Ash and Su, Brits on vacation. Lauren, Tasha, Brett and Dan, the 2 East End couples that took mercy on me when I first arrived and let me tag as a fifth wheel for a week. And Rob, northern England metal guy world traveler. There are many more but I just can't be bothered to list everyone. Fan Club Harry and your Dutch girls, Eric the Viking and everyone else, you're the best.

It's been long days of snorkeling and swimming, leisurely afternoons drinking beer Chang (which tastes remarkably and horrifically like St. Ides) and lots of wandering nights celebrating lunar occurrences and too many buckets (200 baht = $5: A bucket filled with a bottle of Samsun, devilish Thai whiskey, illegally strong red bull, soda and coke and a handful of straws - deadly I tell you). For a minute I thought I might need to change my name to BucketWood.

Speaking of Krabi (so appropriately named), after a day of riding motorbikes I've begun to question the Thai driving system and right of way, which it appears to be based on might is right. Saw a bunch of beaches but have been a bit underwhelmed by the town itself (though to be fair the coast I saw today was truly awe inspiring). Rob and I are headed to Ko Phi Phi, which is supposed to be one of the most beautiful places on earth, as soon as our friends show up (if you are reading this and you know who you are please get here you lazy bastards). Then who knows?

To Ashley, I wish we met sooner, good luck in India... and from here to eternity :). To Ian, you're a twat, get here now. Krabi is boring as fuck and our room's a cave. Victor, go to Laos, she's a sexologist for Christ's sake.

A Crash Course On the Anatomy of Robots

To all of you stateside, Mexico, and abroad: much love, peace, and all that.

Why oh why did I leave Ko Phangnan?
Tuesday, May 23, 2006,

Current mood: 😵Recovering

Ok, so it's been a couple weeks. Let's hit it in summary....

After nearly getting jumped by several Thai bikers and various other mess with Rob, managed to dump my motorbike on an ill-advised 4am cruise around with Rob who managed to get lost for the next 3 hours (Krabi is the size of the Village mind you) and meet up with Ian and pay for the damages which were thankfully fiscal and not medical. Met cool ex spec ops kid James. The 3 of us flee Krabi. Good riddance...

So we take a boat to Ko Phi Phi, supposedly one of the most beautiful spots in Thailand as well as one of the worst hit by the Tsunami. Of 8,000 people on the island, about 3,800 were killed. It was fantastic and beautiful and unfortunately built the hell up and full of trustafarian traveler twats. You know the kind, they just spent 6 months in Australia on mommy and daddy and have spent several months in resorts and backpacker spots and now think they're well traveled. They look at you with a cool arrogance and condescension that makes normal chit chat consist of listing where you've been and where are you going and such shit, mingled with women thinking you are trying to shag em and men thinking you want to sell em drugs. Looking Asian does not help. Went snorkeling in some fantastic spots, read cryptic signs such as "memorable way to descend water" (cliff diving) and "swim with harmless reef sharks" (swim with black tips that will hopefully ignore you). After a few days Rob headed to Laos, Ian back to Bangkok, and James and I headed to Phuket....

Phuket: a beach paradise of Sodom and Disneyland. Lady-boys, prostitutes, go-go girls, and scam artists by the boatloads in a setting that looks like a cross between old 42nd street and *Apocalypse Now*. Add the fact that James is a lightning rod for trouble. Two days of drinking and driving off advances and hanging with terminally unintelligent Swedish girls. Good Irish food though (?!). A shirt they sell there is a perfect summary: (in front in English, back in Thai) "No. I don't want a Fucking suit, girl, massage, tuk-tuk" (expensive motorbike rickshaw). Left alone at 6am after dancing and partying all night....

Spent 6am to noon on a bus to Ranong on the Burmese border. Immigration hell in Thailand, then sketchy boat ride to Burma (now fascist Myanmar and Middle East-style anti-American). More migration shit. Back on boat. Done with new month-long visa 2pm. Wandered through empty Ranong, got 3:30 bus to Bangkok, was assured it would take 9 hours tops. Around 1am started questioning. Around 3am was very annoyed. 4am arrived at Ian's, exhausted and livid...

So Bangkok again. My paranoid theory that any female companion I have will benefit from our time and end up with someone else then casually destroy me once more affirmed. A girl here is now back with her ex and engaged. It can't help but remind me of recent emails, one from an ex telling me she was back with her ex-drug addict boyfriend I had to hear constant condemnation about; and another asking if I would mind if she and her fiancé opened a bed and breakfast together in my small Mexican town. We all deserve what we get...

Now recovering from horrible stomach something with Ian due to eating street shellfish after partying all week. We definitely deserve what we get. Met up with James for lunch today. Rob will probably join me up north in a day or two. James is going back to Arkansas (sorry bro). Ian will maybe meet me in Laos. Off to Chiang Mai in 2 hours to meet up with Van Gogh Steve. See ya at Red Brick bro.

To all who have been tolerant enough to deal with this scattered brain dead listing, cheers, peace and love

Soi Cowboy

How did I end up here?

The ball blasted from the stage past Rob's ear as Damien recoiled from the instinct to catch it (can *one get gonorrhea via a ping pong?*). The sad looking teen dolls swayed to what can kindly be described as Thai Karaoke nightmare in a bored opium daze. Every five minutes or so one would take the spotlight, firing darts from their pussies or blowing out birthday cakes. One exotic, possibly Indian, girl pulled what appeared to be the beginning of a plastic necklace out only to reveal a minimum of twenty feet worth of neon cord which she lassoed a Thai business man in the corner with.

"You want another drink?" Ian bellowed over the Thai equivalent of Brittany Spears.

"Dude let's get the fuck out of here" Rob implored and Damien was inclined to agree.

"We go to Cowboy now?" Georgia asked. Desperate for air, and the last half hour of his life back, Damien nodded furiously not quite drawing the connection.

Patpong is Bangkok's red light district. It is buried in a massive *Blade Runner'esque* commercial center, where Damien's only previous venture had been a futile attempt by Ian and himself to find the makings for Italian food. Georgia and her friends, wicked chefs the lot of them, had cooked for them every day since Damien stayed from his initial arrival and this subsequent passing through Krung

Tep. Ian and Damien had tried to return the favor – unsuccessfully. That day *Patpong* had looked like any Asian market you could find from San Fran to Hong Kong. Tonight it was pure Mephistopheles. Like a mad bazaar in hell, every manner of electronics, libations, flesh and substance was up for sale. Warehouses of dozens of open air bars megaphoned go-go, lady boy, sex show temptation; and above every visible street show were floors and floors of hotel rooms by the hour, brothels with Ma Ma Suns furiously pounding calculators and notebooks, noodle shops and reggae spots, and more Brits than you could shake a stick at. Cornrow Londoners roaming in packs, boys on tour beer in hand, giggling Irish lassies ripped on Ecstasy, and more than a few cousins of Jabba the Hut, a pre-teen on each thigh, cocktail in all hands. The four of them weaved in and out, stopping only at one of the omnipresent 7-11's for some red bull and whiskey, before turning onto Soi Cowboy, the target of choice. Moving past a handful of unconvincing lady-boys (a rarity here, due to cheap plastic surgery), Georgia bantered with a doorman then led them into a second story club where a show was already underway.

The thing about smut, really—if you're from the West anyhow—is that most people expect it to look like smut. Damien had been to shitty dives and outlaw clubs in over a dozen countries on at least three continents. They had a look, a feel, a vibe in fact that was instantly reassuring and repulsive. There was no doubt that the vibe was here. However as they cleared the second set of velvet-covered doors, the four found themselves in what can be best described as a modern multi-million dollar club, tuxedoed wait staff and all, with an ingratiating Maitre D leading them to their front row seats at a center stage. This formal atmosphere, blaring Techno, and industrial strength AC notwithstanding, created an initial impression of misplacement and under-dressing. Damien had barely ordered a Jack and Diet before his sense of discombobulation was further exacerbated and then thoroughly sent into the stratosphere as the tables darkened and the stage exploded. It was a good three minutes of eternity before Rob turned to him and said

"Well that's impressive"

On stage about twenty very ripped and well-hung Thai men were dressed in a Mayan-cum-Africa tribal get-up with Happy House exploding through a clearly mind-blowingly expensive sound system. They were employing all manners of trampolines, ropes, trapeze, and acrobatics – and they were vigorously, manically fucking.

Uh-huh. Must have had to work out a lot.

"Probably a bit of Yoga and Tai-Chi"

Makes sense.

This went on for another ten minutes or ten hours, Damien wasn't quite sure, and they continued to comment as if they were watching a football match - cause really what else can you do as a young hetero male facing what will surely be a scene never to be scrubbed from your brain?

"Is that what I think it is?" Rob mumbled.

"Yeah mate, lots of these guys just do this for the cash. Hell some even become Lady-boys cause it pays better," Ian answered and sucked down another G&T. Georgia was giggling.

Fucking hell.

On the floor in front of them, which he soon noticed were littered all over the stage, were pages of taped down straight porn. All the fuckers were looking at them to keep hard, as all but one fuckee in drag stared off blankly into the distance. That particular she-he was moaning in English what Damien thought were quotes from *Full Metal Jacket* (*"me so horny."*)

Dude…

"Yeah mate we'll go, just let me grab another G and T." Ian signaled over the waiter as the music stopped and the guys bounded off stage.

"Fuck, is that it?" Rob eyed the exit.

On cue the same scarring house track, the one that Damien can hum to you to this day, started up again and once more the stage was flooded with – *pale skinny out of shape guys? What the fuck is this now?* Damien almost said as maybe three-dozen tighty-whitey wearing noodle sellers lined up around the edge and began rotating every few beats.

"Just like the girl go-gos downstairs, pays less, but I reckon you go to the gym less" Ian got his last drink and Damien put it together.

"Fuck me, let me never go broke here" Rob said simultaneously seeing the placards.

Each one of the pasty onstage models had a white number pinned to their undies and were being bought off the stage one by one by clients through their waiters and led to upstairs rooms. The casual immorality of this was currently being outweighed by Damien's realization that they couldn't leave without causing a ruckus till all the boys on stage had been bought.

Can I ask you guys something? How often do you come here?

"Here? Neva" said Georgia.

"I've been to the girl ones once" said Ian.

"Hey man I'm with you" said Rob.

Well what the fuck are we doing here then?

Georgia looked quizzically then said "You American Damien. We thought that's what you like. No?"

As Damien thought of his beloved countrymen and the joy of traveling in their wake the stage had thinned to the last 8 poor bastards who no one wanted to buy. He imagined the MC was doing a bargain basement auction off and noticed the guy standing in front of them was looking directly at him. It must have been his tenth rotation at this point and he looked him square in the eye, smiled and shrugged. Not a *hey you interested*, but more of a *hey it's a life* kinda shrug.

No. Not exactly.

Δ   Δ   Δ   Δ

Cambodia

Holiday in Cambodia....
Sunday, June 25, 2006

Current mood: ☺happy

Check it, I'm actually writing an update on time in a third world country where the Internet is censored and generally crap (gentle pat on my own back).

A Crash Course On the Anatomy of Robots

Why you may ask? Well several reasons, some good, some not so good. Let's go.

I arrived in Siem Reap last week to a flurry of street assault. Like monsters from a zombie movie you are stormed at every turn by a combination of beggars, many with small children or missing limbs from landmines (or kids missing limbs from mines), drug dealers guised as taxis, and taxis guised as dealers. It's all a bit much at first, but I managed to jump on a motorbike and bail the hell out. By evening I found a decent guesthouse, and my Scottish friend Eilidh who I know from Chang Mai in Thailand. Things have been going pretty much up from there. But before I get too pleased let's talk about Cambodia...

The city I'm currently in is a beautiful contradiction of charming river guesthouses, obnoxious luxury resorts, and astonishing poverty. Angkor Wat can account for most of this just outside of town, which along with being one of the Seven Wonders of the World is an unbelievable testament to multiple religions and cultures and rulers from about the 8th to 12th century. It is an ancient city of ruins and worship, stunning in its sheer size and scope. Look it up.

As for the poverty it was within only hours of arrival that I felt like I should set up an outreach program. It is hard to refuse the begging children and I have found myself many a night with a kid on my lap buying a meal or drink that he or she will only take a little of before running the rest off to share with their family.

Last night I saw a man named "Beat" Cello, who is a Swiss doctor who plays Classical Cello music to raise awareness for children's hospitals. He was forced out by the Khmer Rouge in the 70's massacre (3 million Cambodians starved or were murdered for being elitist or educated and it plunged the country into the dark ages). To get an idea of the severity, know that wearing glasses was considered enough to be shot, and keep in mind that Cambodia is roughly the size of New York State that then had a total population of about 5 or 6 million. Look up Pol Pot on the web.

A Crash Course On the Anatomy of Robots

In the 90's the king asked him to return and set up children's hospitals, which have been miraculously done with almost all private funding. The WHO and Queen Ann have complained to him that third world countries should not have sophisticated medicine since it is out of line with the government's progress. This is first world horseshit and they should be fucking shot. About 70% of Cambodians have tuberculosis (which opens the door for the deadly Japanese Encephalitis), and government hospitals are death traps. About 60% of blood bank donations are HIV or hepatitis-infected and without proper labs only more people will die. Also, given that there are still 6 MILLION landmines here (landmines which the US is one of the only countries who refuses to outlaw), the rate of people accidentally being maimed or, without proper hospitals, most definitely killed, is alarming.

Needless to say I was fairly moved and you should read up on it and contribute if you can.

On to brighter things, today I went to a floating village with Eilidh a couple miles down a dirt path where I was, predictably, worried about mines. We found a boat that lead to a city composed of boats and houses in the middle of a lake, created by a meteor, completely full of wildlife. I am still not quite sure what one family was doing but it appeared to me that they were fishing with a ball python. This would be surreal except that I'd already saw a pit of crocs and massive catfish in feeding frenzy. A couple of hours on the lake and a quick stop at an earnest but painfully small environmental center later (i.e. smaller than our room), we headed back to town.

My friend Rob who was supposed to be arriving today has got himself Typhoid and is grounded in Bangkok. I'm going meet him back here in a week when Eilidh has to split. I'm gonna see Angkor again before I bail to the capital of Phnom Penh.

As for now, we're getting on a 6am bus to a 7am boat for a 7-hour river trek to Battambong, Cambodia's second largest city which sounds a lot like Luang Prabang in Laos but not as touristy.

It would seem odd that I am my happiest in Asia here amongst total contradiction and extreme, but any of you that know me also know that is what I thrive on. I love balance, but it is a balance of extremes and for the moment I am at home.

Give me a shout.

To all with peace, love, and all that jazz

Killing caves and fields, Angkor at dawn and bamboo trains...
Tuesday, July 04, 2006

Current mood: ☠restless

I'm in Phnom Penh (which I guarantee I just misspelled) staying at a lakeside guesthouse with Rob waiting for Van Gogh to get in from the north. Yesterday went to the genocide museum (a former school turned death camp/prison/torture facility) and infamous Killing Fields (mass graves, bones and clothes sticking out the dirt, rooms full of skulls). This fun-filled afternoon was followed by a night out amongst the Khmer elite (rich kids with guns) at a club amusingly called "Heart of Darkness" and the first decent pool table I've played on in months. Other than the craziest driving on motos I've ever witnessed (far worse than DF), that's been my experience here so far.

So Battambang and the last days of Siem Reap...

In the wet season the boat down the river to Battambang takes 3 hours or so. I asked around as to the time it would take now and the best answer I could get was somewhere between 5 and 8 hours. With this in mind, Eilidh and I woke up at 5:30am with virtually no sleep and headed out.

The "express" boat, bearing no resemblance to the fine vessel on the ticket, was a rickety leaking contraption overloaded with passengers and a terminally fucked up VW engine. Between bailing water and breaking down, I am shocked we did not sink.

The first 5 or so hours were beautiful, riding through river communities and lakes of water plants, small children waving and screaming hello, and general good vibes. However after 7 or so hours, breaking down maybe a dozen times, alternating between frying under the sun and soaking in monsoon, we were fairly finished.

No such luck.

We fried the engine and the fan belt went out about an hour from the city. This was 10 hours in. A big Canadian guy and I decided it was worth the risk of landmines to wander into the jungle and find someone to get us to town. By the time we actually got someone to understand us, our driver had a new fan belt on and we struggled the last 2 hours down the river. Fuckin Cambodian transport...

So Battambang, Cambodia's 2nd largest city, actually feels much more like a small village. Eilidh and I splurged and got an AC room with a balcony, television and fridge ($7 a piece) and hit the town. It was a breath of fresh air in that apparently there have only been roads built here in the last year or two and they are not very well worn, traveler-wise. There's really only one bar, and for the first time I felt truly foreign (we walked into a Cambodian kickboxing match and essentially 1000 people stopped talking and stared and pointed as we walked around the ring).

Most days we just lounged and walked around exploring. The one day we rented motorbikes with a Canadian/Australian couple was a lesson in Cambodian history and off-road biking. A local guy named Tony rode with us and brought us to a series of caves where the Khmer Rouge did much of their slaughter.

In brief, the 2 caves we went to were about the size of a small Manhattan bar, and over 4 years had over 20,000 people murdered in them, mostly by strangulation, being thrown off a precipice, or being axed to the back (apparently to remove liver, lungs and heart to be eaten). It was needless to say fairly rough to listen to, especially since Tony had a good deal of his family murdered during the time (his father was a doctor).

As hard was hearing about 20 kids getting blown up in his village since they decided to see what would happen when they hit a UXO with a hammer (he described it as walking through "meat" of children then seeing

237

flesh hanging from trees). Totally commendable to the people here and their tolerance and determination to heal as a country was demonstrated meeting some former Khmer Rouge who somehow continue to live amongst their former victims.

All this was spread amongst seeing temples and riding some of the most hardcore off-road I have ever done, especially with Eilidh riding shotgun (think 10-inch wide winding paths on roads with flooded potholes the size of Volkswagens at 50 kph).

A final move: we went to the infamous bamboo train trail. Essentially, where the terminally slow train runs once a day to PP, there are totally wonky tracks by the roadside. Locals build bamboo platforms with motorbike engines and toss them onto axles on the tracks then ferry locals to and from the city. We tossed three motorbikes on one and rode during the sunset through the countryside. It was a pretty fantastic way to end my last day with Eilidh in Cambodia.

So at week's end, at 7 in the morning, I left Battambang for Siem Reap once more, and Eilidh headed to Bangkok on her way to Indonesia. I'll just leave it at this: I had a truly amazing time. It was extremely difficult to leave, and I thought I was going to lose it a bit as I got on the bus. I'll miss you kid.

Back in Siem Reap I met up with Rob recovering from Girardisis (not Typhoid but no picnic). We watched lots of late night World Cup (sorry to my English crew) and went to Angkor Wat at 5am for sunrise (I told you I'd make it babe). It was stunning though I was far more impressed with the Bayon temple with its giant stone faces and catacomb passageways than Angkor itself (I suppose being the largest religious building in the world and one of the 7 wonders almost dooms it for disappointment). I then waited in Siem Reap till Van Gogh arrived then headed to PP where I currently am.

That's the deally. On a completely random note: anyone in Asia right now please drop me a line. It's my 31st on the 12th and I wanted to corral some heads to Sihanoukville on the Cambodian coast for some bonfire beach action.

Peace, love, give me a shout.

Leaving Phnom Penh, Sihaloukville lounging, b-day in Eden...
Wednesday, July 12, 2006

Current mood: 💀anxious

Well then. I've just turned 31 in southern Cambodia. I am currently having a violently disturbing panic-filled hangover, I reckon on account of mixing wine, beer, Jack Daniels, tequila, and whatever else was sent to me last night. Rob and Steve threw me a bash at a beach bar called Eden and that is exactly where I woke up this morning having lost most of the late evening (DJ'ing whilst fending off one of the bar owners' girlfriend is about the last thing I recall). Today I watched *The Beach* for the first time and deeply regretted having read the book first since it made the film almost impossible to sit through. Especially considering that me, Rob and Steve have been constantly taking the piss out of other travelers and being "real" (i.e. with bad American accent stuff like "shit man, that's totally not real braw, I remember back in 89, that was when Cambodia was good dude, I'm heading to Afghanistan to start a yoga commune and get away from all this shit brother. Wanna buy some grass?") Starting the day with X3 and 2 iced coffees did little to quell the nerves either. Just now I had 3 of us on a motorbike and was shaking like a leaf thinking of what a piss poor ignominious end it would be to crash on my b-day.

I've been enjoying Sihaloukville quite a bit. PP was a manic town with insane traffic and shitty bars. We hit the road last week and I slept the entire bus ride on account of being up till an hour before we jet. I managed to forget not only my deodorant but the only disposable camera I have bought so far. Good job. On the plus, it was warm and sunny when we got here, which apparently has not been the case for a good two weeks. This weather continued till yesterday when we 3, my new Austrian friend Martina, and an English couple decided to take a boat over to an island beach about an hour away. I shit you not, a friggin typhoon passed about a kilometer away and the sea was very angry that day to steal a phrase. The beach itself was nice though, though visibility for snorkeling was pure shit. We loaded up sacks of lobsters, crabs, shrimp, chicken, sour soup, and beer and made an afternoon of it. The ride back was also choppy as all hell, but at its end we were treated to a magnificent sunset on one side and a full daytime moon and rainbow on the other. Steve said "shit man I don't even know where to look it's so beautiful" and that about summarized it.

So other than that it's been a whole lot of lounging on the beach, bonfires at night, and an amazing number of birthdays coinciding with or near mine (which if you're Cambodian means free food and cake and a whole lot of intolerable Karaoke). At first we were annoyed we were staying so far down the beach (our moto drivers lied and said we were on Serenity Beach), but in retrospect it's a good excuse to tool around. Other than the water being pretty nasty at the other end, the harassment is considerably less here (kids literally hanging onto you if you don't buy a bracelet, moto drivers constantly trying to grab you or sell you drugs, etc.).

The plan as of now is to ride or bus over to Kampot about 170km away and hang there and in Kep (abandoned former beach resort, now kinda spooky ghost beach, post Khmer Rouge). After that Eilidh is hopefully gonna meet me in PP and we'll head to the wild east (that or I might be making a rather extreme detour to Indonesia or Malaysia). We shall see...

So that's the news, drop me a line, love and miss everyone, peace out

Parting ways in Kampot, cave disasters, haunted casinos, and lounging in Kep...
Tuesday, July 25, 2006

Current mood: 😵 exhausted

OK, lots to update, let's just list it.

Me, Rob, and Steve left Sihaloukville on account of the fact that after 8 days we were fairly sure it was only moments before we would open a bar, guesthouse or opium den. We took a cramped ass taxi 150km to Kampot, which along with Kep is apparently where all the finest black pepper in the world comes from, go figure.

Once in Kampot, we managed to get forcibly removed from our guesthouse for drinking local whiskey and buying mixers rather than buying all our drinks from them. I got in a heated debate with the very young Danish owner about how I too owned a foreign business abroad and could understand her plight but to no avail. Go figure.

The next day I went back to Phnom Penh and met Eilidh at the airport. Trooper that she is, she flew from Indonesia to Kuala Lumpur to Cambodia to meet up. The least I could do was take a two-hour taxi and scoop her up.

After a night in PP we took a cab back to Kampot and proceeded to do a very stupid thing. The town is surrounded by a series of limestone caves. For experienced climbers (which not all of us were) this is dream. Therefore I and Eilidh, Rob and Steve, and our English friends from Bamboo island all got motorbikes and took the shit road out to a nice set in the middle of nowhere. This was a grave error.

Once in the caves we had to crawl through some very wet and dark narrow passages and scale some fairly hairy shit. It was on a 4-meter climb that Steve and I lost track of Rob. I was looking over for him when I heard a dull crash and what sounded like gurgling from the darkness below. I repeatedly screamed Rob's name and heard nothing but a gradual moaning. Like an idiot I suddenly convinced myself I was a superhero and tried to leap to his aid. The first indication that this was ill-planned was when the hold I was grasping proceeded to crumble in my hand and I started a fairly nasty downward fall. Somehow I managed to turn midair and land it, of course not without tearing open my right leg and crunching my left knee and generally scraping the hell out of everything else. The next thing I noticed was that I had landed several inches from Rob and had I turned just a little differently I probably would've crushed and killed him, good job asshole.

So Rob hadn't answered because the wind was knocked out of him and he had fractured and quite possibly broken several ribs on his left side. This was thanks to a boulder that had gently stopped his fall about two thirds of the way down the more than 12-foot fall. Steve was trapped above and everyone else had taken off to another passageway. "Great" I thought, Rob's gonna die in my fucking arms with a punctured lung and it's all cause he was following me and Steve (everyone else had muttered something along the lines of "no fucking way" when we started climbing).

So anyhow, some local kids helped me carry him out while Eilidh and Steve went on to worse climbs in attempts to find an exit. It was a miracle that Rob turned out OK since it took a fucking hour for a car to come pick him up (no way he could've got on the back of a bike), and once back in Kampot, a friend who happens to be an orthopedic doctor, took care of him. Thanks sweetie. Lucky.

So Rob was laid up for a few days whacked out on Valium and Codeine. Meanwhile Eilidh and I took a hellish 4-hour off road trek to Bokor hill, which is a spooky place indeed. Imagine an abandoned luxury hotel and casino and church on top of a mountain with a panoramic view of the city and rolling mist pouring through former guest rooms and dining halls; lots of jungle leeches and other icky things as well.

When Rob got solid enough we headed to Kep on bikes (which is essentially like Bokor except an entire abandoned beach resort) and hired a boat to a small Island. We stayed in huts and built bonfires on the beach, and generally chilled in the nicest water I've been to in Cambodia. Some Irish kids brought some black label while me and a bunch of Australians did manly fire duty. Roar.

So two nights ago was it for the foursome we had become. Steve and Rob are in PP right now on their way to Kuala Lumpur (they both got sick of the rainy season here). Eilidh and I are headed back to Sihaloukville so I can sort my Vietnam visa, then we're off to Kratie in the wild east to check out some endangered freshwater dolphins. We both have to be in PP on the first to fly out, me to Ho Chi Min, Eilidh to Bangkok then Edinburgh. I'm gonna head north from there to Hanoi then double back and catch a flight to Hong Kong.

At a little over 3 months in I'm starting to get a little road weary. I think 4 and a half I'm gonna call it quits and head back to LA then New York then Vermont and Montreal (though I have a sneaking suspicion that the UK is in my very near future). Then of course Guanajuato for the Cervantino Festival and grand reopening of me, and Alex's bar "Ël Fusilado."

Anyhow that's all the news that's fit to print. Sending love from the Far East. Peace out.

Δ   Δ   Δ   Δ

Mortality

"Little early in the day"

Eilidh glanced back at the five Khmer drinking in the lot in front of the restaurant. She and Damien were staying by the lake in Phnom Penh at a backpacker hangout riddled with mosquitoes, from the aforementioned body of water. Other than tuk-tuk and motorbike taxis the majority of locals here were either tour guides or bar owners. Five wasted locals in front of a hippie vegetarian joint did stick out a bit, but hell

We're the tourists here. Maybe their uncle owns the joint.

It had been a long day of embassy nonsense. Getting Damien's visa for Vietnam had been the most annoying so far. On top of that, their plans for Kratie and freshwater dolphin watching had been shot on account of the fact that half of the year seventy percent of the country was completely inaccessible except by boat due to flooding - Battambang had been quite enough thank you very much (Eilidh was still recovering from the sun's effects on her British complexion). Earlier, they had checked into their guesthouse and showered before catching a beer on the water. Damien was starving and a group of scraggly shady drunk Cambodians was of little concern. Still…

They do kinda look a bit out of place.

Walking into the neo-hippy trustafarian restaurant reminded Damien just how safe he'd been playing for much of this trip. Maybe it was the density of languages in the region that made it feel like learning any was a lost battle. He'd blame it on the tonal nature of Asian dialects (*ho* means like ten things depending on the inflection), but Khmer is one of the few non-tonal idioms in the area. In any case, he hadn't gotten past a few cursory words and names of local moonshine and almost everyone he was hanging with was British (Kienyo had already responded to an email he had written about Eilidh with "so you traveled 10,000 miles to find another white girl?"). As pan flutes wafted through the thatched roof courtyard and Eurotrash Nuevo hippies sipped Tiger beer whilst awaiting the inevitable fire show, Damien grabbed a table in resignation and waved over a bandana-wearing Cambodian teenager with a Che Guevara shirt.

Uhh… suor-sdei, uh bir beer Chang sohm, and uh, a menu?

The waiter looked quizzically before saying "You want two beers and menus?"

Uh, yeah, thanks

"You look Khmer. You Cambodian family?"

Uh, no, American, well Chinese, my mother Cantonese

"Ah. Very good mix"

Eilidh chuckled as the waiter sauntered off. In the few weeks they had known each other some version of this question had surfaced for Damien at least three times a day. Brits especially seemed to consistently ask a variation of "but where are you really from" after Damien would say he was from the states. On most occasions his answer was "New York," followed by "Brooklyn," followed by walking away.

It was with these thoughts in mind and the waiter about halfway back with beers that five pops sounded at the front of the restaurant. Despite having been thoroughly inundated with the sound of explosions from his time in Mexico, his New York nature kicked in on instinct and grabbing Eilidh's hand he grumbled

Under. The. Table.

"What it's just firewo-"

NOW!

She let him pull her down and was about to comment on the directness and paranoia of Americans when she noticed the two men lying on the ground shaking about ten feet from them. The three others they had been drinking with leapt into a pick-up and tore ass out of the place. The waiter ran to the bar and dialed out on his cell screaming in Cambodian, and almost without missing a beat the band played on.

"What the fuck was that?"

One to the head and chest; the second got another for good measure. They had no idea it was coming. Damien got up and started walking to the bodies, one of which was in seizure.

"Wait! Where are you going? Are you daft?!" she looked in the direction of the shooters.

They're history. Just gonna see if there's any hope for these two.

She waited under the table, not sure whether to get up again. Several other diners had begun muttering with a few standing up to join Damien. Both men lay splayed out on their backs with their arms out like snow angels. The closer one would have been standing with his back to the table, the other with his left side. They had been the same group they had noticed on their way in, and best she could figure the other three must have produced guns mid-conversation and fired point blank. In morbid contemplation, she realized had it not been a planned execution, the bullets would have more than likely flown in their path.

Damien knelt by the first man, whom in his opinion, had died thoroughly and instantly. Blood pooled in one eye around powder burns and an angry gaping hole where his forehead used to be. He carefully stepped over the body to the next man who was going through spastic convulsions and had an immediate sense of grim déjà vu. The man, probably in his late twenties, stared up at nothing as his lips mouthed alien prayers. Grabbing the man's small rough shaking hand Damien muttered *It's okay now, it's okay.*

He waited a full two minutes for the tremors to stop. By then, a circle of murmuring backpackers had formed around him. He stood up and walked back just as the first police and paramedics began to arrive. They did not require a statement.

Beer Chang sohm, Damien waved down the waiter.

"Are you actually going to drink a beer now?" Eilidh looked in disbelief.

They're gone. I did what I could, which wasn't much. Not like those fucking vampires and dumbfucks.

A true crowd had formed and a whole gaggle of Chavelors and tourists stood around bullshitting and retelling what would amount to the *craziest* exiting part of their package holidays. The cops, in true third world crime scene etiquette, were handling the bodies and casings without gloves and putting egg crates over the blood pools to keep street dogs from lapping them up. It took less than ten minutes for the bodies to be packed up. Unaware, new arrivals filled the tables and business went on.

"Jesus, I can't believe two people just lost their fucking lives and everyone is eating and drinking like nothing happened"

Death is a funny thing; people deal with it very differently. Some of these kids have never seen anyone die, let alone violently. The others may be travel junkies who've seen far too much. Some people eat, some joke, most gossip. I did what I could, which was nothing. Thousands die all over this planet every day in shitty ways, you just gotta keep on living.

There was a long pause.

"That's the first time I've seen anyone die"

You're lucky, and to be fair, from Scotland.

"Fuck off. I'm serious, this is completely fucked"

I know. I'm sorry. Shit humor is my way of dealing with it.

"Well can we at least get out of here?"

Of course, let's go.

They went back to the guesthouse where she would cry and he would write. Later they would get drunk in the Lake District at a club called *Apocalypse Now*, where Damien noticed most of the patrons were packing heat. Wandering the streets of PP he briefly thought about mortality, turned to her and for the first time said that he was in love with her. She told him to shut up and stop being such an emotional fucking American. They both laughed at that - for different reasons. Then they went to their temporary home and had quiet furious intimacy.

Afterward, as they lay in the darkness, the tiny fiery point of an opium-laced cigarette drawing trails and comets through the sky, he wondered if one day his death would bring others closeness. She thought about Edinburgh, waiting with the future, thousands of miles away. For reasons each their own, they held each other closer.

They then passed into slumber, quiet and still as corpses.

Δ   Δ   Δ   Δ

Lost in Translation

Cambodia is hours from being just a memory. Israel is locked in stupidity with Lebanon. Your life is a mess and you want to go to Britain. Strangely feeling at peace in this land filled with such recent violence. Strange to feel like anything is possible and consequence is unknown. Strange to feel free and like the world is at your feet and any direction you head is full of possibility.

A Crash Course On the Anatomy of Robots

You don't even know where to begin.

The flight to Ho Chi Min was about to get under way and Damien was finally ready to bid farewell to the land of Khmer.

Khmer, how the fuck did Kampuchea become Cambodia?

He suddenly remembered dropping Eilidh in Don Mueang International Airport and thinking, amongst other things, about the very Western need to rename shit. Krung Thep Maha Nakhon is the largest city in Thailand. It's full name is *Krung Thep Mahanakhon Amon Rattanakosin Mahinthara Yuthaya Mahadilok Phop Noppharat Ratchathani Burirom Udomratchaniwet Mahasathan Amon Piman Awatan Sathit Sakkathattiya Witsanukam Prasit* which roughly translates to "The city of angels, the great city, the eternal jewel city, the impregnable city of God Indra, the grand capital of the world endowed with nine precious gems, the happy city, abounding in an enormous Royal Palace that resembles the heavenly abode where reigns the reincarnated god, a city given by Indra and built by Vishnukam."

You will notice that nowhere in there do you find the word Bangkok.

After 4 months on the road Damien felt for the most part that Ivy and New York were out of his system. He had done the hard reboot, the exploration of self, the proverbial walkabout - that's what he told himself anyhow as he drank and fucked his way across Asia. At the very least he was writing again.

On a daily basis he madly scrawled illegible notes hoping for inspiration for a new book. The monthly accumulation of notebooks was beginning to remind him of Michael Douglas's character in

Wonderboys. Still, he felt he was making progress. More immediate evidence could be seen on his blog which he updated on a weekly basis and had reached the shocking figure of about 4,000 readers, many of whom keep inquiring if he was planning on using the updates for a novel. To this he simply replied that though did not rule out the possibility, he had no desire to repeat his last book (a memoiresque dive through debauchery in Latin America) and that this journey had been primarily a personal one.

He had once more sought to do a reset on his life and to that end he had been successful. For better or worse the Southeast had been reached and explored. Vietnam and the end of his journey were a month in sight. He had met someone new and entirely different from any past loves (in the very least that she continually slagged on him for all things American, and the very foolish logistics of trying to continue a Mexico/Scotland connection).

Things were looking up.

He would try to remind himself of this several hours later in Saigon where he once more found that bureaucracy is an international consistency, the sound of frustration is the same in any language, and robots can turn on their masters.

Vietnam (but first a little more Cambodia)

August 1

You've been here for five minutes and you're already ready to lose it. Yet another customs agent has wrecked your passport after picking and pulling at it because after seven years you look different from your photo and don't wear glasses. You'll probably have to go to the fucking embassy now. Bullshit. Rejected from Vietnam, well at least you're not the first American to say "fuck this place." Pissload of bureaucratic horseshit. Thought you were going to get shot just now for sneaking off for 20 minutes for smokes, a burger, and a hasty summary to Eilidh. Now you're on a flight back to PP, Cambodia. Fucking great.

August 2

The US embassy is open two hours a day Monday through Thursday. Today is Wednesday and your visa runs out Monday. It takes days, possibly weeks to process a new passport. $100 will speed the process. You are defeated.

Mumbling Englishmen and tutoring Khmers who are opening guesthouses. This is your morning in Narin Guesthouse. You imagine by now she is in a car from Glasgow toward Stirling. You picture green hills and bright sun and thick Scottish accents. You are sitting next to her holding her arm and entertaining some relative who you barely understand about Americans and travel and writing small poems. She looks forward and smiles and perhaps passes a small kiss in the air. It is clean and dry. It is as you imagine it.

When you and she get to her parents' place you slip away for a shower after all the prerequisites and some bit of culture shock. She is a bit formal until you get to her room where you and she lie down clothed on top of comforters and pass out exhausted in the mid-afternoon light.

After waking you'll say that you love her and she'll smile and kiss you, with that look in her eyes. The one that says she's not sure if you should be here, or if she should open up, or if this is realistic, or could possibly last. You kiss her back long and soft and pretend you cannot see the doubt in her eyes.

Back in Phnom Penh

I imagine you are in Bangkok

On your way to the airport

To London and beyond

Still a bit sleepy, from last night's rumble and fumble

Opium laced cigarettes and talking about not putting those emotions

Into so many words

(See Special Features section for more)

EXHILED, Siha again, PP, FUCK Vietnam and still in Cambodia... Wednesday, August 02, 2006

Current mood: 😠angry

I said goodbye to Eilidh this morning.

A Crash Course On the Anatomy of Robots

After some time in Kampot about a week ago, we ended up back in Sihanoukville to get my Vietnam visa. We spent 5 days, drank and smoked, danced and lived. I DJ'd some nights at Eden getting shit from young Irish girls (acting like American sorority brats), and before we left the owner of Monkey Republic tried to convince me to work at the bar.

We then went back to PP; we got a luxurious hotel room on the river, and spent the last two nights together living it up. At 7am yesterday we got to the airport and said our goodbyes (hopefully temporary) and Eilidh went off to Bangkok for a long layover before London then Glasgow. My flight to Vietnam was 4 hours later but I didn't mind.

If these descriptions seem short it is because of the last 24 hours. Rest assured the last 2 weeks have been amazing and lovely and I'd have many wonderful things to report if not for recent events, which are dominating my current existence. I'll reprint part of my last email to Eilidh and you can see why.

"So I've got a minute. I imagine you are riding in a car with a relative from Glasgow by now if not already at home and crashing out from exhaustion. I've had a horrible 24 hours since we departed, and it is no small exaggeration that I could have bought a round trip to Bangkok, spent all day with you, seen you off and flown back for less money and headache.

So, the details...

I spent the 4 hours after your flight waiting for mine in total delirium. I read an *Economist* from front to back and scribbled some journal entries and poems which I can read you some time at the very least for a laugh. I got on the flight, which was too short to sleep on, then walked into customs in HCMC.

The young kid at the counter insisted that I looked nothing like my photo and proceeded to tear at the already fucked cover till the picture practically fell out. They made me sign something, which they also said didn't look right, and then sent me to the chief dickhead who refused my entry. They then assigned armed guards to me.

A Crash Course On the Anatomy of Robots

Between begging my embassy for help (which they said it was too late for) and trying to get back to Cambodia, my afternoon was spent in quarantine.

I finally managed to get in on standby to PP at 7pm. It cost me $100, plus of course the price of my original ticket, not to mention my now useless Vietnam visa. A guard took pity on me and as we walked to the gate gave my passport to another guard to hold while I stopped in the smoking lounge.

I chained through three smokes before I noticed my escort wasn't paying attention and snuck off to find a magazine and buy a burger. It was here that I noticed an Internet place (madly overpriced at $1 every 15 minutes) and decided to risk scribbling a lightning email to you. Reading it over now I apologize for the chaotically burned out tone that must have come across but I really thought any second I was going to get jumped by a squadron of military goons.

Anyhow, got back to the gate where of course there was a gaggle of young guards looking clueless and barking into walkie-talkies and needless to say I didn't get another moment to myself till the doors of the aircraft were locked and the plane started moving.

Back in Cambodia, pissed off and dying approximately the same time you wrote this email, I entered a new hell as Cambodian immigration proceeded to grill me. Once I convinced them that I was indeed Damien Wood, I was given a short leash of a limited visa to get to my embassy, grab a new passport, and get the hell out the country. I think I only managed this since Cambodians despise the Vietnamese and wanted to come off as more understanding than Ho Chi Min customs.

So about to collapse, either to the ground or in tears, I hopped in a cab and told him to take me to Narin Guesthouse, the closest to the embassy according to Lonely Planet. I checked in and found once more that guidebooks are shit since the embassy had moved sometime last year. Too busted to move again I had a beer and some dinner and passed out in a bed bug-laden double.

After some considerably shit sleep (about the time you'd be flying to London), I woke up to knocking from my moto driver. I showered and grabbed my gear (unpacked still) and headed to the embassy which amusingly only sees Americans between 2 and 4pm, Monday through Thursday.

Begging to talk to someone I was put on the phone with a nice lady whom I explained my situation to. She said it'd take 1 to 2 weeks to get the passport. Begging and further explaining that I'd be in Cambodian jail before that happened she offered me an emergency passport (only good for one year) at double the price with an additional fine for mutilating my copy. It'll be done within a few days, which since they are closed Friday through Sunday (and my visa expires Monday and I have no Vietnamese visa), hopefully means tomorrow. I was too defeated to argue.

Right now I am waiting for my photos to develop. I had my camera developed too so when I get the photos I can see your face, take a deep breath, and not kill anyone when I go back to the embassy."

So anyhow that's where I'm at. The first real shit bureaucracy of my trip, hopefully the last (knock on...). Wishing you were all with me to share a drink and reduce my agitation.

Peace love, all that.

Δ   Δ   Δ   Δ

Detour (where fate's wicked sense of humor catches up)

Damien stepped out of the hostel and flagged down a tuk-tuk. The previous day's events had drained him of the temporary joy that

Eilidh had brought to his soul (*a bit dramatic don't you think?*). *Fuck it*, he was, as Rob pointed out in Laos, looking *awfully tragic.*

He knew some good spots near the backpacker pond, Boeng Kak Lake, and if all else failed, there was always *Apocalypse Now*, the third world disco of choice round these parts, where there had apparently been a spectacularly mismanaged gunfight the other night. Across the dance hall, between two rival gangs, opposing groups of 4 and 5 gunmen let loose across a crowded bar and probably about a dozen rounds were exchanged. One shooter was hit – in the leg. An overly armed populace and too many Chow Yun Fat films might be to blame for the trigger-happy youth with less than stellar marksmanship.

As he rode through the city he thought of its dark rep, the child prostitution, human slavery, and all-around offerings to appetites less conventional. There's a book he flipped through in Kampot, something along the lines of *Phnom Pen Confidential,* or some shit like that. Along with *The Beach* and *Southeast Asia on a Shoestring,* they were among any number of books you could buy in color photocopy form for a fraction of their value. The criteria to being put in this exclusive library of homeless hawkers on carts, feeble English bookstores, and hippy hostels across the land, were anybody's guess. He half thought of putting his own travel novel out there just to inject some new life in circulation (unpaid, mostly read by trustafarians, but circulated nonetheless). In this particular sordid little slice of life, the authors had compiled stories from expats in the capital city. Among all the drinking and drugging and spiritual ex-war crap you might expect there was also a bit on two expats talking about fucking tweens up the ass and how much they disliked it - nice.

Why write about love, Damien thought, when I can track how much an infant goes for out of a brothel in Kep? This was a country without moral compass, whose recent history was as evil and forgotten to the rest of the world as any currently-occurring African nightmare. It is an underbelly where ex-military and thrill seekers rub shoulders in bars, and everyone has killed or had someone close to them murdered in their lifetimes. Now they were just tired and dead inside on the frayed nerve endings of what was once a sense of country and self. No wonder he felt at home. Need to blow off some steam? Just drive a little off road, rent an AK-47 and buy some bullets. It just costs you munitions and a target: livestock from $5 a chicken to $100 a large mammal; if you got in the thousands you could get a prisoner on death row; killing cows with Bazookas - how fuckin cosmopolitan of our wartime sociopathic distant stance.

There's no consequence here, and since we live in a world where no one takes responsibility any more, it makes a pretty good playground for those who can and will stray. Why did *he* not feel anything? He had wandered through relationships with Marie, Jez, and Ivy and had left hollow. Was Eilidh just another in a long line of companions he would wander through to convince himself of humanity? Was Southeast Asia just another set of countries where he could lose himself in cities, where the customs and words were strange and alien and somehow comforting to him as a youth, where feeling strange and alien was unfamiliar?

A Crash Course On the Anatomy of Robots

He had experienced love of sorts, and death at arm's length—so close he could taste it. He had wandered the earth like Cain and disappeared in the shadows of his own self-created persona. Like war correspondents who hide behind a lens and pretend they are watching something outside of themselves, he had created a barrier between himself and his own life. Poetry was his own crack, his own private dancer. He had broken the cardinal dealer rule of getting high on his own supply, of confusing the mask for what was underneath. He told his world to himself in fables and convoluted combined truths, and in that way it could never touch him. No matter how horrible, or banal, or tragic, or beautiful, it all just became pretty phrases and spoken words, funny stories and deep lessons – regardless if the extraction of meaning was arbitrary, regardless if it was no more than a defense mechanism, or matter of mere survival.

He walked into a side bar in the Lake District, some hookers shot stick and the owner gave a friendly wave. He had spent a few assorted nights on his two – well now three trips to the city and got to know the locals a bit, including a crew of rowdy ex-marines that kept the flesh and booze flowing.

Howdy James

"No shit? If it isn't Mister Wood, hey guys, you remember that crazy ass Japanese dude I was telling you about that I met in southern Thailand?" (Speaking of ex-Special Ops)

In the flesh, and I'm Chinese James

"Whatever"

Four easily-spotted types sat in front of him. One black, two Latino, and James doing his best Johnny Bravo with Navy tats impression.

They were like the retired armed forces Backstreet Boys. The larger Latino put out his hand and said

"Hey bro, Tuso, good to meet ya, James was saying you're the only guy he ever met that had a prostitute pay him"

I was wasted, we were dancing, and something she saw in me made her think she needed to take care of me

"I'm sure she did" conspiratorial wink follows.

She just paid for cab fare, I'm sure James neglected to mention the infinitely more interesting bit where he had to hide out in my room when the Thai authorities came looking for us after one of his own less-than-prudent interactions with a lady of questionable background

"Hey man, she set me up bro, and they're all of questionable background bro, fuckin Phuket"

Well cheers to that

He pulled up a chair and ordered some rice wine and Ankor beer.

"So what's the word bro?" James gave his patented sleepy eyed Arkansas delivery.

Oh the usual, fell in love with a British chick, got deported from Vietnam, getting piss drunk, etc.

"Those Brits are fuckin crazy carnal" Tuso pulled up.

Yeah, here's to the empire.

They bullshit and drank for a while. Damien bought a couple of rounds for the bar which Chan, the owner, seemed overly pleased at. The two others, Pedro and Artt, shot some stick with the local talent, who to be fair, were extremely fucking talented (I guess when all you do is sell yourself and play pool you gotta be pretty good at both).

The night moved on and many rice wines and war stories later James said

"So what's the deal bro, you gonna hang here forever or what?"

You mean Asia? Naw, gonna head to Vietnam for a month then dip back stateside.

"Naw I mean, you gonna keep rolling like this? It's been what? Like 5 years on the road?"

Technically I have a home base in Mexico, so it's only been like five months.

"You know what I mean man, I mean you've been drinking and druggin and fuckin and runnin for like foreva right?"

Dude, a week in Thailand with me does not make you an expert on all things Damien

"Uh-huh, so am I wrong? You know you can't live without consequences forever right?"

Define forever.

As Damien stepped out of Bikinibar one of the girls followed and slid her hands into his pants.

Sorry not interested, bye bye he smiled and stepped backwards into the road.

The next conscious moment Damien experienced he was crumpled on his side with his face in the dirt. From a million nosebleeds he instantly recognized the smell of rust and salt in his mouth. A slim pair of female legs was doing the childhood pee-pee shuffle in front of him and he had the odd sensation of being unattached to his body. *What the fuck?*

By his guess the car turning the corner must have been going about forty miles an hour and had most likely actually been accelerating when it struck him. James later told him that he had bounced off the front windshield (smashed) and flown completely inverted over the car before landing on the concrete sidewalk. The girl had started screaming as he stumbled to his feet unsure of what had happened, only that his right leg was exploding from where the bumper had struck and that alien pains ran throughout his body. He grabbed onto the weeping girl who was muttering in Khmer.

It's OK, I'm fine, look at me ok? I'm fine don't worry

"My boyfriend killed by car, my boyfriend he die like this, my boyfriend he die" she babbled and embraced him. James and the boys must have exited the bar as soon as it had happened and were now standing with Chan the owner and a bunch of clients around him.

"Jesus Christ man, you OK? You flipped like a fuckin rag doll bro" Tuso put his hand on his shoulder.

Rather than replying Damien put his left hand on Tuso's left shoulder brushed him aside and stumbled to the car. The owner, a medium-sized Cambodian man probably in his mid-twenties was ranting at him in Khmer and broken English.

"Why you no look? Stupid American, you drunk! Why you —"

Damien grabbed his shirt with his left hand and dropped him with his first shot. Lying half suspended by his shirt, the man slumped into semi-consciousness as Damien continued to hammer him in the face with his free hand half bent over.

YOU TRY TO KILL ME MOTHERFUCKER?! YOU TRY TO FUCKING KILL ME AND YOU ASK ME WHY?! YOU FUCKING FUCK!

As the blows continued and the driver's face began bruising and bleeding, Damien was vaguely aware of the crowd that had gathered around him. Their eyes were hungry, lips twisted. He wouldn't be able to recall when the others' legs began to join him, only the image of feet bearing various footwear kicking the man in his ribs and legs, of the dozens of blows joining his own in a grim sort of harmony till he too was at his feet stomping on a now motionless figure.

When it stopped it was James's face that came into focus, standing between him and the body.

What am I doing?

"We got to get the fuck out of here bro. You probably need to go to the hospital"

What I need is a fucking drink.

"Bro, we have to get the fuck out of here. You probably have a concussion or internal bleeding, the fact you're fucking wasted was probably the only reason you're not dead right now"

Fuck that, and fuck him, let's get a drink.

"Damien! Look at me! He's fucking dead man, we fucking killed him, we need to get out of here now!"

What? No… he's just fucked up. We didn't--

"We fucking did man. We stomped on that motherfucker for like five minutes man. Trust me, he ain't getting back up, and we need to get the fuck out of here"

But the police--

"Chan and the rest will cover and say it was some gang shit or a robbery, they already took his wallet, we need to go"

Damien stumbled off with the four others, aware that he was on the verge of blackout drunk and most likely dying. As they turned the corner the girl made eye contact again with her fist in her mouth. He had gone from victim to monster in less time than a karaoke track.

When he woke in an unfamiliar room in oversized clothes, Damien's first instinct was that he had been drugged and kidnapped by a Cambodian prostitute. So when James and Tuso appeared with a coffee, his initial fear was replaced with a hazy kind of dread; that, and a shocking complement of pains throughout his body.

What the fuck happened?

"It's all good carnal" Tuso handed him a cup "We got back here and cleaned you up, plus we got rid of the clothes. James didn't want to let you sleep cause you might have a concussion, but we eventually decided you were just piss drunk and in shock"

Concussion? Fuck that hurts! as he stood his right leg bore testament to what was surely at least a hairline fracture.

"Yeah, and there was some blood in your piss last night so we figure you got a bruised kidney as well"

Fuck, I guess you should see the other guy.

The room held silence for a minute before Damien looked up and James handed him a paper.

I don't read Khmer.

"Just look at the photo."

Cambodia, like many third world countries, has any number of tabloid rags that tend to have executions, car accidents, and other assorted atrocities on their front pages to sell papers. This one had a man beaten to death outside a bar. Just like that, the previous evening flooded back.

Oh fucking hell. What does it say?

"Dunno really, we think it says a local store owner was taken out of his car, robbed and beaten to death by a gang of unruly youth"

Haven't been called unruly in a while.

"Don't worry, we're cool, we're not even sure it's the same thing, but just in case we gotta get the fuck out of dodge"

Great, I've got to get to the damn Vietnamese embassy today.

"Don't worry, communication is garbage in this part of the world. Just get your visa and get out"

What about you guys?

"First flight into Bangkok this afternoon."

Right.

"That guy nearly killed you man, he had it comin"

Right

Damien gave customary hugs and goodbyes shoving the fact that he had initiated and participated in a possible public murder. As he walked out into daylight and flagged down a moto-taxi he caught a glimpse of himself in a restaurant window looking fairly tragic but certainly not like he had been run over by a car and killed a man less than twelve hours before. In fact, with a baggy pair of Bermudas and a yellow t-shirt with a parrot on it, he supposed he looked very much like every other shithead tourist slumming or retiring round these parts.

And who's to say that's not exactly what I fucking am?

Δ   Δ   Δ   Δ

August 6

Saigon...

You feel like death warmed over, cum in a sock, hard and used – the softest bitch on the pole; chillin with Italians speaking mongrel tongues and talking trash while losing pool to punk ass kids at 50,000 dong a pop. Life is so fucking cheap. You should be in prison, the victim of vigilante justice, at the very least a bit fucking moved and torn apart with guilt and sorrow. Instead you are just tired, and you didn't even know his fucking name.

Vietnam, limestone islands, nutty Brits, 4 months down
Sunday, August 13, 2006

Current mood: 😊bouncy

So, I've been allowed into the country, $400 lighter ($200 on flight to and from Cambodia, $100 emergency passport, $50 entry and exit fees). I got into Saigon (now known as Ho Chi Min City) last week and was greeted by the expected chaos I've been warned of this whole trip.

So the deal: yes Vietnam is full of rip off artists. Yes the sellers here are maddeningly frustrating and relentless in their harassment. Yes, you can't even imagine how insane traffic and motorbike driving is. Think if Chinatown was the size of Manhattan, and it was always Sunday afternoon. Now make the road about one fourth as wide, and insert 4 times the number of motos as there are taxis. Got that? Well now remove all traffic lights. There is Saigon and Hanoi for ya. And yes it is more expensive and touristy than all the other countries I've been to on this trip. On the plus...

Vietnam is stunningly beautiful. After hanging with some very nice Italian guys I flew from Saigon to Hanoi, met a loony group of Brits and at 7am was convinced to run off to Halong bay, a series of limestone islands and caves off the coast (being drunk out of my mind, and my new pal Jane repeatedly referring to me as a sexy pirate probably clinched this last-minute decision). After battling a tour guide and bus driver I was finally allowed to join the group and spent the next 4 days on the coast.

So Halong bay was spent between the following activities: caving (nothing so perilous as Cambodia, more like Disneyland presents Vietnam caves, neon-lit trails and all); boating on various craft (including sleeping one night on a surprisingly nice boat with a dozen doubles on it); hiking (a truly challenging 4-hour mountain trek where I was sure some of the weaker members of our group would expire); swimming and kayaking (disgusting, despite being in a desolate area of islands, the litter was everywhere and I nearly stepped on a syringe the first time I headed toward water); and generally getting the piss taken out of me for being an American and mumbling when I spoke to Jane. Thanks kid, had fun, and you've got a pretty funny accent yourself tiger :)

Anyway, spent a night in Halong city listening to bad karaoke on a neon junk and eating more excellent seafood. Saw the Brits off as they headed to China and got a bus back to Hanoi. Once here found an anonymous hotel, did some weird TV interview on how foreigners feel about Vietnam, partied a bit (well a bit too much truth be told, had to get a moto for a 30 second walk cause I was unable to focus on a map) and watched a lot of cable in AC (think Cartoon Network and IFC). Vietnam is either blisteringly hot or raining furiously. It is currently the former.

I just bought an open bus ticket to Saigon. It stops in Hue, Hoi An, and Nah Trang, all of which I'll spend a night or two in before returning to the metropolis. I'm just about skint and since Chase has decided to change its debit cards from MasterCard to Visa (currently my new, functional, card is in LA), I've just got enough to hang for a week or so and fly out to Hong Kong before getting back to the states.

So that's the deal. I've done four months in Asia as of Wednesday and I'm pretty much done. I've made many friends, and fell not a bit in love a couple times, eaten frog, kangaroo, pigeon, water morning glory, banana leaves and most likely dog (though I keep telling myself it was wild boar), hiked mountains and waterfalls, trekked through ruins and jungle, lounged on beaches and rivers, dumped 4 motorbikes (only paid for 1 which was the first in Krabi and the only I didn't pay the extra bit to insure), taken one nasty cave fall (nothing compared to Rob who I was attempting to save), drank and smoked a bit too much, got in shape but haven't lost too much weight (on account of the drinking bit I imagine), and a whole lot more I'm just not recalling at the moment. It has been an adventure I suppose. It has also got me back to center (either that or I'm so frightfully nuts now I can't tell the difference).

Well, that's all the news that's fit to print. Send me some love. Peace from the east :)

August 17

Your room smells like piss and you've got less than 2 million dong left. "Redbull potentially kill you I suppose" says a Brit in Hoi An.

Suffer the little ones in a world of power-mad monkeys running beat up devices into an apocalyptic ground suffer the sex workers and infants born and bred now slavery a Disneyland Kill Bill superman commentary on western desire projected in neon and flesh to bad happy house suffer my children, suffer. It'll make it pass all that much faster and insignificantly to the pulse of our dying civilization.

Tired, motorbike bullshit and porn star Israeli (25 in a month, fuckin Christ.) Bitter orange juice tastes like you just brushed your damn teeth. Airline and airport nightmare ahead, terrorists in England the source of what will surely be a ridiculous headache in Saigon, Hong Kong, and LA.

Killing time before 12 hours south on what you pray will be a comfortable bus. That shit from Hanoi was unfucking tolerable. Smoking like a fool, gotta quit in LA. Lungs hurt. Leg hurts, fucking Christ...

Today is Friday, Saturday in Na Trang, Sunday night leave for Saigon. Monday go straight to Cathay Pacific and try to fly by Tuesday. Just remembered the crowbar thrown tomahawk style at the Irishman last night. Thank god it wasn't a knife or a gun.

Ivy is three months pregnant and Orlando is drinking and why do you need to know that? That means she was back with him and almost immediately got deliberately got knocked up only a month after you left. She should be a victim on her own fucking time. She shouldn't bring a child into it because she feels bad. Well that's your answer: you didn't need to know...

In two weeks you'll be back with Eilidh and back in New York. What have you learned? You've found your personality again, but what does that mean? Why are you so defined by your relationships when you are so relentlessly individualistic once on your own for a while. You must crave support on some level despite your dislike of reliance and being smothered. You guess that in lieu of family and a centrally-located support structure you put all your feelings of nurturing and being nurtured into the women you end up with, who invariably cannot bear the weight of it or expect more than you are willing to give.

Why does no one leave you alone when you're working? Do you look like you need another fucking pair of sunglasses? There's so many French in Vietnam.

This coffee is frighteningly strong even with a half a bottle of water diluted into it.

You haven't been up and running this early in eons. What the hell to do with yourself? *Wonder where Pornstar went.* The worst of first love scenarios engaged in debauchery's immorality. Memories of Alice and Rob calling you "tragic" in Vientiane, open shirt, wacked out eyes, wild hair and all – where to, not-so-young man?

Think India has got to be next, that or South America. Need something radical. Asia was a tease. Maybe Africa, that'd be some shit.

India? Why do you still think of Marie? Are you doomed to compare every relationship of your life to that doomed first? *They Might be Giants* plays and you think of trying to find your way back from Delaware with MOC and Ivy.

Christ that wasn't so long ago.

Done with Vietnam I tell you, Done!
Sunday, August 20, 2006

Current mood: 😖Hung-over

Just finished David Mitchell's "Cloud Atlas," dizzying, read that or "Ghostwritten" ASAP. Also "Unpacked" Lonely Planet writers' nightmare anthology, wanted to write a story to them almost simultaneous to finishing. I'll give you nightmare travel you expense account twats.

A Crash Course On the Anatomy of Robots

L'Etranger keeps bouncing in my head, for reasons too dark to share on this blog, let's just say I feel like Mersault more and more every day...

OK, so clearly unfocused today. Buckets, hopefully the last in Asia, are clearly to blame. Saw bar owner this morning who says "they tried to rob you last night yes?" Vague images of hoodlums and hookers trying to frisk me blur in my mind (ha! wrong guy buddies, no cash, no smokes, no nothing, just a room key and a flyer, fuck off!). In my addled mind I probably thought it funny for them to go to all the effort for a buy one, get two free coupon.

So Hue, Hoi An and Na Trang. Lovely I suppose. Bought a linen suit and three ties for $25 in Hoi An (tailored no less) and mostly have been barflying it for the last week. I'm atrocity and pagoda'd out. Anything with the word "cultural" attached sends me to the hills. Moreover I'm fucking sick of being hustled and harassed by Vietnamese con artists who appear every 5 seconds. Last night I finally advised one particular artist who had approached me like 3 times that very very bad things would happen if he ever spoke to me again (he waited all of 15 minutes to come up again).

Been chillin with Irish kids and Israelis, an odd combo indeed. Pornstar Johnny, Israeli madman, informed me the other night of how he's slept with 25 Thai women since he got here and videotaped some of it which he's emailed to friends in Tel Aviv. He also mentioned how one of them was 15 and he didn't realize it till he saw her student card next to her homework. He kept making clueless comments on how "they always hook up so easy, think they just want place to sleep." Wanted to end him where he sat but he was simply so fucking innocent and stupid in it that I could only sit exasperated with my head in my hands saying "What the fuck bro. Don't you realize it's like that because you're an affluent westerner by comparison, and it's morally reprehensible to be taking advantage of a class and gender and culture divide that's so clearly to your advantage?" He just stared at me as if I was speaking Swahili.

Later that night in Hoi An, him and me, a random Irish bloke, and an Australian decided to find bar on outskirts of town. The clown car of choice was a motorbike with the Ozy driving, me behind, and the Irish on edge, with my hand clapped to Johnny's on a pedal bike dragging parallel. When it was clear that we were in rice paddies and awfully lost, the tire on the motorbike made a sensible decision and blew out. Thinking it lucky it happened in front of an abandoned gas station we walked up and called out. The door opened and closed rapidly. When Irish turned to me and said "I don't get it Damien they just opened the door" a small Vietnamese man appeared, went on one knee and, Last of the Mohicans style, hurled a crowbar into Irish's back. He crumpled instantly, mouthing something along the lines of "JEEZUS WOT DA FOOK!" and upon seeing 3 more shocked white faces; the man instantly reverted to "sorry, sorry." After we managed to get Irish standing, said Mohican gave him a ride to town whilst Johnny and the Ozy and I woke up a villager who could fix the tire.

It was in this shit state, after a bowl of rice noodles and piss beer, that I got on a bus to Na Trang—a 10-hour nightmare I had been dreading for days. Tolerable enough in the end, the climax came with the most spectacular sunrise I have ever witnessed over limestone cliff and ocean as we pulled into town. Most of its beauty was lost to me, as being hung over and surrounded by Kodak-moment French has a way of doing.

So in Na Trang and leaving this afternoon to Saigon to sort ticket disaster. Oh yes that... Well after all my passport shit you would think I had learned to keep all my personals under lock and key with a guard-dog named Spike to watch over, but right after all my nonsense, and unnoticed till Hue, I managed to leave a folder somewhere (most likely the Asia Pacific flight to Hanoi) with my old passport, letters, and of course my return tickets to Hong Kong and the States. I am praying to God that Cathay Pacific will issue me new ones or that someone in Saigon has found the envelope, but we all know the likelihood of that particular pipe dream.

So I'm sitting in an Internet cafe now with an English couple I know from traveling North Vietnam, killing the 7 hours I have before heading to Saigon, and fate, and sure-to-be bureaucratic bedlam. Wishing you all well wherever you may be. Love and peace and all that shit.

PS. I'm in LA with any luck from mid-week till the first. Anyone in that foreboding land, drop me a line. If not I'm in Vietnamese prison.

August 21

Saigon again... The fact you didn't know his name nags at you on a daily basis now. The image of a golem keeps popping in your head. Makes sense, why not an out of control murdering Jewish robot that must be destroyed? You are made of mud and malice. Gotta keep moving, keep distracting, keep running from yourself.

Change focus. What to show Eilidh in New York? Baile Funk one night. Kienyo will be sure to make at least one comment on how you've gone halfway around the planet to find yet another white girl. East Vill and Brooklyn, the best of the easily accessible underground the city still has to offer unless you've totally lost touch. Stamford, see MOC and Ronnie, run past the graveyard and introduce the parents (*hmmm... maybe hold off on that one*). Burlington and Vergennes, do the wedding dance and hope she's not too horrified by Americans caned and dancing to the *Village People* - gotta reserve a room in Vergennes or Burlington - crap, eight nights and nine days. It's gonna disappear so fast.

Need another book for the plane...Baby, baby, you're lost again.

Goddamn lost track of days. It's Monday the 21st. Your father's anniversary (an unbelievable 12 years) passed without notice. You're in HCMC about to embark on your last quest for travel—reissuing tickets to LA ASAP. Dysentery kicking in, standby on its way, currency run out but booze is cheap.

You wouldn't have it any other way.

Out of the Valley (A Crash Course on Terminally Pat Open Endings)

"Out on the road today I saw a Deadhead sticker on a Cadillac. A little voice inside my head said, "Don't look back. You can never look back."

-Don Henley, **The Boys of Summer**

A Crash Course On the Anatomy of Robots

Back in LA and Beyond

August 30, 2006

Hilarious, you're in the same lounge you escaped armed customs guards about a month ago. Not so hilarious for one unfortunate storeowner I suppose. Thank God that you had some emergency cash for the exit visa here. Got 100 minutes until you start your 20-hour, two-stop trek to LA, Hong Kong first stop. Where the fuck is a teleporter when I need one? Last day and night in Saigon? Stopped two fist fights, both initiated by Johnny over pool, drank not enough to feel wasted but enough to feel it now, went on several mad motorbike runs and saw the latest Harry Potter. Looking at the first page of this notebook you wear a bitter grin.

LA here you come again.

In Hong Kong, in the most ridiculous stroke of luck you've been upgraded to business class and are currently drinking some sort of coconut cocktail while reading the *LA Times*. Karma's doing a pretty shit job of accounting these days. Thank God for small miracles.

August 31, 2006

You're jet lagged and smashing through rock and fucking roll style in LA.

Waiting on Alex's patio in the OC. Back in the land of the free baby. Meet Eilidh in two days in NYC and rock the fuck out.

Home baby. Home.

Friday, September 15, 2006
Back in the USSA...

Current mood: ☺busy

Writing from my friend Adena's crib in Brooklyn. Here's where I'm at...

I got in on the 30th. My two weeks of hell standby in Saigon finally ended and I got on an uneventful flight to Hong Kong (which from the air looks insane, kinda like dozens of mini-Manhattans with aerial highways and water everywhere, very *Blade Runner*-esque). In the airport my name was called to which my immediate reaction was simple (of course they've overbooked now I'm trapped in China). To my shock and surprise I was bumped up to first class. My chair folded out to a full bed, I had pay-per-view, cable, and braised lamb with red wine for dinner, and downed maybe a dozen champagnes and screwdrivers before dozing off and waking up above LA.

A little on time travel...

Since Southeast Asia is a 15-hour time difference from LA, I actually arrived in LA 2 hours before I left Hong Kong. This of course completely fucked up my internal (or lack thereof) clock and I am still recovering.

LA was far too brief and typically bizarre. I went from the airport to a b-boy competition and a subsequent after-party full of dancers (more than a little intimidating when I was dragged to the floor). I went straight into barman mode to chill out, only occasionally breaking to dance and play guitar. A very nice group of kids proceeded to inform me they were porn stars, which I thought was a joke then realized I was in LA. Go figure.

I discovered my phone number has been sold to some company in Connecticut. If you wanna call and harass them please feel free.

I spent the next day chillin with Alex out in the OC. It was far too short. I miss you bro, get back to Mexico soon.

A Crash Course On the Anatomy of Robots

I didn't get to record, though my last hours I got to watch Nuno Bettencourt work on a Perry Farrell track, helpless to interact in any way and dealing with conversion problems on my laptop the whole time.

I then got on another plane, and arrived in Newark. I got in an argument with the car rental lady and ended up stuck with a super-grandma-mobile (Dodge Caravan, no baby seats). The blame was placed on Labor Day.

2 hours later Eilidh got in from Edinburgh (minus luggage) and we headed to Kienyo's dungeon studio. About 10 minutes in (Sujihno struggling to clean up), we got a merciful call from Adena saying we could crash. I'll be here till the 26th btw, North Williamsburg if you wanna get up.

Barely in, Eilidh and I started a 4-day whirlwind tour of my New York friends. The fact that a friend who I haven't seen in 8 years is subletting the other room in the apartment left nowhere to hide from partying and catching up.

Wednesday was Stamford with the crew at Tigins. Thursday through Sunday was an awesome wedding in Vermont. That warrants its own blog entry and was beautiful drunken chaos (trying to explain to Eilidh how all my CT, VT and PA crew were interconnected made everyone seem overly incestuous but hell, Stamford was representing. I even got a friend's girlfriend to take a chunk out of my neck and try to shove her tongue down my throat while Eilidh was on my arm. I said something helpless about Americans and drinking). Alcohol-poisoned and burned out we rolled back to the city.

Eilidh left Monday night. It seems we are developing a habit of collecting sad goodbyes in foreign countries. Maybe Scotland in November baby...

So anyhow, now I'm chain-smoking while watching TNT and attempting to finish my new book. I have broken down, and yes, a character in the third section will be spending quite a bit of time in Southeast Asia. At this exact moment I am recovering from a night at Kush where Kienyo was spinnin. I have 0 dollars in my pocket and an unused drink ticket. Fuck.

I'm on MSN messenger, and Yahoo messenger. That's about as fast as I can communicate otherwise shoot me an email. I'll be back in GTO on the 26th. This Cervantino is gonna be a blast, though Belle and Sebastian just cancelled so sorry to the Indy heads. Maybe catch you here or there.

Δ   Δ   Δ   Δ

Loose Ends

September-November, 2006

Damien, after a truly daredevil escape from Brooklyn, fled once more to the Northern Central Highlands of Mexico. There he found himself once more immersed in the exuberant overflow of culture, tastes and sounds that is Latin America. Upon arrival he found that Ivy had attempted to poison his (not quite) good name but summarily failed in these endeavors to all but the most foolish and gullible ears. Five months pregnant with her still-drinking and possible ex-drug addict boyfriend, he still wished her the best though he resolutely believed she had become the first of his significant others that he could give a shit about ever seeing again.

The culture shock that he had avoided in the states, in no small part from being with Eilidh and running into his travel buddy Van Gogh, came down quite unexpectedly when he reached his new home down south. Little had changed since he had left all those months ago to wrap up things in New York and do the masochistic drive to La La land. There were new people, students and travelers of course, and the flow of backpacks and books left him much feeling that the world was a terribly small place, half expecting Ian or Kienyo to pop around the corner. Certainly if Jez had appeared it would have been no surprise. On that particular note, travel through Asia had indeed brought about a reset in perspective and in his most recent times in the city he had been able to enjoy both Jez and J's company with little inner turmoil or angst. They were now deep into their own interpersonal dramas and he wished them both well in whatever highs and lows they might be led to.

As for Marie there was another brunch, one even more cordial and surface than the one nearly a year ago. Her odd desire to open a bed and breakfast in his small town was never mentioned other than to acknowledge that those plans had become defunct. He liked to imagine that she wanted to start some torrid affair behind her faceless new hubby's back that would inevitably end with her realizing what a fool she was to lose him, and his replying, after pause, some majestic line about how he wished things could be different but it was all too late. He pictured himself quite like Hans Solo in this particular delusion.

As for his parents, they still haunted Damien, and he imagined they would continue to for the remainder of his days. The words "cancer" and "AIDS," "gay" and "estate" had forever moved into the darker realms of lexicon for him, but he had begun to forgive, and as with all things, regrettably or mercifully, he'd begun to forget.

As for Robots and social vacuum, the road if nothing else reminded him that he was a fairly social animal (with the aid of libations anyhow), and that the distance he had felt from the rest of the human race in that time, was, well, fairly human. There were far more people living in that valley if he should ever feel like going there again. In his way he ran down it and back out again – triumphant bullshit poster at the top of the mountain and all (insert your own Hallmark wisdoms here). One particular Khmer might be inclined to be skeptical if he were still breathing, and Damien might be more than bit inclined to agree. James has plans to visit him in Mexico (*what a reunion that'll be*).

Kienyo is still fighting the good fight with the aid of bad Brazilian retro. Van Gogh is studying massage and chasing Israelis. Ian is somewhere in the UK saving for his wedding where Damien will surely get drunk and cause Georgia to say "It's not that I don't like you Damien. It's just the effect you have on Ian…" Rob is in the Philippines still cursing his ribs and loading up on "blueys." The rest are all as healthy and sound as their respective personalities will allow them to be.

Which of course leaves the two big fat questions…

After a month in Mexico, which seemed like a constant going away and welcome back party—in no small part aided by a major arts festival and owning a bar (one that incidentally still looked like a bomb shelter)--Damien began to do a bit of thinking, which as you may have discovered by now he does far too much of. It seemed to him that the last three years had afforded him a bit of a second chance at the cost of some hard life lessons smattered with some good old-fashioned immature recklessness. He had gone through nearly a dozen countries on three continents, sold a house and gained and lost an apartment, nearly died from a drinking binge and intestinal fallout, dealt with (poorly) his parents' lives and passing, and quite effectively saw the end to two (if not three) relationships. Throw in a little manslaughter and a dash of homicide and he we are.

A wise man might say it was time to take a rest, but as we have seen, Damien is not all that wise. Therefore at October's end, before everybody in Mexico celebrates the dead and what they had meant, Damien decided to take a chance and celebrate his own dead by moving on and leaping into the fray.

You can of course guess where this is going. Currently it is November and Damien sits in a flat in Scotland drinking Earl Grey and pretending he is British. He smokes outside the townhouse, which is only a mild annoyance as he said he would quit in Asia (and failed, but at $0.25 a pack who can really blame him)? He finds it awful, cold and rainy in this place and gripes that the clichés for once have held true. It's dear, but when you come from New York, nothing really seems expensive again, just fodder for complaining about the high cost of living. He's got to get back to Mexico to renew his visas before the New Year, but this is just scheduling – though we know how that can go. He thinks he like it here.

Eilidh is at work and will be coming home soon. She's at class or work most of the week but it balances with his whole loner self-image (a clear defense mechanism born of loneliness). They've been waking up before dawn every day and he's been trying to shake jetlag. Sometimes it feels as if he's never stopped traveling, and maybe that's true.

They're in love (though he's promised to only say it every 2 days as to not highlight his American propensity to express so much). They share looks, embraces, and mostly healthy meals (though he does manage to sneak the occasional Scottish breakfast). In a country that invented Scotch he has managed to get embarrassingly blasted just once so far, and she seems to like having him around. The feeling is mutual. But who knows, the future is uncertain. But then again what isn't?

If you step far enough back, it eventually makes sense.

Δ   Δ   Δ   Δ

There is a church...

November, 2006

Across from my apartment off Leith walk in Edinburgh. The lights in the back flicker with what seems to be purpose (my Cub Scout days are long gone with any hope of understanding Morse). As I smoke my morning fag (60 cents a piece by my reckoning), I imagine a small child or church worker tied up by a lunatic priest attempting to reach out in the hopes someone will come to their rescue. I've read too much Stephen King and imagine myself calling out and ending up with a cruciform jammed into the back of my head by some mad clergyman with a receding hairline, black catholic get-up, and a serious baring of teeth. I guess I'll just wait to see if anything appears in the *Scotsman* tomorrow.

A Crash Course On the Anatomy of Robots

I went to Bangkok last week for Ian and Georgia's wedding and found that all the poets are still dead, and try as I might, I still feel a bit like a robot with human parts when around certain twats. Maybe it's the other way around.

I heard a rumor that Cambodian authorities now suspect several foreigners were involved in a fatal beating in Phnom Pen in the beginning of August. James strongly advised me never to go back as several mobs of less-than-savory characters have been looking for a foreign Asian backpacker and couple of ex-military types. The man's name was Chankrisna Vichea. I'm going to remember that.

The Ataris' emo version of *Boys of Summer* blares on my laptop through iTunes. I've opened up a playlist called Teenage Wasteland, which includes this track, *Teenage Dirtbag* by Wheatus, Dramarama's *Anything, Anything*, and more than a healthy sampling of Quicksand and Rancid. It brings me back to when I first met Marie, before my father had died, before my first book was lost to drugs, before I knew much outside the city, before I embarked on this silly mission of immortality through publishing glorified journal entries and turning temper tantrums into performance art.

I like to think I've grown, but I still know all the words.

Epilogue

Boldly Going…

January 2007

Damien is in New Jersey – again

Somehow I seem condemned to end up in this state.

They've cut the direct from Edinburgh to Atlanta, hence this pit stop at Newark International airport, which as terminals go, isn't really that bad. Next stop Houston (dubiously dubbed "George Bush International" – gilded statue with airborne midair jacket and all) then finally Guanajuato, 20 hours give or take since Damien left Eilidh's flat off Leith Walk. Just now he's managed to buy season one of *Heroes*, a legal pad and pen, and the autobiography of Michael Knight himself, shockingly with him on the cover wearing a "Don't Hassle the Hoff" shirt. Absentmindedly he wonders if it was released pre- or post- his infamous remarks in Germany and his subsequent suing the press into publicly recanting that he was caned out of his mind (apparently he was experiencing the debilitating effects of "cold medicine").

Perhaps now would be an appropriate time to mention just how much Damien despises airports, airline food, and for that matter flying in general. It's not so much the typical mass transit inefficiency, fear of heights and closed spaces grip-on-mortality thing *(though I do fret over these and the delusion of losing my unpublished Great American Novel in the drink without hope of posthumous debut).* Rather it is the overwhelming sense of loss. Damien is losing, in fact of his own free will departing with, untold dollars and hours toward an experience easily rivaled by a teenage stoner session *Twilight Zone/South Park* marathon, save for the fact the latter results in some enjoyment.

His friends and strangers mysteriously envy his globetrotting. Mysterious in that his destinations never seem particularly appealing to them – too hot, too cold, too dangerous, too not American small town – that he must simply assume they envy the mere act of going from one end of the world to the other. It is both with their interest and humanity's in mind that he feels that someone must invent a functional teleportation device.

You heard me right.

The device so commonly referenced in fiction and film is long overdue. From Stephen King to *Galaxy Quest*, *The Fly* and its Kronenberg re-envisioning (well that didn't work out so well actually), and immortalized by an American playing a Scotsman on a cheesy 60's sci-fi show (Damien happens to love *Star Trek*, but its brilliance lies in its undeniably endearing corniness) – he is sick of a world without one.

It is mind boggling in the same way as the space program and cancer - that one can transmit gigabytes of information (libraries' worth of text and images mind you) through the air via invisible signals within seconds, drive cars fueled by garbage and cooking oil, and watch Forrest Gump have new interactions with long dead people – yet no one has developed teleportation. One comic decrying the current state of technology with iPods yet no jetpacks comes to mind ("What happened to that future?")

Damien imagines at his most cynical that it is the same reason we haven't colonized Mars, don't all drive electric solar cars, and you can survive with AIDS without the slightest inconvenience should you happen to have a bank account on par with Magic Johnson:

Laziness

We are often quoted as a brutal species whose principal strength and evil lies in cruelty, self-preservation, and greed – and though this is all true, Damien believes it manifests itself as a result of an unbelievable species-wide laziness. We haven't taken on space because we haven't fucked up the planet enough to make it imperative. Fossil fuels (however fucked up in their contributions to the environment, war, and generally inefficiency) fuel *(sorry)* far too many economies, societies, fat white guys smoking cigars, and dudes in turbans who go fishing with George Bush and bathe in crystal, to possibly change till we've dried the fucker up. As for AIDS, like everything else, if the rich can buy their way out of it (and make some bucks while they're at it) well – fuck the poor.

All of which is to say that Damien's not holding his breath on teleporting out of this airport lounge (a sports-themed one playing Martha Stewart no less) anytime soon. Richard Branson will have commercial space flight for the ultra-rich long before Bush's moon base collapses in on itself, SUV's only get more popular as oil prices have monks in Burma being tear-gassed, and Africa will be a barren wasteland as Magic publishes his fourth inspirational autobiography.

Please Scotty, please – beam me up.

Δ   Δ   Δ   Δ

As Damien would imagine it…(A Damien Wood Novel)

Damien has started again on the new novel and has no idea where it is going, but for the moment it is in fact going. He hasn't thought of a name for the protagonist yet so for the moment it's just Damien. It starts in Mexico, sort of like this…

the joy of cooking

Olive oil and parmesan on cheap Mexican spaghetti was all Damien could stomach that morning – morning if one defined such times of day by when one roused rather than the restrictions of the sun and clock. Listening to Bob Dylan's less lyrical though infinitely more sonorous son, he began to piece together the events of the previous nights. There had been the prostitute who threatened to tear his eyes out in the cantina. The Norwegian had saved him - that much he did remember. Why she had wanted to maim him in the first place was still a bit foggy, though he suspected he had been sleeping on the table, and being aroused from drunken slumber was often a precursor to violence. He felt pretty good considering, and this fact in itself was thoroughly depressing.

It had been three months now since he had fled to the quiet little fishing village far south of the border and American authorities.

A little less than a hundred days of sun, sea, and far too much fucking mescal had softly made its way into a lithe existence of escapism and immediacy. When every day could be your last you tended to try enjoy it while simultaneously attempting to forget it. He thought of Marie back in New York less and less, but still daily. The way she walked, spoke, touched, fucked, laughed, cried, and all the rest of the shit kept his mind full of doubt. This was especially true on the slow beginnings of the day when the mind would go on autopilot and flit and flounder where it pleased. Those were just a few of the things he thought, mostly in contrast to the viking girl who had saved him from the hooker last night, and the smell of mildew and rot emanating from the bathroom/bedroom around the corner where she now slept.

He hadn't noticed when she walked up and placed her hand on his shoulder. She gave a strong squeeze that spoke of assurance and maybe a little affection but mostly just announced its presence.

"*Ya luke betta,*" her voice was rough, almost a growl, and the morning and lacking command of English did no good to soften the edges. He wondered if she had sounded like that when they met two nights ago. The past three days had been full of uncertainties and half-dreams. Her very presence now confirmed some of those as truth, if this indeed was not yet another delusion.

"*Thanks, it's all subterfuge, would you like some?*" he smiled and lifted the plate of partially eaten pasta. She gave him a look that at first conveyed confusion (what possessed him to use *subterfuge* anyhow), followed by disgust, then reassertion of facial expression control into a polite refusal manifest in a semi-smile and light shaking of the head. Sometimes it is only in the smallest moments that we can truly understand one another, and ourselves for that matter. They come like a rush, a touch, a kiss, or a look, and pass like shudders briefly, insubstantially, and intimately known. At that moment, as she looked very much like a little blond girl offered candy rather than the fierce woman carefully watching him, he realized in that short, furious time, why he had picked her up, why she had let him, and what they meant to each other.

On the one dirt road in town wild dogs run amuck while young girls point giggle and wave. He puts on his most sincere little kid smile and returns the gesture. How long till they are someone's baby, or hurt someone else's baby? How long till they are waiting for someone long gone on the run, or letting strange drunken men pick them up and offer them poorly seasoned spaghetti in the morning?

Upon arriving at the tienda that crossed the Puerto Angel road, Damien spotted two things, or rather one and the absence of another. The Federali pick-up sat unoccupied in the midday sun, idling with the driver side door open, shotgun still locked in the dash. With a quick scan he surmised its occupants were inside the store (maybe they just want a beer), and upon closer inspection spotted three of them in full get-up: AR-15's, jumpsuits, ammo belts — true fucking cowboys. There was one truth with law enforcement in Mexico, and that was that you simply did not fuck with it. Run, hide, bribe — whatever, just don't cross it. Especially in areas like this — 50 miles from the most liberal definition of civilization — federal law enforcement was a trouble at best, and much more likely someone's personal hell realized. Damien made a slow retreat as to not appear freaked if spotted. In a town of less than a hundred permanent residents, it would not take them long to find the one Asian gringo who had been lolling about. As the shop grew distant and out of sight and no roar of tires or shouts followed, he began to run. The little girls laughed and waved as he passed as if it was some new exciting game. Despite the absurdity of it he waved back and beat a path into the jungle and his cabana.

"Ju need ta leeve? Vy, are ju in trouvel?" in the closest approximation of softness he'd yet seen, she expressed concern he could not address, and demanded explanations he did not have time for.

"Just trust me babe I need to get the hell out of here yesterday. If the lady at the tienda hasn't given me up yet the cats at the cantina surely will, and I don't have the money to bribe my way out of this. Extradition to the states then Cambodia is the last thing I need" he forced the last of his belongings into the sack pushed it down and cinctured the opening.

He abandoned his art, music, and some random toiletries. In a far recess of his mind came an image of a local fisherman wearing Brut cologne and listening to "Blood on the Tracks" with Munch's Madonna hanging on the sunny side of his thatched hut. It was strangely assuring.

It wasn't Ivy, the Norwegian, or the tienda owner for that matter. As Damien looked out the back of the camionetta and the village disappeared in the distance, the best he could figure it was the prostitute. She probably was all hot and bothered after the other night and sent news of the troublesome gringo to the nearest authorities. This inevitably connected with some mistaken pre-historic wanted ads from some half-ass border patrol description from six months ago and finally manifest in a Federali patrol going to check it out. God bless communication.

He wouldn't miss the town; there were a million like it all along this coast (though he might have to move inland a bit just to be safe). He certainly could do without that fucking cantina and its turncoat whore. But the girl – well the girl he did regret a bit. She was quite beautiful in an odd utilitarian way, if such a description can be used, and it's not every day you find companions willing to argue on your behalf of your drunken, most-definitely-in-the-wrong self. It was also refreshing having a communication that could be so continuously – well, interesting.

Just then a sensation struck Damien that in its own way was the perfect answer and summation. It was not fear, or regret, or nostalgia, or love lost or anything so poetic. It was only something much more primitive and simple and mundane than that. Hunger, plain hunger punched his gut. He had never finished his pasta that morning but had instead given it to her, who looked upon it like a dead rat and refused anyway.

Somehow this made perfect sense and he turned about to the open winding landscape to the west. He then watched the sunset and, in a beat up pickup full of farmers bouncing like hell to and fro on the road to oblivion, rode off into it.

Special Features: Deleted Scenes, Alternate Ending, Credits, Propaganda on the Author (Just Pretend it's a DVD Made out of Paper)

Examples of Confessionary Literature

Dorothy Allison - Bastard out of Carolina

Jonathan Ames -What's Not to Love?: The Adventures of a Mildly Perverted Young Writer

Jim Carroll – The Basketball Diaries

Dave Eggers – A Heartbreaking Work of Staggering Genius

Kent Evans – Malas Ondas: Lime, Sand, Sex, and Salsa in the Land of Conquistadors

James Frey - A Million Little Pieces

Nick Hornby – High Fidelity

Zoe Margolis - Girl with a One Track Mind

Henry Rollins - Solipsist

David Sedaris – Me Talk Pretty One Day

Hunter S. Thompson – The Rum Diaries

Elizabeth Wurtzel – Prozac Nation

I told Alex I was scared

Those were the exact words

"Alex, I'm scared."

It must have been six — seven
in the morning
on a lazy Guanajuato night
turned dawn.

I remember
after some
particularly heroic
benders
(the kind that take
a good part of a week
multiple partners and successive blackouts)
that vomiting could produce
a little
(just a little)
the lining having worn thin
from cocaine,
puking,
excess.

A Crash Course On the Anatomy of Robots

There it would be
a little red line,
a tiny mucus membrane
amongst bile and liquor.

But now

as my friend slowly woke

it came bubbling out.
unaided mouthfuls
of crimson
and just a little
saliva
(too little saliva.)

Like the loser
in countless Kung-fu flicks
before his last shot,
or that kid slinging
crack in Clockers
constantly drinking Yoo-hoo
to quell the inner-city fires
that burn in his fictionally
realized mind.

But I'm no Sonny Chiba

A Crash Course On the Anatomy of Robots

or fictional urban dealer
and this is no film
this is life.

This is a studio overlooking
the valley at 6 or 7am
with my confused friend
mirroring what must be panic on my face.

He had given me some
sort of stomach-coating laxative
and a squeeze on the shoulder
before I lay down
and hoped for the best

Like the time I thought
that I would die on mescaline
and simply accepted it.

But how can you really
accept a thing like that?

The last time I saw
someone spit blood
it was not my face
I saw in the mirror
but my mother's.

A Crash Course On the Anatomy of Robots

The day my first book was published
Five after she found out she had cancer
One before surgery —
unsuccessful.

It was just a little

just a little bubbling out
with so little saliva.

"Damien, I'm scared," she said.

Those were the exact words.

Later there was so much blood,
so much black, blood and bile
And it came not just from her lips

but nose
and wounds
and stitches
and tubes.

I had never seen
something so small
bleed so much.

A Crash Course On the Anatomy of Robots

By then she was too far-gone
to really be scared —
only desperate

And her words
"There's something wrong,"
spoken to no one
in particular.

They did not see me.
They did not ask me.
They were a statement
to a world no longer in reach,
no longer seen or able
to return to.

So that night I slept
and hoped
and dried out.
And sometimes when I'm alone
in the darkness
listening to scorpions and thinking
of lovers far or long gone,
those words sit
and they echo.

"There's something wrong."
There's something wrong
and I am scared

Battambang with Eilidh

On a bamboo train amongst rice paddies
And smiling children who scream "hello!"
I felt the heat of my motorbike
Against my back
And the curve of your hip
In my side.

As the sun set I thought silly things
And remembered last night
And that sometimes bourbon
Makes me more
American
Than usual

That is to say
I don't know when to let
Emotions stay silent
Or practical
Or acknowledge the specifics
Of time's passing
Which is all to say

A Crash Course On the Anatomy of Robots

That I regret not,
Saying I loved you
Even as I knew
The response
Would be measured
And sane
And solid
And all those things
Which escape me
Sometimes

On the road
The life
The existence
I live in
That so many drop
In to visit
As the children who wave
As we ride on by

The taste of quinine and mint
And salt soaked sop soap
Mingled with cigarettes and the brief
Touch of your lips

Have you ever noticed
Everyone's unique

A Crash Course On the Anatomy of Robots

Taste and odor?
Like equilibrium only felt
In its absence

Your small quick tongue
Feline curves which dance
Cross musculature
Skin
And wistful eyes
Disinterested as you have left
To the next place and time
Yet furiously intent in cataloguing
The present
Your fingers coy
Brushing glances
Light holds
Your voice commanding
Beyond your frame

Baby I'm lost in Cambodia
Dodging landmines and street urchins
Crushin cycles and chewin time
But baby without you
Baby it just ain't the same

All in all said
I will miss you too.

the beginning of the end of pre millennium blues

sitting in butterfly pad Clinton hill
mind creepin like virtual flashback usherin in the new year

pre millennium apocalyptic hiatus
the taste of a girl fresh on my mind
the chemical imbalance
rewind
of ecstasy overload rippin temporal havoc
on my senses in this consensus
of mass apathy

in this city of itty bitty spiders
rhymin and climbin to the top of the world
found twirled and unfurled on the finger of god
or me
or a dog with a bone

alone in the nexus of transformers abraxis
or death before taxes
or thoughts which have racked this mind
all too long

sing me a song dear
sing me a song

A Crash Course On the Anatomy of Robots

about love and redemption
and cancer driven irony.

move it along

like hate and exception
and rancor bitten bigotry.

cause sex is an extension of love
but you still like to fuck
and you can worship conventions above
and still think it sucks.
when a man asks for change
in model filled soho
and your heart says rearrange
but you mouth says "no bro"
keep it on with the flow on the go
to the end of humanity in the sanity
of a killing jar.
or madness from afar we call society
treasurin sobriety over statistical calamity
but still buryin the city like so many grains
of capitalistic dust.

rust in pieces electro jesus.
your cathode eyes

A Crash Course On the Anatomy of Robots

and spoon fed lies
have rotted my brain
with pepsi spice girl
g.i. joe fatalism.

we deserve what we get.

we deserve what we get when it comes if it comes
in this static age of self sabotage
this frantic stage of utopian mirage
this moment of time
just for you
just for you

just for you.

cause six hours
interlocked in the corner of a loft with burning eyes under an exit sign in
Brooklyn.
your jaw rolling like heroin hiccups
a forcing tongue tasting like camel lights
I swallowed my gum for you
I swallowed.

A strange moment when I brushed her arm
like a revealing recoiling viper

A Crash Course On the Anatomy of Robots

"Happy New Year!!!"
screams champagne in my eyes
as the damaged one kisses me and I know
I'll live to regret it as
the vultures circle and chemicals take effect.

clarity
my kingdom for clarity
and chickenless scenes.

cocaine the bunny cries
and holds me in desperation
as her friend pleads
about fuckin my brains out

an oxymoron I think
my mind is already absent.

every year an excuse toward Sodom.
again I am your victim
I have no more drugs
I have no more love
yet you still come with buckets
to draw mud
and evaporate
the last drops of my well.

A Crash Course On the Anatomy of Robots

somewhere in Seattle with Osh-Gosh suspenders
greyhound one way, one week warning
(I hope the stars in your eyes have not died yet)
I'm not nice.
stop tellin me before I believe it.

almost back to center
you said the new year would renew you
burning ginger ale
Snapple Newport olfactory feast.
too many thoughts
improper timing.
(it's never right.)

a cat plays with my pen and won't let me write
it circles my bed and leaps on my back
craving attention.

I didn't say love,
I said attention.

And as it digs in its claws
it purrs in delight
cause this is your fun
this is your fun.

never malicious or angry or planned

A Crash Course On the Anatomy of Robots

the game is the game to keep me from writing
and you'll sit on my pad if the scratches don't work
till I finally pet you and then you'll run away.
and it's funny I think,

not ironic little one
I said it was funny.

water sign warning, we are funny
I don't believe in the stars
but I know I am cancer.
once you asked what I meant and never understood
till they told you it spread and couldn't be stopped.
though it burned bad I knew it would come
and still said I loved you
as radiation reigned.

so springtime come save me
from nosebleed burn heaven
seven long seconds till I lose my cool
what can I say that won't be
selfish, opportunistic or cruel?

rule with me
this universe
till the end
of the world.

Back in Phnom Penh

I imagine you are in Bangkok
On your way to the airport
To London and beyond
Still a bit sleepy
From last night's rumble and fumble
Opium laced cigarettes
And talking about not putting those emotions
Into so many words

Motion
It actually slows the impact of things

Lying alone in the guesthouse
No longer near the embassy
I feel your absence as acutely

I see you sitting
Thinking of flying
While all I can think of
Is lying next to you

My email said "love deeply"
While yours said "take care"
And in counterpart they spoke

A Crash Course On the Anatomy of Robots

Of our separate mechanisms

If I had not been detained
In Ho Chi Min's customs
Sent back on my ass
And escorted by security
I'm sure I could have snuck
Something longer than those words
Something deeper
More significant
The sentiment the same

We are rare birds of prey
Vampire cats
And gecko pixies
So strange to have found
And danced
And found closeness
And the casual intensity
Of brief lifetime loves

A Conversation on Spirit (Alternate Ending)

Battery acid rained and burned eyes like Brooklyn in September. The poet watched the lady shake off the season and pull into a booth while her younger friend approached the bar. She ordered two Bombay and Tonics in broken Spanish. He pulled the gin out the cabinet and ice out of the antique cooler by hand before measuring with a hand-blown shot glass and cutting a lime. The older lady winced when he returned the mixing spoon to a cloudy glass on the wooden bar top. He smiled while his hair hid his expression and thought *Americans on tour, gotta love em.*

Algo mas?

"Ummmm…. Pear don, no comprendo?"

Sorry, will that be all?

The older lady gasped and said "You speak English, oh thank God; we've been struggling all day"

Where you two from?

"New York, we're on a little celebratory vacation."

No kidding, I'm from Brooklyn.

"Really? So how did you end up here?"

Long story, here and handed them a copy of Estranjero.

"You're an author?"

Please don't call me names.

The younger one giggled, while the older pored over the back cover and flipped through briskly.

"Who's your press?"

A small one in Canada, thankfully. I can't stand that damn book and it's been far more successful than I wanted.

"Why would success be a problem and why do you hate it?"

That's two questions, and to answer both, it really doesn't reflect me as an artist.

There was a long pause.

"So how come I've never heard of you?"

How come I've never heard of you?

"You've read *The DaVinci Code*?"

Yes

"Then you've heard of me."

I thought Dan Brown was a man.

"Well he is, but I represent him."

So you're an agent.

"Well a bit more than that but yes."

Well by that logic you know me.

"How's that?"

You're drinking a gin and tonic?

"Yes."

Well I bought the ingredients and now I've sold it to you.

"Well that's not quite the same."

Isn't it then?

His manager and barmaid looked up from the bar where they were currently taking a liquid lunch. She gave an *oh not another one of these* looks whilst he attempted to suppress one of his patented guffaws.

OK then, Miss, correct me if I'm wrong, but you get many solicitations daily?

"Well I get many queries yes."

And you have an assistant or team who reads them or maybe even you yourself decide whether the pitch is something marketable.

"Well, of course, and there's no way to read all the queries and...."

In any case you try some of those out asking for samples?

"Yes"

And based on how they fit your, let's call it palette, you decide whether to take on the whole work, yes.

"Yes, if the first 30 pages catches my attention."

who can sell a whole lot more and take a tidy chunk for your troubles, then you agree to represent the writer.

"Well that's an oversimplification, but yes."

Well, I'm in the exact same business. I own this place. All the alcohols you see behind me are the ones that I've picked. I mix and sell spirits to clients such as you lovely ladies then make a profit. But I would hardly say I'm brewing and distilling the stuff yet. And in any case I only sell stuff that I myself would drink.

"Well, that sounds like your limiting your profits."

Perhaps, but it is very important to me you see, that I be able to drink and enjoy anything I have chosen to sell. I go to the market and see what's out there. You look at queries, I look at labels, one catches the eye and you try it, if it goes down well I buy the whole bottle and then try to sell it in my bar. The thing is, sometimes I can only appreciate a good bottle after a couple tries. Also, I find labels notoriously misleading. There are some beautiful labels on shit bottles, and crappy labels often show not a lack of quality in the spirit, but in the distillers' ability to properly market. I have an inherent distrust of flashy bottles, and a personal love of those that look a bit rough on the edges.

"Well surely your customers prefer recognizable brands in nice bottles."

Not always, though that would certainly be true of certain people. I'm ashamed to say many of our countrymen who know no better since they haven't been exposed to anything else, or worse, their exposure has been to bad bath tub brews and shitty tequilas.

"But surely you want to make money and stock what people buy?"

Well to be truthful, if they want to drink swill and piss they can just go across the street to Manuel's joint, it'll make both of us happier. Still, as you point out, I do want to make money and please people.

Hey, he called to his barmaid, *Camila, what you drinkin?*

"A White Russian"

Why?

"I like how nice they are"

Alex, he called to his manager, *what are you drinking?*

"Dos Equis Lager"

Why?

"To get fucked up."

Very eloquently put. Now my barmaid and manager have just begun to illustrate a point for me.

"You allow your staff to drink?"

Of course, it would be somewhat stupid to have people who didn't drink buying and selling booze for me wouldn't it?

"But they might get drunk on the job."

A risk of course, but so many people do hate their jobs, and I feel that in the end it is the public that suffers their bitterness and displeasure so why encourage it by having non-drinkers working for you? Anyway, the point is that Camila drinks White Russians cause they're sweet and creamy and undeniable strong. Kahlua is Mexico's only indigenous liquor did you know that?

"What about Tequila?"

That's a spirit as is Mezcal but we'll get to that.

"OK."

So here we have a lovely unique little cocktail of Kahlua, Vodka and cream over ice. It's a bit too heavy for some, and certainly too sweet for most, but Camila likes it and I'm happy to serve it. Alex on the other hand likes the uncomplicated taste of a good solid lager. Let's do this rough; if Camila is nursing some Zadie Smith then Alex is kicking back to some Bukowski.

"That is rough."

Sorry bad hangover.

"Goes with the territory I suppose."

Anyway, I happen to like both drinks depending on the occasion. You meanwhile are drinking a gin and tonic. I myself find both gin and tonic water disagreeable, whatever juniper berries are I never want to run into them, and on principle I do not drink things which once were considered medicinal such as tonic.

"How is tonic medicinal?"

Well I won't bore you with the details, and the name is obvious enough, but back when Malaria was a real problem for the imperialists and the great empire couldn't get anyone to take their meds they made a simple realization. Although their members abroad would often forgo their meds and succumb to illness, they quite rarely would forgo the afternoon or evening nip. Since gin and soda with lime cordial were all the rage at the time the government decided that by simply creating a concoction of soda, sugar, and quinine, the most basic of all anti-malarials, that they could make the colonials drink their meds without even knowing it. Hence tonic water, which to this day has that distinctly other flavor you only need to read the back label to discover as quinine.

"Fascinating."

More disturbing probably, and possibly a myth, but who knows. Anyhow, I have on rare occasions, trapped in an airport or some tropical beach, imbibed the stuff, and though I can never call the experience so much as satisfying, it did do the job. Your Mr. Brown on the other hand is a bit of a different story. He's more of a rum. Now while I must concede that there are indeed some fine rums out there, they are more often than not mixed in cocktails which disguise their taste. You could say that people who dislike drinking in general tend to order such cocktails. Malibu and Pineapple, Pina Coladas, those would be fine examples. To me Malibu and Pineapple tastes like cheap perfume smells, and a Pina Colada should never be drank anywhere less than 80 degrees outside, where a stiff whiskey would simply prove to be too challenging.

"But some people love them. They're both very popular and who are you to judge those who drink them?"

Yes they do, and I am not judging them. I go only on my own tastes. I do however judge those that push such concoctions for a quick buck, since I have the distinct feeling that they only drink them cause they don't know better stuff is out there.

"And you think you should be the one to show them."

Well, of course, there is a time and a place for all of that. But many non-drinkers go out and order them in regular bars in the middle of the winter. If I can steer them toward something better, nothing too radical mind you, maybe a Melonball, then I will.

"What's that?"

Vodka, Midori and fresh OJ, you can always count on those Russians.

"Is that another literary allusion?"

To Nabokov, raises his glass. Anyhow, your Mr. Brown is like rum and the overpowering mixture of cliffhanger narrative meant to hide his presence. You could substitute any number of low-quality rums and few would notice.

"I seriously doubt that."

Look, maybe you're right to some degree. Obviously Crichton can tell the hell out of a story without making me wince at his prose, but the story still gets me where it gets me. In the end, the difference, or hangover as it were, is I don't feel so particularly used after him.

"So what's the problem if he so popular?"

Look, I often get people ordering the highest quality rum to mix with Coca-Cola, another former medicinal incidentally, not realizing that though it might indeed reduce the hangover, if they drink enough of the cocktails it generally tastes exactly the same as my shelf stuff. And the stuff does sell like wild of course. The combo of spirit and caffeine and sugar makes people start acting like the proverbial pirate of one of the more popular spiced varieties.

"I still don't get the problem. You make money and the clients are happy."

The problem my dear madam is that I would make money anyhow, admittedly less, with higher-quality product. The other problem is the type of clients I get. Not unlike my staff who drink what they do cause they like the taste or want to get hammered, I want to do both and I genuinely appreciate the stuff. I'm not one of these Nazi bartenders who thinks people who drink rum and cokes are fools, or that only a sommelier should be able to order wine in my joint. Quite the contrary, should the former walk in I will try and be as helpful and informative as I can allowing them to sample various mescals, and to the latter I will listen patiently, attempting to sort what can be learned from the bullshit. What I will not do however is ever push rum and cokes. Why would I try and convince people to buy something I myself would almost never drink and some frat bar across town will do anyway?

"Well someone has to make money…. You mentioned Mezcal again, what's that?"

Ah, yes, so we come to it. Mezcal is a generally unrefined cactus spirit from Mexico. It is our specialty as you can see in all the various unlabelled bottles of various color and depth that line the walls behind me.

"I thought that was tequila." said the younger.

Tequila is a type of Mezcal that must be made from blue agave and is generally manufactured in the small state of Jalisco to the west of us. Think champagne as a type of sparkling white wine with only the specific French varietals deserving that name. Mezcal however can be made anywhere in Mexico from any cacti and is still mostly a private thing done in private homes scattered throughout different regions.

"Do you buy that from the market?"

I go about once a month into unknown states looking for private haciendas to try and find undiscovered types. The ones I like I buy and bring back here where I bottle and age and infuse them with various flavors to both keep the tradition alive, support the growers, expose a new generation to the spirit, and as you will probably point out, make a tidy profit.

"That sounds like a lot of effort when you could just buy tequila down the street."

Anything worth it is, and unfortunately, Tequila has gone down in quality greatly as the international demand has overwhelmed the small state it comes from, which now generally produces watered down, nearly undrinkable or horribly expensive export-only versions.

"So you sell Mezcal. Is it any good?"

To many, Mezcal is at first too rough a drink. Unlike most spirits it is by nature cask grade, that is to say it has not been watered down to reach the magical 80-proof mark. Practically no alcohol on earth naturally and consistently comes out like that. They are often lower and must be distilled or fortified, or in the case of most distilled spirits such as Scotch or Bourbon, quite higher and must be brought down to make them suitable for the masses. Mezcals come from private haciendas and are individually made with care. They are not made for mass distribution and I suppose that is why I enjoy them so much. Some are too bitter, some too sweet, but if you can find a good one, well they are far better than any tequila you have ever tasted I would reckon.

"Well I don't like tequila, but I guess I could give it a shot."

Well, I think I got into a little bit about that, but more to it I'm sure perhaps you feel that way because you have only had it forced upon you, usually when drinking something else and it may have been of questionable origin to begin with.

"Sounds familiar." the younger one said.

The point is the growers who spend years to produce a batch do it because they enjoy it and are providing something to a community that both appreciates and enjoys it. But it is a dying art. Were you to talk to younger Mexicans they would far more often order a rum or brandy cocktail and view Mezcal as something of a drink of the past - not unlike someone who reads your Mr. Brown over David Mitchell because everyone else on earth has. It is not so much because they really like rum or brandy with coke as that they have been clubbed over the head with it. Every local disco and obnoxious pick up joint pushes the stuff on you. You could say the same of many of our own pubs and nightclubs where trendy cocktails are shoved at you on a list and 50% of the room is drinking the Cosmo of the month cause Paris Hilton had one the other night.

"Well they sure make a bigger killing than some little scotch bar."

Quite, and they have no shortage of other establishments ready to jump on the bandwagon to cash in. The difference is in a hundred years when all that remains of the Cosmo is a footnote in Wikipedia next to Long Island Iced Teas under the byline of "cocktails of bygone eras," people will still be drinking Mezcal.

"Do you think?"

I hope, but I do fear it may be forced out of existence by a lack of exposure and distribution with its former makers forced to sell their ranches and go on to making something of a lower quality and easier marketability.

"That would be a shame," said the younger.

A loss, and a quiet one. I am the only bar of my kind left in this region, though I have heard others are starting up again.

They sat quietly for a few moments all taking in each other. Camila had long tuned out and Alex seemed to be actually trying to contemplate. The older lady sipped her G & T whilst the younger stared into hers, as if she was suddenly no longer sure if she wanted it. Finally the agent looked up at the poet, now lighting a cigarette and sipping a light brown concoction, and decided to break the tension.

"Well then, sir. What are you drinking?"

A double espresso cappuccino with Bailey's and Kahlua.

"What?!"

I haven't thought of a name for it yet.

"But after that whole bit about Mezcal and how Dan Brown was like a shitty rum and coke and improving the masses and all that…."

Well, while I enjoy a tough challenging drink now and then, and a lighter simpler thing like beer at other times, or both alternatively, which lessons the blow of one and enhances the other, sometimes I like something a little messy myself. Here I've got my sweet and creamy with a bit of fast sitting on top of a thick bitter which could undoubtedly give me a nasty hangover and quite possibly an anxiety attack if I drink it too quick.

"Then why are you drinking it?" said the younger.

Well, as it's still early in the day, in the right dose this drink is the exact cure for what ails me. The bitter espresso will get my blood going along with the Kahlua and its sweetness will take away a bit of the shock. The Bailey's mellows it out a bit and I froth the whole thing to remind myself it's better to act like a pretentious twat than to be one. It might not stick with me like an excellent scotch, or burn me like a night of Long Islands, but it gets me where I need to be and does its job. More than that, I should probably want another one tomorrow.

They sat as an uncertain nervous laughter was shared. The older lady wondered what the hell the kid was on about and decided to dismiss the whole thing other than to mention as a wacky Mexican anecdote at the office.

"So this unnamed thing, is it very popular?" she asked.

Not yet, but a lot of people have been asking about it. I sometimes let them have a sip, and the more that try it, the more that they order and continue to. I'm afraid it'll never be as popular as our Cuba Libra, rum and coke with lime, orders, nor receive the acclaim or disgust of our Mezcal samplings, but nonetheless it's a start.

"I see, well then maybe you should name it after yourself…" She couldn't see where she had put the poet's book, no damn good anyhow, she figured.

"Well then, Mr. Double Espresso Bailey's and whatever, what was your name again?"

Damien, said the poet.

Then the rain stopped. Damien grabbed his bag, nodded at the slightly confused looking ladies, hugged his barmaid and headed out the door with his manager to his car.

Southeast Asia was waiting.

He had a plane to catch.

Acknowledgements

To all the early readers who fought through drafts and had the kindness to read more and my fellow writers who were critical in edits and feedback: Tony Cohan, Jamie Salazar, Kevin Brink Nielson, Lizz Huerta, Ethan Lombardi, Drew Trudeau and most especially Jillian Medoff and my editor Carolyn Fireside, whose patience and suggestions were invaluable.

To my friends that lived with me through it: Jessica Grotfeldt, Kienyo Timothy, Marc Phillipson, Nicholas Wood, Tom Walsh, Ian and Georgia Moss, Steven Michel, Rob Nichols, Camelo Castillo, Leopoldo Umberto Enrique Balderas (or just Polo for those who know him), Jules Foles, Michael Severens, Karen Deer, Heather Masterton, Wendy Rowe (R.I.P.), Carl Restivo, Alex (Chander) De Graaf, Rachel Atschultler, Damon Yetka, Tim Piedmont, Gillian Glover, Daphne Brunneceeli, Steve Mendizibal, Holly Anger, Fred and Lori and the whole Decarlo Clan (yes you too Tony), Angie Morena, Joanna Lawson, Steve Lightner, Marc Smith, Hector Garcia, Verena Wacker, Ramon Hernandez, Moises Ruiz, Walter Friedman, my family at Fusilado, and everyone that I'll once more have forgotten to include yet again – THANK YOU!

Finally I dedicate this book to all the people who helped inspire and nurture it.

You are my Crash Course on life

Propaganda on the writer

Kent Evans is the author of *Malas Ondas: Lime, Sand Sex and Salsa in the land of conquistadors* a semi-autobiographical novel about self-destruction throughout Latin America and finding that corniest of motivators – love. He was a fixture on the spoken word scene throughout the 90's till he grew tired of writing slam pieces about being a homeless gay Asian man. (Though Kent is part-Asian, he is neither homeless nor gay - not that there's anything wrong with that.)

Lately he chooses to pursue his craft through music and fiction (well sort of fiction anyhow). His performance of choice involves gathering non-traditional musicians (DJ's, classical players, Latin funk bands) and performing poetry in a live Jazz/Trip-Hop format. The Original Soundtrack for the Novel (written, performed, and composed by Kent) is currently available from all major distributors.

In the new millennium Kent has done shows throughout the states, Europe and Mexico, including the *International Arts Festival of Cervantino, RAI* in Spain, and the *Artery* in Houston. He had appeared on NPR for shows including *Nuestra Palabra, the Front Row*, and *Living Arts showcase.*

True to his nature, Kent has been traveling much of the last few years hence the (ahem) delay of this new novel. Rest assured he has plenty of poetry collections ready to go should his fan base grow truly bored and want something to fill the time between shows and works of (ahem) fiction. Kent is fully aware that no one reads poetry other than aspiring writers and failed ones who teach English (both of whom have the propensity to describe his work as "self-important" and "childish smut," about which Kent believes they are simply missing the point).

Kent was born in New York City under no choice of his own, in 1975. He is half Cantonese and half UK mongrel (mostly Irish one might assume based on his drinking habits). He grew up between New York, Connecticut and Rhode Island and has traveled extensively throughout the US, Canada, Mexico, Europe, Asia, and the Caribbean.

So now you can desist with all that *but where's he really from* bollocks.

www.ingramcontent.com/pod-product-compliance
Lightning Source LLC
Chambersburg PA
CBHW020609270626
47155CB00022BA/350